SUFFICIENT CERTAINTY

A Novel About School Violence

By

Stephen Woodfin

Formatted by Enterprise Book Services, LLC

"For all they that take the sword shall perish with the sword."

Matthew 26:52 (KJV)

Chapter One

I dreaded it when I glanced out the window of my law office and saw Logansport Panola approaching the front door. I dreaded it not because of who she was, but because of what had happened a month earlier. Thirty-three days ago, her grandson, the boy she had reared from childhood to young manhood, had brandished a gun in his high school fourth period class in our small East Texas town. Seconds later, he and two of his classmates died in a flurry of gunshots, bullets Coach Jim Briscoe, his teacher, fired with the Colt Government Model .45-caliber semi-automatic pistol he wore on his hip at school every day under color of Texas law.

I opened the door for her.

"What brings you to see me this fine morning, Momma L?"

"Red told me to come by and visit with you about a matter, Etch."

I ushered her to a straight-backed chair and sat down across from her at my desk.

Her few words had already set my mind racing. 'Momma L' was what everyone in town called Logansport Panola, the closest thing our community had to Mother Teresa. She stood five-feet two-inches high, measured about four-feet across at the shoulders, had hair darker than night, sparkling white teeth, and iridescent skin of polished bronze. Her age was indeterminate, although at least three generations of kids had sought shelter in her two-bedroom, shotgun house located on property on the south edge of town that had been in her family since Reconstruction. Despite her age, she still worked

1

as a teacher's aide at the elementary school and pastored the Peavine Church of God in Christ. She was as inscrutable as the wind, intolerant of pretense, willing to forgive a contrite sinner, and forever the sworn enemy of injustice.

The person she referred to as "Red" was the legendary lawman and private investigator Red Roper. After a stint in a Marine rifle unit in Vietnam, he came home, earned a Texas peace officer certification and worked nights on patrol while he took a degree in philosophy from Stephen F. Austin State University in Nacogdoches. In his law enforcement career, he had been a Dallas homicide detective, a special investigator for two district attorney offices, turned down an invitation to become a Texas Ranger, and served as the go-to trouble shooter for sheriff and police departments across the country.

For the last ten years, Red had made his living freelancing as a private dick. I'd used him as an investigator on criminal and personal injury cases and over the years, we had developed an understanding: I had his back, and he had mine.

I knew if Red Roper had suggested Momma L come to see me, the shit was about to hit the fan.

Although my given name was Daniel Danielson, Momma L called me 'Etch' because of an incident thirty years earlier when I was a young lawyer representing a woman in a divorce and child custody case. The estranged husband blindsided me one night in the mall parking lot, planning to cut my throat with a box cutter. I deflected his blow and, instead, he slashed a swoosh that ran from my chin to just south of my right ear. I grabbed his wrist and flipped him over my shoulder and head first onto the parking lot. Then, I stomped the shit out of him until mall security arrived.

Attired in his jail uniform and handcuffs at the final divorce hearing, my assailant took the stand, pointed at me and said, "If Etch-a-Sketch over there had left me alone, I'd still have my kids." I let my beard grow after the box cutter wound healed, but my right jaw looked like an Etch-a-Sketch smiley face drawn with iron shavings.

"What matter is that, Momma L?"

She reached into a file folder that rested on her lap, drew out an eight-by-ten glossy photograph and slid it across the desk to me.

I studied the portrait of her grandson, Carmel Sideout, in his cap and gown, a shot taken at a photo op for graduating seniors a few days before the killings. In it he smiled, his lips closed, yellow horn-rim glasses slid part way down his nose, his head cocked as if he were about to make a smart-ass remark.

"I need for you to help me clear Carmel's name."

I knew from former dealings with her that she expected me to give it to her straight, not pull my punches or dance around the issues. "What makes you think I can accomplish that assignment, Momma L? The facts as I know them are that Carmel made the first move and the rest of the deal was on him."

"Those aren't the facts, Etch."

"He pulled a gun and waved it around. What was Coach Briscoe supposed to do, wait for Carmel to start shooting?"

"Carmel never owned a gun in his life, never handled one. I raised the boy from birth, and I know what I'm telling you is righteous."

"Kids have ways of hiding things from their parents and grandparents. Maybe that's what Carmel did with the gun."

Momma L wasn't having it. "Etch, he was going to graduate as valedictorian of the class. He was all-state on the trombone. His classmates picked him as most likely to succeed. Half a dozen schools of his choosing had offered him scholarships. He worked nights at Starbucks and saved enough money to buy a used car two weeks before he..." She took a Kleenex from her purse and pressed it against her forehead, wiped her eyes. "I'm telling you it was not in him to do such a thing as this."

She paused a minute before she added, "And the other kids who died that day-"

"Maria Juarez and Benjamin Cohen."

"Yeah. Maria and Carmel had been going together for six months and getting serious. Carmel, Maria and Benjamin were talking about sharing an apartment at college. They had already begun scouting out places, talking about what furniture they'd need, planning how they could make the deal work. They died together because they always sat as close to each other as they could. They were a team. Does that sound like kids who wanted to end their lives?"

I hadn't seen any of these facts reported about the incident. "You're right that Carmel doesn't fit the profile of a school shooter. But the fact remains that he carried a pistol to class and gave every indication he was about to open fire with it."

"Have you seen the gun?"

I thought about the news reports. "I remember images of a Glock 17, a nine-millimeter."

"Everybody's seen those pictures, but none of the reports ever claimed the one they showed was the weapon Carmel had with him that day. I've asked the police to let me see it, and they refuse. Say the case is 'still under investigation.'"

"Are you telling me you think he didn't pull a gun? I thought some of the other students in the class had corroborated that part of the story."

"A couple of the kids said they saw something in his hand that might have looked like a gun, but they couldn't be sure. That's why I've been trying for a month to get some answers."

"And that's where Red Roper comes in?"

"I went to see him and told him the police had a lid on it. He made some calls. That's when he told me to come see you."

"OK, Momma L, I'll talk to Red about the investigation, but I still have some questions about my role. You say you want me to clear Carmel's name, right?"

"That's right."

"The law's not much good at that sort of thing. On the criminal side it deals with guilt and innocence. That doesn't apply in a case like this where the would-be shooter is deceased. On the civil side, the law is about money, who owes whom for a wrong committed. If a court determines Carmel's death was wrongful it can award damages to his beneficiaries. Under Texas law those beneficiaries are his parents, his wife and his children. Since Carmel had neither wife nor children that leaves only his parents, not a grandparent like you. In other words, you don't have standing to bring any kind of legal action on Carmel's behalf."

"It's not about the money, Etch. If anything ever comes of that end of the thing, I would want it to go to the school to set up a scholarship fund in Carmel's name." She reached into the folder and slid two more documents to me.

I studied them a minute. One was Carmel Sideout's birth certificate. It listed his mother as Caddo Panola of Kilgore, Texas, and his father as Hobo Sideout, address unknown. Carmel's eighteenth birthday would have occurred the day after the shooting.

The other paper was an adoption order dated sixteen years before Carmel's death. It recited that Caddo Panola had relinquished her parental rights in favor of Logansport Panola and that Hobo Sideout had never responded to the adoption proceeding, so the court had terminated his parental rights by default after he had received due process of law.

"What happened to Caddo Panola?" I thought back and pulled an image of a striking young Black woman from my memory banks. I saw her as a teenager, her black hair streaked with gold highlights, her swag, her presence that filled any room she entered. I remembered handling a case or two for her: minor in possession of alcohol, caught with a couple of joints in her locker at school.

Momma L took a deep breath, leaned against the back of the chair, gazed at the ceiling for a second before she answered. "I couldn't do much with her. Lord knows I tried. She went from bad to worse. She was just too damned good looking for her own good. She worked here and there, but eventually decided she could make more money turning tricks than she could flipping burgers. A few months before her thirtieth birthday, she came up pregnant. She wouldn't tell me who the father was, just said he wasn't in the picture."

"The birth certificate identifies him as Hobo Sideout."

Momma L allowed a laugh. "She made up that name. A 'sideout' is hobo talk for a section of track where the train stops to let another one pass. It's where hobos jump on or off, where they don't have to deal with a moving boxcar. She listed Hobo Sideout as the daddy as a joke. It meant the father was someone who passed through town and took the next ride out. Carmel never had a daddy."

I thought about a fatherless child whose mother had abandoned him, and I re-thought the notion that he didn't fit the school shooter profile. I kept those thoughts to myself. Momma L had enough on her plate.

"Where's Caddo now?"

"She left Kilgore when Carmel was two. That's when I adopted him. She's lived all over, but I haven't seen or heard from her in over ten years. Last I knew she was somewhere in California."

"She didn't come to Carmel's funeral?"

Momma L didn't answer. I understood. Every family with a saint in it must have a sinner or two to even things out.

I thought about the situation for a minute as we sat in silence. "Have you spoken to anybody else about the case?"

"Just you, Red and the police."

I stood up, and Momma L took the cue and rose from her chair. We shook hands. "I'm going to talk to Red and snoop around a bit. After that, you and I can have another meeting, and I'll let you know if there's a way to move forward."

She handed me a slip of paper from her purse. "That's my cell. I appreciate you hearing me out, Etch."

I hugged her and escorted her to the door. As I watched her walk to her beat up '89 Toyota Corolla, I wondered what the hell I had gotten myself into.

Chapter Two

A few minutes before ten o'clock that morning, I pulled off U. S. Highway 259 South onto a gravel driveway that ran through three hundred yards of red clay and pine trees to Red Roper's cabin. The early June sun beat down on its tin roof raising the temperature to the low 90s and producing waves of heat that wrinkled the bright blue sky. As I approached the house I heard the unmistakable explosion of gunshots and spotted Red at his homemade firing range, a revolver the size of Houston in his right hand, noise-protecting ear muffs on his head.

I parked in front of the house and walked to his firing range out of his line of fire. He had hung paper targets the shape of human silhouettes on bales of hay, and I saw closely grouped bullet holes in the human heads and mid torsos. Red holstered his service revolver, a Smith & Wesson L-frame .357-caliber with a six-inch barrel, took the ear protectors off, donned his trademark Stetson, and gave me a nod of recognition.

He was old school through and through and packed a world of hurt into five-feet-ten-inches, one hundred and sixty-five pounds. His hair, once fire engine red, had aged to rusty silver, shaved to a half inch. His freckles had paled and deepened into a permanent ruddy complexion, a fitting contrast to his Cool-Hand-Luke blue eyes. He spoke soft and slow in a Lufkin accent, had a steel trap mind and wore a peace sign necklace his brother had sent him while Red was fighting in Vietnam. His circle of trust was microscopic, and I counted it one of my greatest life achievements to be in it.

We walked to the shaded front porch and Red poured two glasses of iced tea for us before he spoke.

"I suppose Momma L came to see you," he said.

"She did."

"The deal doesn't pass the smell test, Etch. Something's rotten."

"Care to share?"

A feral hog darted out of the tree line a good fifty yards from us and ran across the drive. Red stood, drew his revolver and fired one shot. The pig collapsed, kicked its hind legs a couple of times and expired.

"Sumbitches are a goddamned nuisance," he said as he sat down again. He grabbed an expandable file off the plank floor, set it in his lap and thumbed through the tabs. I figured it contained everything anybody knew about the school shooting thus far and was still a work in progress.

He took out a yellow legal pad, reviewed his notes. "I spoke to Quasimodo at the PD. Off the record."

"Of course." Quasimodo was Red's nickname for Kilgore PD's chief detective, although he wasn't a hunchbacked bell ringer, just an odd bird. "What did he have to say?"

"Not much. He had interviewed Coach Briscoe and gotten the same story everyone heard on the news. I asked to see the gun Carmel supposedly brandished, and all he would tell me was what he told Momma L."

"'Still under investigation.'"

"Bullshit. I can't count the number of times the PD has asked me to examine a gun tied to one of its investigations. Usually they want to know what light I can shed on things. Not this time, though. Best Quasi would do was show me a picture of it, not a very good one either. I believe it may have been intentionally out of focus."

"What could you tell from the picture?"

"In my expert opinion?"

"What else?"

"If that picture was all I had to go on, it would be my opinion that it was a plastic model of a Glock 17, maybe even a toy BB gun."

"Which is why the PD doesn't want anyone to examine it?"

"More than likely. The PD is caught between a rock and a hard place. If it's a toy gun, Coach Briscoe may have overreacted, and he may have committed a serious crime, possibly a capital one.

Meanwhile, the American Gun Association, the AGA, wants to make Coach Briscoe its national poster boy for the movement to arm teachers and is breathing down the PD's throat to clear Briscoe and conclude the investigation. Slim Atwell, the elected Criminal District Attorney of Gregg County, is waiting for the smoke to clear and hoping none of the victims comes calling. The school district is hunkered down, sticking with the party line that Coach Briscoe acted heroically in a tragic situation. The irony of it all is that the people in the best position to know the facts have fed the public a crock of shit, and three kids are dead for no good reason."

"But if the gun was a good enough facsimile of the real thing to cause confusion, wouldn't the law still protect Briscoe and the school district? I haven't studied the statute in detail yet, but I believe it says a teacher can use deadly force if he has 'sufficient certainty' that a shooter may be about to open fire."

Red reached for another file, drew out a sheet of paper and handed it to me. "This is Briscoe's right to carry permit. Check the date of issuance."

I read the date aloud. "May 17th."

"That's two days after he shot the kids," Red said.

"He'd been carrying a gun on his hip for three months or so without a permit?"

"Bingo. The law requires the school to have the permit on file before a teacher can carry a gun on campus."

"Do you know if Briscoe had received any training in firearms before he received his permit? If so, I imagine Texas courts would say he was qualified to carry, even if the permit didn't issue until after the shooting."

"The plot thickens, counselor."

"Let me hear it."

Red was on a roll. "Dud McGill does the firearms training. He signed the permit. I talked to him yesterday. Guess what? Dud says Briscoe is a regular at the firing range, the AGA sanctioned one in the Sabine river bottom."

"I know the place."

"McGill says the permit was just a formality because Briscoe was well-versed in all sorts of guns and was a crackerjack shot. He could hit a bullseye at twenty yards with the Colt 1911 .45 he carried at school."

I played the devil's advocate. "It's one thing to hit a paper target in a controlled environment. It's a whole nuther thing to be accurate under the extreme stress of a situation like what happened at the school."

"You're right about that, Etch. But those kids weren't more than ten or fifteen feet from Briscoe in the classroom. He fired five rounds. How could he miss twice from that distance and hit the wrong target two other times? He wasn't a rookie with a gun. He should have been able to hit Carmel in the chest with his first round and finish him off with round two if he needed it. And by the way, his fifth shot, the one that killed Carmel, was a head shot. That was after Carmel probably had time to be dodging and taking cover. And there's one other thing about his target practicing habits."

"I'm listening."

"To access the firing range a club member must swipe his membership card at the front gate. I checked Briscoe's swipe records. From February through April of this year he went to the range a total of three times. In the first ten days of May, he went every night."

"You're saying he was getting ready for action, honing his skills?"

"Exactly."

I talked my way through the analysis. "So, he's a crackerjack shot, has a target at close range, and he misses it four times before he delivers the perfect head shot."

"Yeah."

"Are you saying he missed Carmel on purpose?"

"It's the only conclusion I can draw from what I know about gun fights." He paused a second. "And the other thing is that I don't believe he shot Maria Juarez and Benjamin Cohen by accident. They were intended targets, too."

"It's just too much to believe, Red. We've gone from Coach Briscoe being a knight in shining armor who did a great job containing a horrible shooting spree to a scenario where he intentionally killed three high school kids who weren't doing anything wrong.

"I've been around Coach Briscoe a few times through the years at school events, parent-teacher conferences, stuff like that. He always struck me as a guy just putting in his time, doing enough to pass muster and have his contract renewed. He's smug all right, a small-town know-it-all, but I never had him pegged as dangerous."

Red shook his head. "I know, Etch. It's a lot to take in, and we don't have half the information we need to draw any conclusions."

"I guess that means we owe it to Momma L to do some more digging."

We discussed the division of labor for the investigation, but before I left Red I had one more thing to say.

"All of our digging doesn't amount to a hill of beans unless there was an innocent explanation of why Carmel had that gun, real or fake, in his backpack. That's the whole case. Even if it was just some crazy prank or child's play, if he brought that pistol into the classroom unannounced and surprised Coach Briscoe and his fellow students with it, he sealed his fate and the fate of Maria Juarez and Benjamin Cohen. The rest of it is nothing but window dressing."

Red nodded. "That's the way I see it, too."

"Let's find out what really happened at the high school that day."

We shook hands and got down to business.

Chapter Three

First, I went back to my office and pulled up on my legal research software the law the Texas legislature had passed in late February in the wake of the Parkland, Florida, shootings. It popped up as The Student Protection Act ("SPA").

Under the SPA local school districts had the option of arming teachers and other designated classes of employees. To carry a gun on campus the employee was required to obtain a permit that demonstrated he or she had completed a full day of training in firearms handling, including two hours of practice on a firing range under the supervision of a licensed instructor. Although the SPA provided that each local district had the discretion to implement the Act, the legislature had built in a provision that made the decision to opt in a no-brainer. If a district adopted the provisions of the SPA, the law shielded the district from any liability associated with the exercise of rights the SPA created. But it specifically stated that any district which did not comply with the SPA could be held liable to "the full extent of any damages incurred as a result of a school shooting."

The SPA also created an operative test by which the actions of an armed teacher or employee must be judged. That test was that the school employee was justified in the use of deadly force whenever he or she had "sufficient certainty" that a student was about to engage in violence towards another student or was actually engaged in such violence. The SPA did not define the term 'sufficient certainty,' which meant the courts would have to establish the parameters of the term if and when specific cases arose.

And, as Red had said, one requirement of the SPA was that the district must have a permit on file before it could allow any teacher or employee to carry a gun. The custodians of those permits were the principals of each school.

The SPA also contained a provision about the warning to students required under it. It gave school districts this guideline: Districts shall post a notice in substantially the following form on any campus where district employees carry guns as permitted under this Act. WARNING! DISTRICT EMPLOYEES ON THIS CAMPUS CARRY FIREARMS. THEY ARE AUTHORIZED TO USE DEADLY FORCE WITHOUT GIVING ADDITIONAL WARNINGS TO ANY PERSON WHO ILLEGALLY POSSESSES A GUN ON THIS CAMPUS.

In other words, public school campuses in Texas were a free fire zone for teachers who had a permit under the SPA. A teacher with 'sufficient certainty,' whatever that meant, could open fire on students and ask questions later.

School districts around the state were quick to adopt the Act's provisions, largely because they wanted the liability shield it provided. However, what few articles I could find on the subject indicated that most districts which adopted those provisions had no takers. Apparently, most teachers weren't interested in toting guns to school.

Perhaps we now knew why.

As I was finishing my research, May Ellen, my wife of thirty-two years, stuck her head in the door. She knew my moods and the look I got when a case grabbed hold of me.

"Permission to come aboard, Captain Danielson?"

"Permission granted, my lovely."

She came around my desk, gave me a hug, glanced at my notes. "Whatcha working on?"

May Ellen was the truest barometer I had ever known of what constituted justice, what was fair, what love and human compassion demanded. If she was ever wrong about things it was only because she led with her heart and still believed in the possibility of a good, if not perfect, world. I gave her the skinny about Momma L and my meeting with Red.

She grew quiet. I knew that meant she was analyzing the situation, the human cost of our involvement, how high the stakes were for everyone in the mix, the sorrow of the bereaved parents, the stigma of tilting at windmills. Finally, she broke the silence.

"Do you really think you can clear Carmel's name?"

"I don't know yet, baby. If the facts shake out, I might have a shot."

"And if the facts don't shake out? What then?"

"I tell Momma L we can't get there."

"I've never known you to back down once you've set your mind to something."

"That's why I have to be damned sure we have at least an even chance. That's all anyone can ask for."

"I've heard you say a hundred times, 'follow the evidence and trust your instincts.' This time's no different. Momma L came to the right man."

She patted me on the shoulder and headed for the door.

"Thanks, baby. I needed the pep talk," I said to her on her way out.

She winked at me and closed the door behind her.

A little before one o'clock that afternoon, I pulled up to the security check point in the parking lot of Kilgore High School, and the guard cleared me through to visit the principal's office.

As I walked up the steps of Old Main, I stopped in front of a makeshift memorial dedicated to the students who had died only a few weeks before. I bowed my head, mumbled a prayer, not knowing if God cared to hear it.

Inside, the halls were quieter than usual because of the summer session, the chatter and clatter of teenagers muffled at the far end of the corridor. As I approached the door to the principal's office, I saw Mr. Poteet, a long-time janitor for the district, pushing a wheeled-plastic garbage container next to a wall that contained rows of student lockers. He was wearing a school-issued full-length red jump suit with a black capital K embroidered on the front right pocket. A blue cleaning rag draped out of his left rear pocket.

"What's up, Mr. Poteet?" I asked.

"Hey, Danny. Good to see you."

He and I went back a long way, long before anyone called me Etch or Mr. Danielson.

"I'm just cleaning out the mess the kids left in these lockers when school was out," he said. He inserted a master key into a lock, opened the door, stood back and held his nose for a second to signal how rank the contents smelled. Then he put on a pair of latex gloves, stuck both hands inside the locker and dragged the entire mess into his garbage bin. "If they don't take their stuff home at the end of the semester, it's toast." He waved at me, then stuck his pass key in the next lock.

Sometimes you look for one thing and find another, I thought.

I walked over to him. "Mr. Poteet, Momma L came by this morning to see if I could help her with some final things about Carmel Sideout."

"That poor woman," he said as he took off his gloves.

"I was headed to the principal's office to see about picking up Carmel's stuff from his locker. But if you can unlock it for me I guess I can save Principal McEntyre the trouble of dealing with it."

"I would be glad to help if I could, Danny, but the police already got it. I opened the lock, and the evidence people from Kilgore PD inventoried, tagged and bagged it."

"Just so I can report back to Momma L, can you tell me what the police took from his locker? They haven't told her much of anything yet."

"Nothing out of the ordinary. A couple of notebooks, a textbook or two, a few scraps of paper, like candy wrappers and such. Nothing that I could see that would have anything to do with the shooting. He had his backpack with him in class when the shooting broke out, so I assume they confiscated it, too."

"But you didn't see any bullets or such in his locker?"

"No. Nothing like that." He thought for a second. "There was a picture."

"Of what?"

"He had Maria Juarez's senior photo taped inside his locker. It had smudges on it."

"Smudges?"

"Yeah, like maybe he'd kissed it a time or two." Mr. Poteet's eyes misted. "Carmel was a good boy, Danny. Please tell Momma L how sorry I am for her loss."

I nodded at him and watched as he returned to work.

I went to the principal's office. When I walked in, Marcie Brumbaugh, Principal McEntyre's secretary, looked up from a stack of papers on her desk and greeted me. She was in her early twenties, her hair dyed bright red, white-framed eyeglasses last in vogue in the late 1950s dangling around her neck on a chain made of paper clips. Her blouse was a print of equatorial foliage and a spider monkey eating bananas in a palm tree. Sleeveless, it allowed me to see the pale white skin of her arms. She had painted yellow smiley face emojis on each fingernail.

"Hello, Mr. Danielson. What brings you to school today?"

"Is Ms. McEntyre in?"

"No, sir. She's out of town at a training seminar. She won't be back until next week."

Perfect, I thought.

"Is there something I can do for you?" Marcie said.

"Momma L came to see me this morning about winding up Carmel Sideout's final affairs."

At the mention of Carmel's name, the smile on Marcie's face disappeared, and she took her eyes off me, focused on the stack of papers again. "I'm not sure what I can do for you on that account," she said, speaking to the floor.

"She wanted me to inquire about the process of establishing a scholarship fund."

"Oh," Marcie said still diverting her eyes. She slid a file drawer open and rifled through a tabbed set of files. She pulled out a two-page form and placed it on the edge of the desk nearest me. "It's all in there," she said as she pointed at the form.

"Nice ring," I said.

At that she looked up at me again. She held the hand with the ring at eye level and admired it. "Merlin Hostetler gave it to me." She tinged with pink, as if she had made too much of a confession.

"So, you and Merlin are engaged?" Hostetler was a second-year teacher who served as Jim Briscoe's assistant coach for the boys basketball team. In his two years on staff at Kilgore High School, he had notched three semi-permanent romances. The ring probably came out of a Crackerjacks box.

"Not engaged. More like promised to be promised." She came back to the moment and let her hand with the ringed finger drop out of my sight into her lap. "Is there anything else I can do for you, Mr. Danielson?"

"One other thing. Is Coach Briscoe on campus today? I'd like to visit with him for a minute."

"He's on paid leave."

"For how long?"

"Until he comes back."

"Back from where?"

She squirmed in her chair. I could tell my audience with her was about over. "I don't know the details, Mr. Danielson." She paused for a second as if she was deciding whether to give me one last tidbit of information. "All I can tell you is that I heard he is visiting family out of state." She stood up to signal it was time for me to leave.

"Thanks, Marcie. And congratulations on being promised to be promised."

"Please close the door on your way out," she said.

On my way back to my car, I stopped again at the memorial to the shooting. But this time the sign directly across the sidewalk drew my attention, the bold black letters of the SPA warning. What made me notice it, however, was the large red X spray-painted across the length of it. I walked next to it, reached out my hand and touched the red paint, still wet and dripping to the grass below it. I heard a car screeching out of the parking lot. I turned and saw a maroon, late model Mustang, its dark-tinted windows hiding the driver and any passengers. I pulled out my cell, pointed it toward the car and snapped a picture.

I didn't realize Mr. Poteet had come up behind me. "What the hell?" he said.

"Vandals," I said.

We watched the Mustang jump the curb and race out of sight. "What's the world coming to?" the janitor said, more to the wind than to me.

"I really don't know, Mr. Poteet. Who can say?"

I left him with his thoughts.

A block from the school I pulled over in a convenience store parking lot and texted Red the picture of the Mustang.

"See what you can find out about this car." I knew Red would take it from there.

Chapter Four

My meeting with Momma L had been in what I called the back room, the four-hundred-square-foot office out of which I practiced law. It was attached to a two-story, historic red brick home near Kilgore College that housed a project dear to my heart, a bookstore and coffee shop. May Ellen, my daughter E. J., and I ran the store Tuesdays through Saturdays from ten in the morning until six in the evening, come hell or high water.

The first customer in the bookstore the morning after Momma L came to see me was Levi Cohen, Benjamin Cohen's dad and the sitting president of the Kilgore ISD school board. I got up from my chair at the cash register, walked to him and shook his hand. "I'm terribly sorry for your loss, Levi," I said.

He nodded and hung his head.

"Can I talk to you a minute?" he asked. He glanced around the store to check for other patrons. "In private, if you don't mind."

I asked May Ellen to watch the front of the shop, and Levi and I walked out to my office. I closed the floor-to-ceiling plantation shutters on the front of the room so no one could see us talking, motioned for Levi to take a seat, and sat down across from him.

I had known him for at least twenty years, done business at his jewelry shop, sat in bleachers next to him at football, baseball and basketball games, served a four-year stint with him on the school board. I had last seen him at his son's funeral, and, in the few weeks since, he had aged ten years. He was in his mid-50s, a coat and tie type of guy who wore a starched long-sleeved white cotton dress shirt, even at outdoor events in the summer. His khaki pants were pressed, his shoes shined. He was slight of build, but fit, possessing the compact, muscular physique of a long-distance runner.

This morning, however, he wore faded jeans, frayed at the cuffs, a University of Texas burnt orange t-shirt. A dried mustard stain blemished his shirt's Longhorn logo, two-days' worth of salt and pepper stubble sprouted on his chin. He had a severe case of bed head, and his wire-rim glasses didn't conceal his blood shot eyes. I noticed a tremor in his hands before he scooted to the edge of his chair and placed his palms on the top of my desk.

"What do you need to talk to me about, Levi?"

He pushed himself against the back of the chair, folded his hands, took a deep breath.

"I heard you've been asking questions at school."

That didn't take long, I thought. I knew it wouldn't. The only subject anyone talked about in town these days was the school shooting, and I had no doubt that my trip to the high school the day before would set tongues wagging.

"Momma L asked me to handle a few things pertaining to Carmel. I am sure you are one of the few people who can understand what she's going through."

"I know her grandson was responsible for Benjamin's death, if that's what you mean, Daniel." He was one of the few people who had never adopted my nickname. "It is a clear case of a kid who threatened danger receiving what the law deemed justified. Coach Briscoe couldn't save my son, but he had sufficient certainty that Sideout planned to empty the Glock's seventeen round clip at the students in his classroom. Jim's actions possibly prevented a dozen killings or more. Logansport Panola needs to get her mind around it and let it lie."

"A plastic BB gun doesn't have a seventeen-round clip." I waited for Levi's reaction.

"It looked like the real thing," he blurted out. "That's all that matters."

He had confirmed Red's expert opinion.

"Why would a kid as smart as Carmel bring a toy gun to school knowing that if he pulled it in front of Coach Briscoe he would likely be a dead man?"

"Look, Daniel. I'll never be able to get inside Carmel's head. Neither will you. Briscoe didn't have to guess right about the gun. He only needed enough certainty to believe things were going south. No one can second guess a decision like that." He closed his eyes a second while he regained his composure. "Lord knows I've thought about the scenario every day for the last four weeks. I've put myself in Briscoe's shoes a hundred times. I've tried to convince myself he could have acted differently and still stopped the situation from escalating, but I always come back to the same thing. He had no time and no good choices. He did what he had to do."

Levi was making the exact argument I would hear from opposing counsel in court if I ever took the case to trial. I felt his pain, but I didn't buy the pitch.

"Police officers often confront citizens with guns in their hands. They follow protocol and tell the armed person to drop his gun, get on the ground, or whatever. They don't just open fire."

Levi wept, his hands pressed against his face. I bowed my head and let the storm of his emotions pass. After a couple of minutes, he spoke to me again.

"Daniel, you and I both love our kids and our school. I know that. It's just that we seem to have lost our way. We don't know when our children leave the house in the morning for school if we shall see them again. We don't know if we should turn our schools into prisons with bars on the windows and doors, or if we should keep our kids home. Some people say the answer is more guns at school, some say take all guns off the market. Mental health experts say we must identify the problem students and conduct interventions for them, but the state provides no funding and teachers have enough trouble already just maintaining some semblance of order in their classrooms. The school can't be the parent many of our children never had. And then something like this happens. It happens in small town America where people want to believe they are safe, where folks believe their neighbors are decent law-abiding citizens."

He took a handkerchief from his back pocket and swiped his face with it. I knew he was spent, that the words that had boiled up from within him reflected the hell he now occupied.

I cleared my throat. "Levi, I hear you. Please believe that I do. I've had the same thoughts. Here's where I come down on it. All we can do is to take a step at a time, to address the issues one by one.

Maybe if we do that we can find a workable solution to the epidemic of school violence."

"What does that mean for you and Logansport Panola?"

I knew he would circle back to my intentions as an attorney working a case for a client. His position demanded it.

"As I see it, it means I must examine what happened at the school through the only lens I have: the law as it exists here and now. That's what I plan to do. I will follow the evidence where it leads. If the evidence shows Coach Briscoe was justified in the use of deadly force in his classroom, if it shows the school followed the law, then so be it. Momma L wants no more than what the law provides and no less than justice requires."

"Benjamin, Maria and Carmel were friends, Daniel."

"I know."

"Maybe before you go too far in your search, you should explore their friendship. Maybe if I had done that, I wouldn't be sitting here having this discussion with you. Maybe I wouldn't have buried my boy four weeks ago today."

He stood and extended his hand to me. I shook it.

"Godspeed, Daniel," he said as he left my office.

I had just closed the door behind Levi Cohen when my cell rang.

"Morning, Red."

"How's it hanging, counselor?"

I gave him the skinny on my conference with Levi.

"I can't imagine what he's going through," Red said.

"Me either."

Red got to the reason for his call.

"I tracked down the driver of the Mustang. Paid him a visit a few minutes ago. I need to brief you on the chat I had with the kid."

Red wasn't much for talking on the phone.

"Come on down. I'll be here."

"See you in a few, Etch," he said as he ended the call.

I went back into the bookstore and May Ellen caught me on the way in.

"Levi Cohen brought in a package for you before he left," she said. She handed me a large mailing envelope. The address box bore words hand-written with a black Sharpie: Mr. Daniel Danielson,

Attorney and Counselor at Law, Personal and Confidential. The flap to the mailer was sealed and taped. I took my pocket knife and cut the seal. I glanced inside the envelope and saw a sheaf of papers held together with a black clip.

"I'd better look at these in my office," I said to May Ellen.

She nodded. "Take your time, Etch. We've got the store under control."

I went back to my desk and pulled the papers out of the envelope, laid them in front of me.

I couldn't believe what I saw.

Chapter Five

Red arrived thirty minutes later and let himself in my office door. I was still studying the packet Levi Cohen left me, taking notes on a yellow legal pad. I pointed at the chair, and Red took off his Stetson, sat down and waited for me to take a breather.

A couple of minutes later, I looked up at him.

"Who wants to go first?" I asked.

"It depends. What are you reading?"

"Levi Cohen brought me a gift. You won't believe it."

"Then, tag you're it."

I handed him a copy of the packet. I had separated the papers into exhibits and placed numbered stickers on them, so they would be easy to follow while we reviewed them. It was an old habit learned from many years proffering evidence in court.

"Before he left this morning, Levi dropped these items at the front desk."

"Makes you wonder why, doesn't it?" Red asked. He was already reading ahead to see what we had.

I laid it out for him. "From what I have seen, these papers are the results of the investigation the PD has provided to the school, or at least to the school board. Except for the last one. We will get to that in a minute. Exhibit A is the incident report Quasimodo prepared. It's dated five days after the shooting. Attached to it are Exhibits B, C, D, and E. Those are witness statements from Coach Briscoe, Levi Cohen, Principal McEntyre and a student named Marcus Wellborn.

"Exhibit A takes us through the time line from the first 9-1-1 call to when the PD determined the threat was over and the school was secure. In it you will also find a description of the gun police seized at the scene, which is identified as the one Carmel brandished. As you suspected, it was a plastic BB gun, a replica of a Glock 17, although it was somewhat smaller than the real thing."

Red studied a picture of the gun included with the report. "That's a lot better photo than the one Quasi showed me. There's no doubt it's a cheap imitation, not really a toy because a BB gun can put an eye out in a heartbeat. But it wouldn't meet the legal definition of a deadly weapon. Although, as you and I discussed, I doubt it makes much difference if the ordinary person on the street would have thought it was a real Glock."

I continued my run down of the exhibits. "B is Coach Briscoe's hand-written statement, dated the day after the shooting. It's consistent with what we have heard in news reports with a couple of exceptions. He says they were about fifteen minutes into fourth period when he saw Carmel grab his backpack off the floor and fiddle with it. He says he didn't think anything of it at first because students were always doing that in class. After a few seconds of observing Carmel, Briscoe says he saw him make a face like he had found what he was looking for in his backpack. Immediately after that, Carmel reached his right hand in and pulled out the gun, held it up and waved it in the air. According to Briscoe, the first thing he did when he saw what was happening was that he yelled at Carmel to put the gun on his desk and stand away from it."

"We've never heard that before," Red said. "I've seen news footage from the day of the shooting of Briscoe's account of the events. He never said anything about issuing a warning to Carmel."

"Right. But maybe after he had a chance to reflect on it over night, he remembered it more clearly."

"Possible, but not likely," Red said. "The freshest account is usually the most reliable."

"I'm with you on that. But if we ever question him about it in court, I'm sure he will stick by this statement. It would just be a matter for the people on the jury to decide if he was telling the truth about giving Carmel a warning."

"And the law doesn't require a warning anyway."

"Right again. Which makes me wonder why he added it to his account. My guess is he just thought it made him look better. That he went above and beyond what the law required."

"What's the other thing that doesn't match with what we've heard?" Red asked.

"It's a big one. Briscoe says after the warning he stood up and drew his Colt forty-five. When he did, Maria Juarez and Benjamin Cohen dove at Carmel, apparently attempting to disarm him. Carmel knocked them away and swung the gun in their direction. That's when Briscoe opened fire."

"And, inadvertently, Maria and Benjamin had placed themselves directly in the line of fire."

"Yeah. According to Briscoe their heroism was what cost them their lives," I said.

Red shook his head. "What a world we live in."

"You haven't seen anything yet."

"Continue then, counselor."

"Exhibit C is Levi's statement. In it he admits that the school board learned after the shooting that Coach Briscoe had not filed his SPA permit with Principal McEntyre's office until two days after the killings. The board met with their lawyer in executive session to discuss the situation. Executive sessions aren't open to the public or the press, so that would explain why we didn't see it reported. Ms. McEntyre was also at that meeting. Her statement is that a change in personnel at the principal's office caused the snafu about the permit. She also says that Coach Briscoe had come to her office in late February and inquired about the new law, the SPA. She told him the school board had opted in to the SPA at its February meeting. He told her then that he already had a right to carry permit and wanted to be sure of the district policy, to be sure he could carry a gun on campus. She told him he could as soon as he filed his permit with her office. She says he promised to file the permit the next day. A few days later, McEntyre says she saw Briscoe wearing a gun on his hip on campus, and she assumed he had filed the permit as he said he would. She had delegated the actual receipt of right to carry permits to her secretary, and she had no reason to believe Briscoe hadn't followed through with the filing."

Red raised his hand to stop me. "But there are several things wrong with McEntyre's statement. First, the permit I saw didn't issue until after the shooting. Second, I can't imagine a teacher would show up with a gun on his hip and the principal in charge of the deal wouldn't double check to make sure she had a permit in her file at the office."

"On the first point I guess it's possible Briscoe earlier obtained a different right to carry permit from someone other than Dud McGill."

"Yeah, it's possible. But why would he get two of them? Doesn't make sense."

"I agree, but I'm just trying to cover all the bases. On the second point about McEntyre double checking the permit filing, I'm with you a hundred percent. She says it was a new procedure instituted with the adoption of the SPA and her office hadn't had time to implement all the ministerial steps. So, the permit deal fell through the cracks."

"Yet another example of contrived bullshit."

I had to admire Red's mastery of the language, his clarity of expression.

He continued his analysis. "If what McEntyre says about the timing of her meeting with Briscoe is accurate, then we know Briscoe was focused on carrying a gun to school months before the fatal shootings."

"According to McEntyre, he is still the only teacher at KISD who carries a gun to school," I said.

"What are the odds that the only teacher armed with a gun would be the one in whose class a student brandished a weapon? It is beyond surreal."

"Yeah, wherever surreal is, this turn of events is on the other side of it."

I picked up Exhibit E, the statement of Marcus Wellborn.

"The final statement in the packet comes from one of the students in the classroom who survived the shooting. He says he was two seats to Carmel Sideout's left. Maria sat between him and Carmel. He saw Carmel pilfering around in his backpack. He said Carmel saw something in it that puzzled him, and he mouthed the words, 'What the fuck' before he stuck his hand in to check it out. Wellborn says he thought Carmel didn't know what he had until he pulled it out and got a good look at it. At the same time Carmel saw the gun, Coach Briscoe did, too. Carmel had a deer in the headlights look on his face.

Briscoe crouched into a firing position, chambered a round. Maria lunged at Carmel to knock him to the floor, Briscoe opened fire and continued shooting until he struck Carmel with the head shot. Wellborn says Carmel never brandished the gun. As soon as he saw what he had in his hand, all hell broke loose."

Red wrinkled his forehead, pursed his lips. "Two things strike me about the kid's statement. First, he is a disinterested witness. He was just minding his business and doesn't have a stake in the outcome of the investigation. That makes his testimony much more believable than anyone else's. It's like a guy standing on the corner who witnesses a car wreck in front of him. He's not involved in any dispute that may arise between the drivers of the cars. He's just telling what he saw."

"Right. But it's still a hell of a deal. If Wellborn is right, then Briscoe gave Carmel absolutely no time even to drop the gun. It's like Briscoe was primed and ready to go, like he was waiting for the bell to ring to start the race. But you said, there were two things that struck you. What's the other thing?"

Red slid a paper I hadn't seen before across my desk to me. I scanned it and knew what it was. "This is the information on the driver of the car who vandalized the sign at school yesterday?"

"It is. That maroon Mustang belonged to and was driven by none other than Marcus Wellborn. I tracked him down at his folks' house just a few blocks from here. Decent kid. No problems with the law, 'yes sir,' 'no sir.' I asked him why he vandalized the sign. You know what he said?"

I shrugged.

"He said that the new gun law declared open season on kids at school. He said Carmel, Maria and Benjamin would be alive today if Coach Briscoe hadn't been a trigger happy sonuvabitch. 'Sorry, sir,' he said after he called Briscoe that name. By the way, I told the kid I'd keep the spray paint business to myself. 'Thank you, sir.'"

I summarized what we knew so far. "Briscoe's and Wellborn's versions of the events don't jive. Wellborn's is more believable, but Briscoe's is probably good enough to allow him to skate. It never hurts to have a believable disinterested witness, though."

"That's about the size of it. But why is it I feel like you may be holding something back on me, Etch? I thought you'd consider Wellborn your ace in the hole."

Red was right as usual. Exhibit F wasn't in the stack of papers I gave him. I reached into a desk drawer and pulled out a sealed envelope. "I didn't show you the other document Levi left with me."

I handed him the envelope and continued with my explanation. "I held it back because right now, where we are in the investigation, I don't know if we have enough to move forward. If we don't make the case, then Exhibit F need never see the light of day. You know what I mean, Red?"

"I've seen a lot of things I wish I could unsee, Etch. But it doesn't work that way. Once the genie is out of the bottle the world changes forever. I'll just put this envelope in safekeeping until you tell me to open it."

"Thanks, old friend. I may feel different about it tomorrow, but I need to sleep on it first."

"Sure thing."

"There is one other thing, though."

"There's always one other thing."

"The principal's secretary told me Briscoe was on paid leave and was out of state visiting family for a while. I think that's a crock of shit."

"You think he's on the run?"

"Makes sense to me. Why else would the police department still consider the case 'under investigation'? My guess is that they and Slim Atwell will sit on it indefinitely unless someone forces their hand. Maybe the way to do that is to put some heat on Briscoe."

"How about I track him down?" Red said.

"You haven't already done that?"

"I've got a lead or two," Red said as he donned his Stetson.

Chapter Six

I had found that the best way to allow my brain to work out the kinks in a case in my subconscious was to shelve a few dozen James Patterson hardbacks, some Janet Evanovichs, and a few Dave Robicheauxs. If I was really stumped, I'd rearrange the Classics section and sort business books by author instead of title. I had done all that and read a few pages of *Fahrenheit 451*, a poem by Carl Sandburg, and the epilogue of *The Devil in the White City* when it hit me.

Or rather an early case of mine came to mind. I had been appointed on a burglary of a habitation and sat across from the defendant in an attorney-client cubicle in the Gregg County jail. The accused was a serial knucklehead, a habitual screw up. A tall, skinny white guy in his early thirties named Thomas Lee, he had a black afro and eyes out of focus. His rap sheet was three pages long, consisting mostly of disorderly conduct, criminal trespass, shoplifting. He had no convictions for violent crimes and my professional opinion, after thirty seconds of keen observation, was that he was crazier than a bed bug.

I had read the indictment and couldn't make the legalese about burglary of a habitation, a first-degree felony that carried potentially a sentence of life in the pen, fit the man across the K-Mart plastic table from me.

"Tell me what happened, Mr. Lee."

"I hitchhiked from Dallas. My ride dumped me out on the side of I-20 in the middle of the night. It was cold, and I was hungry. I wandered through the woods until I came on a cabin. There were no vehicles parked near it and the lights were off. The front door was unlocked, so I went inside and turned on the lights. The place was empty. I opened the fridge and found some eggs and bacon, went to the stove and cooked them up. I was halfway through breakfast when the law busted in and arrested me."

"That's it?"

"Yes, sir."

"The indictment says you entered with the intent to commit theft. What was it you supposedly stole?"

"I guess it was the eggs and bacon."

I went to my office and prepared a competency motion, a legal maneuver that requires the state to have a psychiatrist examine a defendant to determine if he is competent to stand trial. Nine times out of ten the state-paid shrink finds the poor sumbitch competent. In Mr. Lee's case, the doc's report indicated the defendant was nowhere near competent. With the report in hand, I paid a visit to the assistant DA handling the case.

"Really? Eggs and bacon," I said.

The prosecutor was an old head guy. He knew the county would have to house Thomas Lee until he regained competency, which would probably be sometime in the twenty-third century, if then. "How about we just have a deputy haul him to the county line and point him east?"

And that's what happened. We decided to punt, to kick the ball down the road, to let the next county over, or the next state over, deal with Mr. Lee. He was harmless. And incorrigible. Nothing the system had to offer would change a thing. Thomas Lee was bat shit crazy and about to become someone else's problem.

Why? Because the legal system wasn't built to handle guys like Thomas Lee.

The application of the Lee principle to Coach Briscoe was simple.

The legal system, criminal or civil, was not designed to handle school shootings, especially one where a teacher fires the gun. The longer Jim Briscoe was out of sight the better. Maybe the whole thing would blow over, recede from our collective memories, scab over and only itch a little from time to time.

But school shootings weren't a bad dream, a horror movie. They were the cold hard truth no one cared to face.

Momma L had said all she wanted was to clear Carmel Sideout's name. But her singular request was outside the box in which the courts, schools, and people on the street went about the routines that defined them. It would take a lot more than a short ride to the county line to clear Carmel's name.

I put *The Devil in the White City* back on the shelf and decided to pay a visit to Slim Atwell, the duly elected Criminal District Attorney of Gregg County, Texas.

Chapter Seven

The DA's office was in Longview, about a twenty-minute drive from the bookstore. When I was half-way there, Red called again.

"I know where he is."

"Briscoe?"

"Who else?"

"The suspense is killing me."

Red laid it out for me. Briscoe was on paid leave, so the school had to know where to send his check. Briscoe arranged a wire transfer to a bank in Tulsa. That wire bounced to another bank in Seattle, to another in LA, to another in Chicago, and so forth until it ended up at a Chase Bank branch in Natchitoches, Louisiana.

"Briscoe thinks he's slick. But my IT guy tracked him down in thirty seconds of button punching on his laptop. He says Briscoe is using a debit card on his account that allows us to pinpoint his location," Red said.

"Does he have family in Natchitoches?"

"Not that we can tell so far. He grew up in Phoenix, came to Texas on a football scholarship to Tyler Junior College, transferred to Stephen F. his junior year and got his teaching certificate. He coached in Lufkin three years, Mt. Pleasant for four. Kilgore hired him twenty years ago."

"Your guy got all that scoop on Briscoe in thirty seconds on his laptop?"

"If you throw in accessing his cell phone records and the background check on his family history, it probably bumps the time up to near three minutes."

"He looked at his cell phone records?"

"Didn't I just say that?"

"Any fun calls?"

"He orders a lot a pizza."

"But no contact with friends or family in Louisiana or old cronies in Kilgore?"

"Negatory. Are you ready for me to rouse him?"

I thought about it a minute. "No. If we have his location and can find him when we want, let's focus on the other pieces of the puzzle before we confront him. I'm on my way to see Slim Atwell. I'll update you when I've had a chat with him."

"10-4," Red said as he ended the call.

An apex deposition. That's what Briscoe was in the case. First you learn all the facts you can about the deal, then armed with that information you talk to the head man. You can't pin the guy at the top unless you already know more about his business than he does.

So far, we didn't know nearly enough about Jim Briscoe.

Which reminded me of the other people we knew precious little about: Caddo Panola, Carmel Sideout, Maria Juarez and Benjamin Cohen.

I called Red back.

"Quick meeting, huh?"

"I haven't made it to Slim's office yet."

"What's up?"

I gave him the names of the people we needed to research, and I added one.

"I'd really like to know what happened between Caddo Panola and the mystery man she identified on Carmel Sideout's birth certificate as Hobo Sideout. You think you can dig up anything?"

"Does a wild bear shit in the woods?"

Five minutes later, I parked near the Gregg County courthouse. I went through the metal detector at the front door, rode the elevator to the third floor and presented myself to the receptionist at the DA's office.

"Etch Danielson to see Mr. Atwell," I said to her.

She was in her late fifties, last smiled in the early 1990s. She had controlled access to Slim Atwell for the last eleven years and guarded the DA's office like it was Fort Knox. She wore a Gregg County Sheriff's Office navy jacket, eyeglasses with frames that covered her gray eyebrows, and had a yellow number two pencil stuck behind her left ear. Three portraits of her pug hung on the wall, and she was sipping a caramel macchiato in a Dave Ramsey mug.

"He know you're coming?" she asked.

"I doubt it."

"You need an appointment. He's a busy man."

"Humor me, Alice. Just buzz him and tell him I'm here. Tell him it's about Jim Briscoe. That should clear up a little time on his busy schedule."

"Humph," she breathed.

I'd seen her face change when I mentioned Briscoe. It was one of those other-shoe-dropping moments. She pressed a key on the phone system, stuck the handset next to her ear to muffle the voice on the other end of the line. "Etch is here to see you about Coach Briscoe," she said. She listened a second and placed the handset back on the hook.

"You know the way," she said and turned toward her pug gallery, her back to me.

By the time I got to Atwell's office, his first assistant, Dave Schmerz, sat across from the DA, jawing with him. Neither man stood to greet me. I sat in a matching chair next to Schmerz and waited. They finished their discussion of LeBron James's athletic prowess before they acknowledged my presence.

"You got a beef with Jim Briscoe, Etch?" Slim Atwell asked. He had his sleeves rolled up a couple of turns above the wrist, the knot of his red neck tie loosened, a gray Trump comb over glued tight against his scalp. He took a Marlboro Light cigarette out of a box pack and fidgeted with it between the thumb and middle finger of his right hand.

"What makes you think that, Slim?" I asked.

"Alice said that was why you were here."

"I told her I was here to talk with you about Briscoe. I didn't say I had a beef with him."

"Let's have it then," the DA said. He leaned back in his high-backed chair, crossed his legs and angled himself to face Schmerz not me.

"Logansport Panola came to see me a few days ago. She wants me to help her clear the name of her grandson, Carmel Sideout."

Schmerz insinuated himself into the conversation. He was about thirty-five years old, the current hot-shot felony prosecutor in Atwell's office. He had tried just enough cases to think he knew something. He wore a navy blazer over his pale blue shirt, his collar unbuttoned. "That'll happen right after hell freezes over." He laughed at his remark, but it fell flat.

"Maybe not," I said. "The police say the case is still under investigation. I suspect that could mean several things. Maybe it means the DA's office has no zeal to prosecute Coach Briscoe because no one considers his actions illegal. Maybe it means the evidence doesn't shake out that well for Briscoe and he may have criminal culpability. Maybe it as simple as the fact that Briscoe is in the wind."

"Let's go back to that 'clear his name' part, Etch," Atwell said. "How could anyone do that? A kid pulls a gun in class and a teacher shoots him before he can use the gun against his classmates. What am I missing here? I know good and well you aren't the sort of lawyer who promises more than he can deliver. Momma L is heartbroken. I understand. It's one of those situations where a person's wishful thinking will never become a reality."

"Unless it was a setup," I said.

"By whom?" Schmerz said. "Coach Briscoe? He was just chomping at the bit for a kid to pull a gun, so he could OK Corral him?"

Cute, Schmerz, I thought. Real cute. What an asshole. I decided it was time to break him from sucking eggs.

"Have you read the file, Schmerz?" I asked him.

"Cover to cover," he said, bowing up at me.

"Me, too. This is how I read it. A kid is surprised to discover a toy gun in his back pack. As soon as pulls it out to see what it is, his teacher opens fire, not on him but on two other students. When the dust settles three students are dead and the teacher is a hero. That same teacher has been practicing at the firing range for a month making sure he can hit his targets. He's also the one who doesn't file his right to carry permit until two days after the killings. Does that sound like a joking matter to you, Schmerz?"

Schmerz jumped up and charged me.

"Back off, Dave," Atwell yelled at him before Schmerz could throw a punch. "Get yourself under control."

Schmerz walked to the corner of the room, never taking his eyes off me. He shook his shoulders so that the wrinkles in his jacket caused by his outburst smoothed.

"Everybody settle down," Atwell said. He sat up straight and faced me now. He dropped his cigarette on the desk and opened a file folder, studied it a second while he gathered he thoughts. "You're right, Etch. Nothing in this deal is funny. I don't like it any more than you do that three kids are dead on my watch. But Dave, in his less than artful way, has made the case for Briscoe. Everyone's initial reaction is that he did what he had to do."

I sensed that the DA had thought through the case and considered more than knee jerk reactions. It was not what I had expected from a career politician like him, one who knew where his bread was buttered.

"Sometimes people change their opinions when confronted by the facts," I said.

"Yeah, but only if the facts are virtually indisputable," Atwell said. "This case is about what was going through Jim Briscoe's head when he was confronted with a sudden emergency. Even an expert marksman can produce collateral damage if he has a split second in which to act. I don't believe we can fault him for being off target. If he is culpable, it's because he already had a plan in mind before Carmel Sideout pulled the gun out of his backpack, before Briscoe fired the first shot. And, like I said, the only way to prove his state of mind is to get in his head. Since he doesn't have to testify, I don't know how you prove what he was thinking."

I took the bait. "You prove it just like you do in every other case. You stack up the facts which demonstrate his state of mind, and you let a jury decide. It's like a case where a guy murders his wife. If he took out a million-dollar life insurance policy on her a month before she dies, a jury may believe he killed her, even if he takes the stand and denies it."

"I understand, Etch. But the amount of proof necessary to swing a jury in Briscoe's case is massive. If there's any wiggle room, if there is a likely scenario other than premeditated murder, a jury will take that way out. People in this county won't vote against the guy who coached their kids in football on a dare."

"You're talking politics now, Slim. That's not a prosecutor's job. Just like it's not his job to carry the AGA's water, or to protect a school district if it's in the wrong." I knew I was bringing the five-hundred-pound gorilla out in the open. But, what the hell.

Again, Atwell surprised me. "The AGA will be in this case, one way or another. The school district knows it was technically in the wrong because it didn't have Briscoe's permit on file. I see that as nothing but a ministerial matter, that it would be unlikely for a court to stick it to the district on a glitch like that. I have to consider how the deal would play out before I make a move. That's not politics. It's me bringing thirty years of experience to the table."

"Damn straight," Schmerz mumbled from his corner.

I had to admit I agreed with Slim. Atwell was in a tough spot, and, to his credit, he had analyzed the case and saw that Jim Briscoe might be in deep shit.

"So, what does 'under investigation' mean? Are you planning to indict Coach Briscoe, or are you waiting for the whole deal to blow over?"

"It means we are still investigating the matter. I haven't made a decision yet," the DA said. He paused before he continued. "Etch, do you remember the Martha Higgins case?"

I searched my memory banks until I uncovered a distant recollection. "That was a long time ago, Slim. But, I remember her."

"Why don't you think about that case for a day or two. Maybe we can talk again after that."

Schmerz looked at both of us like he had no clue.

Atwell stood and shook my hand. "Today's Wednesday. How about you drop by to see me Monday afternoon? I'll have Alice slot you in at two-thirty."

"Deal," I said. I walked over to Schmerz, and he leaned away from me when I got close to him. I extended my hand. "No hard feelings, Dave."

The young prick shook my hand.

But he didn't make eye contact.

Chapter Eight

As I had promised, on my way back to the office I called Red to brief him on the details of my meeting with Slim Atwell. He answered on the first ring.

"How was Slim Pickens?" he asked.

"It was not what I expected." I filled him in on the conversation and mentioned my sparring match with Dave Schmerz.

"Don't be too hard on Dave," he said. "He's a young lion with an attitude, but he comes from good stock."

"How so?"

"I knew his dad, James Schmerz. We worked some cases together when he was fresh out of state trooper training. He was a rising star, a straight shooter. At least until a meth head smoked him on the side of Highway 59 a few miles south of Lufkin. He'd stopped the asshole on suspicion of DWI, and James didn't see it coming. The guy had a snub-nosed .38 tucked inside his jacket, and he pulled down on James the second Schmerz approached the driver's window. He left a twenty-eight-year-old widow and a two-year old son. That was Dave. He's grown up with a chip on his shoulder for the bad guys. He gets a little carried away sometimes, but his heart's in the right place."

"You just never know, do you?"

"Never," was all Red said.

"Slim mentioned an old case to me and said he wanted me to review it and get back with him next week. I think he has something up his sleeve."

"What's the old case?"

"It involved a woman named Martha Higgins. I've got the file somewhere in storage. I have a vague recollection of it, but I need to refresh the details."

"Keep me posted, brother." Red signed off.

I had fibbed to Red about the Martha Higgins case, but I knew he wouldn't mind. He understood it was my way of letting him know I wasn't ready to talk about it yet.

I remembered the case well.

Some thirty-odd years before, I had served a hitch as an assistant DA before I left the DA's office to hang out my shingle. Slim and I had overlapped in the DA's office for a year or so, but he stayed put, choosing the path of a career prosecutor. We tried a few cases against each other when I was handling criminal appointments. He called me one day and said his boss, the DA, wanted to see me about a matter.

That matter was Martha Higgins.

Martha was the legal secretary for Evans VanMeter, an old time, establishment lawyer. VanMeter was in his eighties, and was the undisputed, universally accepted dean of lawyers in East Texas. He was a slight man, not more than five-feet-six-inches, one hundred and thirty pounds. He was a natty dresser, always buttoned down, wore a Sam Spade fedora to cover the thin gray fuzz on his balding head. His voice was soft and gentle, and I thought it impossible to imagine he ever told a lie. A scholar of the law, he had written the standard textbook on civil procedure used in every law school in Texas.

Martha Higgins, a grandmotherly figure, had worked for him for over forty years. VanMeter was a solo practitioner, and Martha handled the day to day affairs of the office. She answered the phone, set appointments, paid the bills.

And, she had full access to VanMeter's check book.

Therein lay the problem the DA wanted to discuss with me.

At my appointed time, I went to the DA's office and Slim met me at the front and escorted me to my audience with Scofield Morgan, the DA. Morgan had logged more than fifty years of trial practice by then. He reminded me of the granite cornerstone of the courthouse building, hard, square, unflinching, weathered. He shook my hand with the grip of a vise, his jaw set even when he said hello. Slim stood in the corner where Dave Schmerz would retreat so many years later.

"I'll get right to it, Mr. Danielson," Morgan said before I had even settled into my chair across from him. He told me about the 'predicament,' as he put it, Evans VanMeter faced. "The state bar has received a complaint against Evans because of what his secretary, Mrs. Higgins, has done."

"What's she done, Mr. Morgan?"

"She's embezzled a lot of money, son. Over forty thousand dollars. To make matters worse she took the funds out of VanMeter's trust account, not his operating account."

I knew that was bad, real bad. Lawyers are required to keep a trust account where they deposit money that belongs to their clients. For instance, if a case settled and the funds arrived, the money remained in the trust account until the attorney disbursed the client's share to him. It was only after the client received his money that the attorney could pay himself out of the remaining funds. The first thing a law student learned was that the surest way an attorney could lose his license to practice law was to play fast and loose with trust account funds. If he was caught with his hand in the till, it was don't pass go, go straight to jail. The state bar had zero tolerance with trust account issues, even if a lawyer like Evans VanMeter was the one who screwed up.

"Evans has already made full restitution to the client whose money was purloined," the DA said. "But the client is a stickler for the law, hence the complaint."

To this day I've never heard anyone else say 'purloined.'

Morgan continued. "Once the state bar receives a complaint about misuse of client funds, it can't sweep it under the rug. It has to have its pound of flesh. Evans has been in negotiations with the bar association lawyers. They say they will not suspend his license if we prosecute Martha for theft."

"The pound of flesh is Martha's not VanMeter's," I said.

Scofield Morgan bristled at my remark. "It's a victimless crime, and Evans has already made the client whole. He isn't in favor of Martha taking the fall."

"But he's less in favor of taking it himself." I was stating the obvious.

"If that's the way you want to put it, Mr. Danielson."

"So, what is it you want from me, Mr. Morgan. I don't see where I have a dog in the fight."

"I've known Evans for half a century. I count him one of my best friends. I have often dined with him and Martha Higgins. Each of the district judges in this courthouse shares the same sort of relationship with Evans as I."

The good ol' boy system, I thought. But I kept that observation to myself this time.

"I suppose you plan to recuse yourself," I said, finally understanding my role. If the DA disqualified himself from prosecuting VanMeter, a special prosecutor would be appointed to handle it.

"I plan to recuse myself as do all the district judges. That means we need a special prosecutor who will take over the case and handle it in front of a visiting judge. If you want the job, I am prepared to recommend you for it," Morgan said.

"Is the deal already cut with Martha Higgins?" I asked.

"No. The disposition of the case would be strictly up to you. You could offer her whatever deal you think best, take the case to trial to make a point of it, or dismiss it."

"If I dismiss it will the state bar consider that its pound of flesh?"

"You'd have to discuss that with the attorneys for the bar association. They are waiting to hear how we propose to dispose of the case."

His reply told me that he had already made a run at the state bar lawyers, probably told them he didn't think the case deserved his office's time considering VanMeter's payment of restitution in full. My guess was that the state bar lawyers had told him that dismissing the case wasn't an option. Either Martha faded the heat, or VanMeter lost his license.

Morgan wanted me to handle his dirty work for him.

"What the hell," I said. He stood and shook my hand again.

Three weeks later Martha Higgins entered a guilty plea to third-degree felony theft in front of a visiting judge. He sentenced her to five years deferred adjudication probation, which meant if she kept her nose clean for five years, the charge would be thrown out and she would never be convicted of a crime.

At the hearing Evans VanMeter sat at the back of the courtroom crying.

I knew why Slim Atwell wanted to meet with me.

Chapter Nine

By Friday word was all over town that I was looking into the shooting, and curiosity seekers were at the door of the bookstore. Some came in and hung out hoping to overhear a few words about my investigation, others approached me directly. I played dumb for the most part, deflecting their questions with remarks like, "I'm just trying to get some answers," or "We're all in this together," or "Time will tell." Those who wouldn't accept my initial response received the one designed to shut them down: "I really can't talk about the details. It's an attorney-client privilege thing."

The irony of the Paparazzi bit was I soon realized it was a two-way street. As people sat around and drank coffee, browsed the bookshelves, wandered around the store, they talked about what they had heard about the shooting. They dropped tidbits about the victims, school personnel and Coach Jim Briscoe. Most of it I knew was only gossip, fake news. But every now and then I picked up a nugget.

For instance, I eavesdropped on a group of thirty-something women sharing old stories of flirtations that went both ways with Briscoe. They all giggled when one of them came out with, "He was such a hunk back then," and another added, "Still is."

Likewise, there were conversations about the victims, many of which made reference to Carmel and Maria's blossoming romance. Others spoke of Benjamin Cohen and his way with words, his plans to study creative writing and his hopes to go to LA and make it as a screenwriter.

I was harvesting what I could from the crowd, when a fortyish woman walked in. She was tall and slender, a natural blonde. Despite her designer clothes, she wore no makeup and covered her eyes with dark sunglasses. She wandered to the coffee bar, ordered her drink, left a nice tip for my daughter. Eventually she climbed the stairs. I could hear her footfalls on the hardwood floors and could tell she had found a quiet spot in a corner room where May Ellen conducted a water color class on Tuesdays.

"Wasn't that Patty Douglas?" I heard a woman say to her friend.

"I believe so," her friend replied.

I recognized the two women as occasional customers and went over to them. "I heard you mention the name Patty Douglas like I should know who she is. But the name doesn't ring a bell."

"She's Maria Juarez's mother. Poor soul," one of them said.

"Bless her heart," I said to them and excused myself from their conversation.

I considered going upstairs to speak with Patty Douglas but decided not to intrude. A few moments later, I heard other footsteps from the second floor and then the hushed sound of two people talking. I could make out just enough to know May Ellen had happened upon our guest. I thought I heard the muffled sound of crying interspersed between their words. And I knew May Ellen's soft heart would serve as the best salve for Patty Douglas's wounded heart.

Fifteen minutes or so later while I was discussing mindfulness with one of our Buddhist customers in the front room, May Ellen interrupted us.

"Can I have a second, Etch?"

The Buddhist offered a slight bow to me and shuffled off to the coffee shop.

"Patty is Maria Juarez's mother," May Ellen whispered.

"I heard."

"She's a basket case, Etch. But she said she had a couple of things she wanted you to know. She started to tell them to me, but I suggested she give you the information to keep it confidential." May Ellen understood the sanctity of privileged communications between a lawyer and client. Even though no attorney-client relationship existed between Patty Douglas and me, I appreciated what she was doing, going above and beyond for a grieving mother. I gave her a hug.

"I'll talk to her," I said and headed upstairs.

Patty Douglas was still alone in the small corner room. She looked up when I came in, and I shut the door to ensure we had privacy.

"I'm Etch Danielson, Ms. Douglas. I'm sorry for your loss."

She had removed her sunglasses, and she wiped her eyes with a worn tissue.

"Thank you, Mr. Danielson. Your wife was a great comfort to me."

"She's that kind of girl."

Ms. Douglas's face brightened just a little at my remark.

"I could tell that about her," she said.

"May Ellen told me you had a couple of things you wanted to share with me."

She blew her nose before she spoke. "Maria was head over heels in love with Carmel Sideout. He felt the same way about her. I could see it in their eyes, the way they held hands, the way he did little things for her, brought her cheap flowers because it was all he could afford. They were making plans for a life together."

"How did you feel about that, Ms. Douglas?"

"I thought they were too young, but that's the way love is. Right?"

"It can be right, Ms. Douglas. The world is full of people who were childhood sweethearts and lived long full lives together."

"That's what I thought lay ahead for them." She fought back her tears.

"I know a few things about Carmel from his grandmother, but I don't know much about Maria. Please tell me about your daughter, Ms. Douglas."

"She was a helper, the kind of girl who took in stray dogs and cats. She always wanted to be a nurse, and I told her to go for the whole thing, to keep her grades up so she could enter medical school after she got her nursing degree. That's what she had decided to do, and Carmel was all for it. He wanted to teach English literature."

"I heard that Maria, Carmel and Benjamin had plans to room together at college."

"They were talking about it. I think Benjamin was afraid he might be a third wheel, but Maria and Carmel didn't see it like that. They were so looking forward to being the three musketeers, to venturing out into the world together."

I felt she was giving me the rosy part of the picture first, waiting to fill in the shadows. I gave her an opening. "How did Maria's father feel about her plans? I assume since your last name is now Douglas that you are no longer married to him."

"That's right. He and I divorced when Maria was seven. I remarried three years ago, but Raul, Mr. Juarez, has remained single. He lives in Houston and has been an absent father to Maria most of her life. Maria took Carmel to meet him about three months ago, though."

"How'd that go?"

"She was tight-lipped about it. I took that to mean that her dad and Carmel didn't hit it off."

"Any idea why?"

"Are you asking me if Maria told me about it, or if I have my own opinion?"

"Which ever one you care to share with me."

"Maria had little to say about their trip to see her dad. Frankly, I thought Raul probably didn't like Carmel because he was Black. I know that's a terrible thing to say, but I lived with Raul for a long time and knew how he felt about such things."

I took that as an invitation to ask her a hard question. "Did it bother you that Carmel was Black?"

She didn't flinch. "Honestly, I could have cared less. What mattered to me was that Carmel was the kind of man who would treat Maria right. From what I knew of Carmel, he was devoted to her and would have done anything to make her happy. That's all a mom could ask for in her daughter's partner. Isn't it?"

I still didn't believe I had gotten to the core of what brought Patty Douglas to see me. I probed one more time. "Ms. Douglas did anything you saw or heard between Carmel, Maria and Benjamin make you suspicious that Carmel might do something violent, something like what happened at school a month ago?"

She paused, a split-second delay, that told me more than her words.

"I never heard anything that hinted of violence. But, in the weeks before the shooting they kept more to themselves than usual. It was like they were harboring a secret. As I look back on it, I wonder if they had formed a pact between them." Her eyes glazed, as if her mind was reliving her last months with Maria, searching for clues she had missed.

"What kind of pact, Ms. Douglas?"

"At the time, I made myself believe they were just consumed with their planning and scheming about the days ahead. What school to attend, how to set up housekeeping, how to realize their dreams and build their careers. Now I think there was much more to it."

"What was the 'much more'?"

"I tell myself I am crazy to think it."

"Crazy to think what?"

She raised her head so she could see out the second-floor window and watched the cars that passed on the side street next to the store, ticking them off one by one. Her gaze settled on a cardinal on the branch of an oak tree, and she waited for it to fly. Before she answered my question, she shut her eyes.

"I wonder now if maybe they were working on an exit strategy."

After Patty Douglas left, I retreated to my office, made notes about our conversation, stuck them in a file folder and added it to the case file. All the while, my thoughts were elsewhere, as hers had been at the end of our meeting. The one thing about which I was certain, however, was that Ms. Douglas had never seen what I had seen.

She had never seen Exhibit F.

For if she knew about it, she would have told me. And if she had seen it, she would have confronted Maria, and Carmel, and Benjamin.

And she might have saved their lives.

Chapter Ten

Off a rutted red clay road, sequestered in a half-acre clearing amid loblolly pines, a white frame building fought a relentless battle against human despair and provided respite for its parishioners. Three whitewashed two by eights formed the front steps of the sanctuary. A makeshift steeple sat atop the ridge of the steep-sloped roof, a beacon to ships navigating the rocks, for mariners on their last short journey to home port.

The structure had remained the same as long as I could remember. I made it at least eighty years old. Never had I seen it without a fresh coat of white paint, never a weed in the church yard, never a misplaced obscenity uttered within earshot of the tall windows, raised during worship services as a sign of welcome to the inhabitants of a harsh world. It was a house built on a rock as Jesus said so long ago.

About ten minutes after one o'clock Sunday afternoon, I parked my forest green Ford F150 in the shade on the side of the road across from the Peavine Church of God in Christ and waited. By my count, thirteen vehicles populated the parking lot. A few minutes after I arrived, the front door opened, and supplicants filed outside, a shimmer of holy ecstasy still on them. They smiled the good humor of deep understanding, of years spent together, of common joys and sorrows, of close family ties, of extended community which cared not how much money a person had in the bank or hidden in the back yard.

The last person out the door closed it tight, left it unlocked, a sign to me that she believed the building and its contents belonged to God, not to the inhabitants of this world.

I stepped out of my truck and waved to her. She saw me, walked over and shook my hand.

"You got a minute to talk, Momma L?" Beads of sweat were half-dried on her forehead, the last vestiges of the vigor of the sermon she had delivered to her flock.

"Sure, Etch."

"Let's sit in my truck and enjoy the air conditioning." It was mid-June, already near a hundred degrees.

"I'm down for that."

When we settled into the cabin of my half-ton Ford, I brought her up to speed on the status of the investigation into the shooting. But the purpose of my meeting with her stretched beyond a review of the facts developed thus far. I needed answers.

"So, your investigation has confirmed that the gun wasn't real?" Momma L asked after she had processed the information I gave her.

"Yes, ma'am. But that doesn't mean Coach Briscoe overreacted. If he had sufficient certainty that Carmel was about to open fire, he was justified in using deadly force."

She nodded. "I understand, Etch. But it still doesn't make sense that Carmel had a gun in his backpack. He would never have done such a thing."

"That brings me to the heart of what I need to talk with you about today."

"I'm listening."

"The most reliable witness is Marcus Wellborn. He confirms Carmel had the gun, even though he said he thought Carmel was surprised to find it in his backpack that day. The question I haven't been able to answer so far is why the gun was there." I paused a second and considered how to handle my next move. "Momma L, there is an old saying among trial lawyers that every mother has a constitutional right to take the stand and lie for her son." I let the remark soak in. "Is there something you haven't told me? Now is not the time to hold things back. If I hope to move forward, to try to do what you want and clear Carmel's name, I must know everything, the bad with the good."

"I ain't lied to you, Etch." She crossed her arms, looked out the passenger window.

"I know you haven't. At least not on purpose."

"What do you mean by that?"

"Sometimes the most important evidence is what people leave out when they tell their stories. What they think is unimportant may turn out to be the key fact to cracking a case wide open. It's what I don't know yet about Carmel that puzzles me. I have heard at least two accounts that lead me to believe Carmel, Maria and Benjamin were plotting more than their college plans."

"What two people told you something like that? Folks who held grudges against those kids?"

"Patty Douglas and Levi Cohen."

The names hit her hard, threw her off balance.

"Oh my," she said. "Lord have mercy. What did they say?"

"Patty said that looking back on it she thought maybe the kids were planning a big exit. Levi told me to investigate the relationships between the three of them. He said he wished he had done so before it was too late. It's because of my conversations with Patty and Levi that I want you to dig deep. Did you see any tell-tale signs that the kids were up to something, signs that everything wasn't rosy, dark things?"

"Kids that age are always dark one day, bright the next. It comes with the territory. But if you know them, really know what makes them tick, you understand what is real and what is just a passing mood. I knew them, and all three of them had good hearts." She stopped for a minute before she continued. "I will never criticize Patty and Levi. I suppose they are doing just what I've done a thousand times since that day. They feel like they are somehow to blame, like they did something wrong, or didn't pick up on the signs, or should have been better parents. None of that means the kids were up to no good. I just don't buy it."

I knew Momma L was talking straight from her heart. "Let me ask the question another way, the way Coach Briscoe's lawyer will put it to you if we ever sit in a courtroom and try the case. He'll go at it like this: 'Ms. Panola, did Carmel ever play violent video games?'"

"Yes, sir, he did. Just like every other kid in the school." She was under oath.

We acted out the scene. "Did you ever talk to him about the connection between such games and actual violence?"

"Don't believe there is one," she said. "Just like I don't believe John Wayne ever turned anybody into a gunfighter."

Pity the poor guy who had to cross examine Logansport Panola, I thought. I ended mock court.

She was still in her role. "Any other questions about my son, counselor?"

I held up my hand, palm towards her. "I get it, Momma L. You are convinced your grandson is blameless. But you haven't answered the question. Why did he bring a gun to school?"

She was back to herself, not acting out a part. "I've thought about it and thought about it. There's only one explanation that makes sense. You'll think I'm crazy."

"Try me."

"He didn't bring a gun to school. It was a plant."

She was right. I thought she had lost her mind.

"You think someone put the gun in his backpack without Carmel knowing it?"

"Your best witness testified that Carmel was surprised to discover it," she said. "How else could that happen? Carmel wouldn't have been surprised to find his own gun, if he had knowingly brought it to school."

Sometimes it's hard to see simple answers, as obvious as they may be. At that moment, I knew the truth was one of two possibilities. Either Carmel Sideout planned an attack on his classmates, or he was set up. Under the first scenario it was shame on him, he got what he had coming. But if the shooting was a setup, Carmel and his friends had died in vain and someone else, or several other people, had conspired to commit murder. And those perpetrators were standing in the shadows laughing at their victims and those who loved them and the rest of us who had taken the bait.

"Momma L, you may indeed be crazy, or you may have solved the puzzle."

I saw hope enter her eyes.

"Let's think about it together for a minute. If Carmel had a gun in his backpack when he arrived at school that morning, how could he have smuggled it through security?"

"The kids have to open their backpacks for inspection when they pass through the main entrance. There's a full-time officer who supervises that process."

"So, if the officer is doing his job, he would discover any contraband a student had. That would include weapons and drugs, right?"

"Yes, sir. And even stuff like porn."

"Which means to get a gun on campus a student would have to make an end run around the checkpoint."

She stopped me. "I just remembered something else about the day of the shooting, Etch. Carmel and the other art club members had a field trip first thing on the day of the shooting. They'd been to the art museum in Longview. The museum has tight security, including a metal detector."

I'd been to that museum and remembered feeling like I'd been stripped searched when May Ellen and I had gone to an impressionism exhibit.

"Did Carmel take his backpack with him on the field trip?"

"I don't know for sure, but he took it everywhere."

"That gun might not have set off a metal detector, I'll have to check that out. But the staff at the museum would visually have checked the contents of his bag. If we assume he passed the shakedown at the museum, then it makes sense he didn't have the gun with him then. Was there a way he could have grabbed the gun when he got back to school and before he went to Coach Briscoe's class?"

"I wouldn't think so. The school transported the kids to the field trip on a bus, and they came straight back after the museum visit. They hadn't been on campus but about a half hour when the shooting broke out."

I tried to put the pieces together. "Somehow the gun got in his backpack during that thirty-minute window."

"That would have been the only time it could have happened," Momma L agreed.

"All right. I will need to sort through the scenarios. But there's one more thing I have to discuss with you."

She waited for me to drop a bomb.

"Slim Atwell asked me to come see him tomorrow."

"I know. I talk to him a couple of times a week, and he told me about your visit and the follow up appointment."

I should have known she was wearing out Slim's phone, working all the angles. "I have an idea of what he wants me to do. It probably involves criminal charges arising from the shooting. I don't know the details yet, but I'll let you know as soon as I do."

"Fair enough, Etch. I trust you on that."

As I drove away from the Peavine Church of God in Christ, my hope was that Momma L's trust was not unfounded.

Chapter Eleven

I went to Red's house and found him sitting on the front porch. He had a copy of *The Art of War* in his left hand and was scratching his Chesapeake Bay retriever Hank behind the ears with his right. The old dog barked a warning at me before he settled back into bliss.

I walked up the steps and sat down across from Red.

"A penny for your thoughts," the lawman said.

I brought him up to speed on my conversation with Momma L. When I mentioned the possibility that Carmel had been set up, he thought about it a while before he responded.

"If it wasn't for the Wellborn boy's statement, I'd say you were out of your mind."

"And I would agree with you."

He worked through the steps aloud. "I've spent considerable time on the high school campus. From a security perspective it's Swiss cheese. There are unguarded entrances everywhere. Students must enter through the checkpoint, but most everyone else comes and goes unhindered. There are back and side doors galore."

I nodded as he mapped it out for me.

"If Carmel didn't have the gun on him when he got back from the field trip, then someone had to plant it without him knowing about it, and they had a short window of opportunity."

"My guess is that the kids went to the cafeteria first thing when they returned. Carmel probably would have taken a potty break, too."

"He stored his backpack in his locker before he ate and went to the John?"

"Probably fits the time line."

"The lockers at the high school have combination locks on them."

"That's right. But I bet students share those combinations with their buddies."

"And their sweethearts," Red added.

Red's remark jogged my memory of my chance encounter with Mr. Poteet, the school janitor. "You can also use a master key to open those locks."

"The school conducts random searches. It keeps the kids on their toes."

"Makes you wonder how many people have access to a set of master keys, doesn't it?"

"It sure does," Red said. He patted the old dog's head, and the retriever laid down on his back so Red could scratch his tummy with the heel of his boot.

I stood up to leave. "Remember the sealed envelope I gave you?"

"Exhibit F?"

I nodded. "I believe it's time you opened it."

"I'll get right on it, counselor."

"Call me when you've had a chance to digest it."

I bent down to pet Hank, and the Chessie snapped at me.

"It's old age," Red said. "Makes him a little out of sorts."

"I know the feeling," I said.

Chapter Twelve

Every big case I have handled becomes an obsession. It's a necessary evil because such cases consist of hundreds of questions the answers to which range from obvious to speculative to opaque to just plain unknowable. The unknowable ones are the most fertile because if no one will ever know the actual answer, the reason something happened the way it did, then I am free to offer my own explanation, knowing the person on the other side of the case cannot refute it. He may suggest his own solution to the conundrum, but his answer is no more certain than mine. Juries love open questions, especially when they go to the heart of a case, particularly if the stakes are high. They love them because they want the attorneys to help them solve the puzzle. And the best way to aid them is to tell a better story than the one opposing counsel concocts.

The Kilgore school shooting was a case riddled with unknowable questions. I knew that at the end of the day, regardless of what happened in a court of law, we would never plumb the depths of its tragedies. At best, I could peel a layer or two off its hard coating of despair, maybe arrive at a point where some shred of justice, a shard of decency appeared in the wreckage. Maybe.

I had learned that the best way to embrace the obsession was to ignore it for a little while, to go about the ordinary affairs of life while it churned in the back of my brain.

So, it was that May Ellen and I spent the rest of Sunday afternoon and evening knocking around antique stores in the nearby town of Gladewater and dining at our favorite Thai restaurant in Longview.

We binged on a few episodes of *Bosch* on Amazon Prime before we hit the hay.

By three o'clock in the morning, I was at it again at my desk at home, juggling the facts, wondering what I didn't know about Carmel Sideout and Coach Jim Briscoe.

At 4:33 a.m., my cell vibrated when Red called.

"I read it," he said.

I knew he was referring to Exhibit F.

"Either we find a way to answer it, or we're toast," he said.

"I know," I said. But Red had already ended the call.

Monday afternoon at the appointed time, I stood in front of Alice again at the DA's office. She ignored me for seven minutes. Finally, without looking up from the papers on her desk, she moved her head a fraction of an inch toward the hall that led to Slim Atwell's office. I took that as permission to pass by her.

This time Dave Schmerz was nowhere to be found, and when I entered Slim's office he was standing next to the window, smoking a Marlboro Light.

"Close the door," he said. He leaned closer to the window to get a better view of something happening on the street three floors below.

I sat down across from him.

"Did you review the Martha Higgins file?" He hadn't looked at me yet.

"Didn't need to. I remember it."

He turned away from the window, walked to his desk and took his seat. "I knew you did."

"I figured you might prefer to have this discussion in private."

"You were right about that." He crushed the hot end of his cigarette into an ashtray full of butts, tapped his middle finger a few times on his desk before he plunged into the conversation. "This case is everything a prosecutor hates, Etch. A terrible killing of innocent kids, grieving parents, terrified students and teachers, a defendant who's apparently a pillar of the community, local politics involving a school district, national politics about one of the most controversial and thorny issues of our day."

"I know, Slim."

"My job as criminal district attorney is to seek justice, not revenge. But justice is one slippery son of a bitch."

"Always has been, Slim. I've come to believe that justice is nothing more, nor less, than whatever a jury says it is. You lay the facts out as best you can, and you take your chances, and you live with the results. It's all we can do, and all we've ever done. The hard part of your job, as I see it, is deciding whether to play the game at all, whether to file a case, or let it die a slow death on its own."

"Which brings us to a Martha Higgins decision, doesn't it?" He opened a file folder and flipped through a few pages while he waited for me to respond.

"I think I understand where you're going with this, Slim. But you need to come out with it. What do you want me to do?"

"I want you to take over the case as special prosecutor. The local judges and I will step aside, you will be in charge and you will handle it in front of a visiting judge."

"That's what I thought. My question is what case you are talking about?"

"The State of Texas versus Jim Briscoe," he said. "Capital murder."

I didn't blink, but I swallowed hard. "Hold on, Slim. Last week you were throwing rocks at me for even thinking I could make a case, any case, against a popular coach people consider a hero. Now, you are telling me I should lead the charge and indict him for capital murder. To use a line we've both pulled out of the bag on cross-examination, 'Were you lying then, or are you lying now?'"

Atwell laughed under his breath. "I prefer to think of it as misdirection, not prevarication."

"Can you give me that in English?"

"I've been looking at this case since day one of the shootings. With each new thing I learn about it, I believe there is more to it than meets the eye. Briscoe is not in the wind, I know how to reach him if necessary. But he has made himself scarce, and his statements are self-serving, evolving over time as if someone is prepping him for prime time. Before long, if we don't stop him, he'll be wearing a Superman outfit."

I still wasn't buying it.

"If that's the way you feel about it, why aren't you taking the lead? Why pawn it off on me?"

"Do you think Momma L came to you by accident, Etch?"

"What do you mean?"

"I sent her to you. I did that because you're not like me."

"How so, Slim?"

"You're still a true believer. I've sat in this chair so long that I've lost my inner fire for justice. It's just another day at the office for me."

"That's bullshit. You know the score, Slim. To me it sounds more like this one's a messy battle you'd just as soon avoid. If you drop it in my lap it's a win-win for you. If I fall flat, it's on me not you. If I prevail, you shake my hand and slap me on the back."

"It might work out that way all right."

I had to get to the bottom of Slim's move, had to know why he wanted to play the deal this way. "Capital murder is a last resort charge. It's reserved for the worst of the worst. Even if I could prove Briscoe intentionally killed Carmel, I don't see a jury ever giving him the needle. Unless, of course, you know something I don't."

Atwell got up and walked to a conference table on the far side of his office. He motioned for me to join him. He slapped the top of a banker's box. "It's all in here. At least all I know so far."

I took the lid off the box and checked the contents. The files were tabbed like mine, well organized. One marked Levi Cohen caught my eye. I pulled it out and examined the notes inside, handwritten, I assumed, by Slim Atwell. The last document in the file was the one I wondered if Slim had seen. It was the one I had labeled Exhibit F.

"Have you read this document, Slim?"

"Levi Cohen gave it to me personally."

"Me, too," I said. "You've seen this, and you still think a jury could find Briscoe guilty of capital murder?"

"If it was easy, anybody could do it, Etch." He patted me on the shoulder, put the lid back on the box. "Are you in or out?"

I shook his hand, loaded the box under my arm and walked out of his office. On my way out, I stopped at Alice's desk and waited for her to acknowledge my presence. She cut her eyes at me. "You might want to check with Slim to make sure I'm right, but I think for the next few months I'm your boss, Alice. Can I get an amen?"

Her face turned a pale shade of green, like she'd eaten a bad oyster, or a vending machine egg salad sandwich..

Chapter Thirteen

Exhibit F, a draft of a one-act play by Benjamin Cohen, lay on my desk. It was dated eight weeks before the shooting which took his life and the lives of his two closest friends.

A Bad Day at School
By
Benjamin Cohen

(BENJAMIN, MARIA and CARMEL huddle outside the classroom door just before the last class of the afternoon is to begin.)

BENJAMIN

Is everything in order?

(MARIA and CARMEL nod at him)

BENJAMIN (Continued)

Let's roll.

(They enter the classroom and take their seats near each other.)

TEACHER

Please turn to page 117, the section about school shootings, how to prevent them and the protocol to follow if an active shooter is on campus.

(Students flip through their books to find the section.)

TEACHER (Continued)

Benjamin, what's the best way to avoid school shootings?

BENJAMIN

According to the book the best way is to keep a watchful eye on our classmates, be aware if we see erratic behavior, and report it to school officials if we do.

TEACHER

(He addresses BENJAMIN.)

Do you agree with that?

(MARIA raises her hand to interrupt.)

TEACHER

(He calls on MARIA.)

MARIA

It's not that simple. Students may have a lot of reasons to strike out at people. They may keep those reasons packed tight in their hearts, so no one really knows how they feel. How could we ever know something bad is about to happen? We can't read their minds.

TEACHER

Maybe not, Maria. But you spend a lot of time with your classmates. Here we are near the end of the school year and you've been with them for months. Don't you think you'd have some indication if one of them was about to explode?

(CARMEL picks his backpack up off the floor and rests it in his lap. He raises his hand for the TEACHER to call on him.)

TEACHER

Carmel, do you have something you want to add to the discussion?

CARMEL

Yes, sir. It wouldn't surprise me if some of the students in this class thought I was crazy.

(The classroom erupts in laughter.)

CARMEL (Continues)

See what I mean?

TEACHER

Point taken, Carmel. But they might be right about that.

(The students laugh again.)

CARMEL

Maybe so.

(CARMEL reaches into his backpack and pulls out a pistol.)

But they aren't laughing now.

(CARMEL stands and shoots the TEACHER first, then opens fire on his classmates. Before his gun is empty, he turns it on himself and pulls the trigger.)

THE END

My God. What were those kids thinking? I put the draft of the play back into its folder and sat at my desk for a long time, my head in my hands.

Then it hit me.

They weren't bringing the play to life on the day of the shooting. If they had been doing that, Carmel would have brought a real gun to school, not a plastic BB gun. And if the school shooting was Benjamin Cohen's play made flesh, Carmel wouldn't have been surprised to find the gun. No, the play meant something else, the exact opposite of my initial reaction to it.

I thought about Gerry Spence and his defense of Imelda Marcos. She had been widely ridiculed because while many people she governed lived in squalor, she amassed over a thousand pairs of shoes. It was a terrible fact for the defense. But Spence turned it on its head. His investigation uncovered a well-known Philippine tradition. In the Philippines, if a person wished to show love and respect for someone, he gave them a pair of shoes. Those thousand shoes Imelda had in her closet were the sign of how much her citizens loved her, not a sign of her greed.

Benjamin Cohen's one-act play wasn't the smoking gun of premeditation. It was his heartfelt call for America to wake up, to put aside its old ways of thinking about school violence and its causes and to search for the hard answers that lay deep below the surface. His play was the purity of youth, tempered with a desire for action.

Chapter Fourteen

I called Red. First, I brought him up to speed on my meeting with Slim Atwell.

"Sounds like he wants you to fade all the heat," Red said.

"I had the same reaction. But he led me to believe that the facts he has developed, or that he believes we can develop, will ultimately justify a charge of capital murder against Briscoe."

"Does anything in the box he gave you make that case?"

"I haven't plowed all the way through it, yet. My guess is that it contains some tidbits we haven't seen and some clues for us to flesh out before we see the whole picture."

"So now we will be the ones answering all the questions with 'still under investigation.'"

"For a while at least."

Next, I shared my epiphany about Exhibit F.

"There's one big problem," Red said.

"Let's have it."

"Even if the gun was a plant, it doesn't matter."

"I thought we'd already worked through that analysis and come to the opposite conclusion."

"Yeah. But I've given it more thought."

"OK. What am I missing?"

"Here's the deal. It all comes down to how the gun came into Carmel's possession and what Briscoe knew about that chain of events. Let's suppose one of the other kids had the combination to Carmel's locker and slipped the gun in his backpack. If Briscoe is ignorant of that fact, he is still justified in using deadly force against Carmel. It doesn't matter how the gun got in Carmel's possession or who put it there. Briscoe may have overreacted to the situation, but it certainly isn't capital murder and it may not be anything criminal at all."

As usual in such matters, Red was right on the money. He'd spotted the big hole in our case. We had to prove that Briscoe knew ahead of time that the gun in Carmel's backpack was a fake.

"Let's prove Briscoe knew the details of the plant," I said.

"Piece of cake," Red said and was gone again.

Hunches. All good legal work consists of hard work, blind luck and hunches. Not necessarily in that order. A good hunch is worth its weight in gold.

It was a hunch that led me to park at Chandler elementary school an hour before sundown Monday evening to wait for kids to arrive to play a game of pick-up basketball. It was a ritual as old as I was. They assembled at the elementary school because the goals were eight feet tall, not regulation ten feet. On those eight-foot goals, kids of ordinary skills could pretend to fly. They could twirl and dunk, hang on the rim, goal tend. For an hour or so every summer evening the players became giants.

The mustang arrived as if on my cue, and four kids, including Marcus Wellborn, got out. In a minute, a beat-up Chevy pickup rolled alongside the Mustang and two more teenage boys piled out.

Three on three. The quintessential game of pick-up basketball.

As I watched them play until it was almost dark, I thought about the simplicity of the moment, how life for those young men should be lived on an elementary school basketball court, or at a part time job flipping burgers after school, or on a church trip, or at a dance, or holding hands with a first love, or lying in the grass in a pasture looking up at the stars, or reading a book about the worlds beyond this one, or making plans for college, or taking a place in their parents' businesses.

I was leaned up against the fender on the front driver's side of the maroon Mustang when the game broke up and Marcus and his buddies lounged their way back to their rides.

I extended my hand to him. "Marcus, I'm Etch Danielson. If you have a minute, I'd like to follow up with you about your conversation with my investigator, Red Roper."

His firm young-man's handshake told me he was ready to get some things off his chest. He nodded toward his buddies, and they huddled among themselves far enough away from Marcus and me to give us some privacy.

"I'm not here to bother you, Marcus. I just need some help understanding what led up to the shootings. The DA has asked me to take the lead on a case against Coach Briscoe, if there is one. Red said you labeled Briscoe a trigger-happy son of a bitch. I am wondering what you meant when you called him that."

A six-foot-two-inch, 165-pound, olive skinned scarecrow, Marcus had his shock of collar-length jet black hair tied into a ponytail with a rubber band. He wore a red KHS basketball jersey with a large white number eleven on the back, palmed a basketball in his left hand and looked at his Michael Jordans while he spoke.

"Carmel was harmless. He was the class smart ass, for sure, but we all knew he was good hearted. He was smart in a kind sort of way. He was going places."

"You're not answering my question," I said.

He raised his eyes. "Carmel and his crew took the Florida shootings hard. They followed the kids who survived and listened to their interviews on TV."

I interrupted him. "Who was Carmel's crew?"

"Him and Maria and Benjamin. They were always together."

"All right. Go on. Did they have any plans to visit the students from Parkland or anything like that?"

"They wanted to start a chapter. Our own group that could speak out about the violence."

"Were you in the group?"

"I told them I was down for it. Just let me know what to do and when to do it."

"Did anything come of their planning?"

"They met with Ms. McEntyre and discussed the project. Benjamin told me Ms. McEntyre encouraged them. She was supposed to run it by the school board at the March meeting."

"What came of that?"

"Nothing."

"Nothing?" I asked.

"Yeah. Benjamin said the school was dragging its feet about helping them organize, so his crew decided to do it on their own. They sent texts to us about the first meeting, and we got together at Starbucks in Longview."

"When was this?"

"Mid-March, I guess. We had about ten people, and Benjamin gave us our assignments. Stuff like call the newspapers, contact radio stations, chat it up on social media."

"And what was the group's message? What were you supposed to tell your contacts?"

"Benjamin handed out some talking points for us. Get guns off the street, get a handle on bullying, reach out to kids with issues. Stuff like that."

My admiration for Marcus Wellborn grew with each word the young man spoke. He was articulate, sensitive, and he was being eaten alive by his pain and frustration. He was our future, and he didn't know which way to turn.

"What else happened with the group before the shootings?"

"We met a couple of other times, talked to some kids from other schools like Gladewater and Gilmer. Benjamin told me he was working on a one-act play about school violence and he wanted us to perform it at a rally to draw attention to the movement. We basically had decided to make a big push this summer, but..." His voice trailed off. "Well, you know, sir."

My gut told me he knew a lot more than he was telling. I decided to cut to the chase. "Marcus, from what I've learned so far, I agree with you about Carmel and his crew. But the fact I can't get around is that Carmel had a gun in his backpack. That seems totally out of character, but there it is. Do you have any explanation of how that happened, other than he just decided to shoot up the school?"

He squared his shoulders, held his head erect. "I know this much, sir. Carmel was not a killer."

"Then why did he have a gun on him?"

"It wasn't his gun. It was mine, sir."

Then he told me about it.

Chapter Fifteen

At eight-thirty sharp the next morning, I entered the office of KHS principal Beryl McEntyre. Marcie Brumbaugh was nowhere to be seen. The door to Ms. McEntyre's private lair was open and the room was dark. I had decided to wait her out when three minutes later she walked in with her purse over her shoulder, and a bunch of notebooks clutched in her arms.

"Morning, Etch," she said.

I grabbed the notebooks to lighten her load and followed her inside her office.

"Just dump them over there." She pointed at a six-foot plastic folding picnic table already laden with what looked like a couple of hundred years of junk.

I pushed the other papers around on the table and made a spot for the notebooks, stacked them as best I could. I noticed the labels on the folders that identified them as packets from a national conference on school violence. It jogged my memory that Marcie had told me her boss was attending a program out of town last week. When I finished placing the notebooks on the table, I saw Ms. Entyre seated behind her desk. I sat across from her.

I knew something of her story. She had risen through the school ranks, first teaching English to sophomores, then doing a stint as the high school counselor. She earned her administrator certificate, took a position as the assistant principal at the middle school and, eight years ago, was promoted to high school principal. At fifty-three, she retained a sparkle in her eyes. Her brownish-black shoulder-length hair was dulled by streaks of gray she didn't hide. She had recently adopted half-glasses that perched on the ridge of her nose and accentuated her high, Native-American cheekbones. She still wore a plain gold wedding band although I knew her husband had died three years earlier from an aneurysm that came out of nowhere. The kids at school loved her because she was fair, even when she called them on the carpet.

She didn't waste time with small talk.

"Is it my turn in the hot box, Etch?"

"I prefer to think of it as the time for truth telling, Beryl."

"The truth about what?"

"About what happened to Marcus Wellborn's gun."

She never took her eyes off me, didn't blink, didn't squirm in her chair. "What did Marcus tell you?"

Fair is fair, I thought. I'd come at her with the whole deal at once, and, as far as I was concerned she deserved to know what I knew. She'd learn it now or at trial.

"He said he talked to you about Benjamin Cohen's one-act play, how the kids hoped to perform it at school before the end of the term. He said you were open to the idea, and that Benjamin had already given you a draft of the script."

She nodded her head, made no reply.

I continued. "Marcus had volunteered the use of his mock pistol, but he was worried about how to get it on campus. He didn't want to get in trouble trying to sneak it through security. He knew he if was caught, he would be expelled, no questions asked."

She picked up the story. "So, I agreed to handle it for him."

"That's what he told me. He said you stopped by his house after school one day, and he gave you the fake Glock, the BB gun he'd received as a birthday present four or five years ago. That's the last time he saw it until the day of the shooting."

Her face was ashen as she listened to my account.

"Here's what happened, Etch. I felt like Benjamin's play was too much, too soon. I admired what Benjamin, Maria and Carmel were doing, trying to organize a group of students to speak out about school violence and to show solidarity with other kids around the country. But I thought, as a lot of people my age did, they needed to take it slow. I thought holding Marcus's gun for safekeeping would give me some control over the timing of their project, allow me to micro-manage their passion."

I could tell she had spent a lot of time second-guessing her role, wondering how it all went so wrong. "So how did the gun get in Carmel's backpack?"

"I don't know."

"How can you not know? You volunteered to take control of it. Help me out here, Beryl."

"I brought the gun here to my office and stored it in my desk drawer." She opened the top drawer. "It was right here." She pointed to the spot.

"Was?"

"I checked it every day, even though I didn't believe anyone knew it was there. When the report of the shooting came in I was sitting where I am now. Before I did anything else, I jerked this drawer open."

She lived the moment, her body's involuntary response to the news.

"The gun was gone." She slammed the drawer shut. "I swear to God I don't know what happened to it, Etch." She was crying now, her face in her hands, her body bent over with sobs. "Someone stole it, and somehow it ended up in Carmel's backpack."

I waited while she took deep breaths to regain her composure.

"Who had access to your drawer?"

"Marcie, for sure."

"Anybody else?"

"You know how it is, Etch. I have an open-door policy. Half the kids in the school have been in here at one time or another, not to mention the teachers and the staff. Never in my wildest dreams did I think any of them would rifle through my desk. Why would they? They had no reason to suspect I had a gun in my office."

"People talk," I said. "Marcus knew you had it, and several members of the new chapter the kids were organizing knew at least something about the play Benjamin was working on. They could have put two and two together and guessed you might have the gun stashed somewhere in your office." I thought how ridiculous her actions looked in hindsight, how innocent they may have seemed to Beryl at the time. She thought she was protecting Marcus and his friends. Instead, she became the instrument of their destruction.

I wanted to let her up off the mat, but I pressed ahead.

"Who have you told about your role in bringing the gun to school?"

"No one. Of course, Marcus knew I had picked it up from him, but I didn't say where I planned to store it. I just told him I would hold on to it until we scheduled the play. You're the first person I've told about it being in my desk."

"You said Marcie had access to your desk."

"She did."

"But you didn't ask her about the gun?"

"Like I said. She didn't know it was there."

"So far as you know, right?"

"Yes. So far as I know."

"You didn't tell the police about the gun?"

"No." She paused. "I was afraid to admit it. I felt like such an idiot, like the whole damned thing was my fault, Etch."

She was in good company. By my calculation, about half the people in town felt the same way.

"It wasn't your fault, Beryl. Someone snatched the pistol out of your desk and planted it in Carmel's backpack. Whoever that was probably banked on you not knowing the gun was missing until it was too late."

"So, what do we do?"

"I'll send my investigator over here to see what he can find. Keep a lid on our conversation for right now, if you don't mind."

"OK, Etch."

I got her cell number to give to Red and told her she'd hear from him shortly. Before I left, she had one more question for me.

"Am I in trouble, Etch? I mean going-to-jail sort of trouble?"

"Not unless you're lying to me, Beryl," I said, and I turned and walked out of her office.

Chapter Sixteen

I rolled into Red's driveway a few minutes after I left Beryl McEntyre and parked next to his white 1993 Crown Vic. I didn't see him outside, so I knocked on the front door. He yelled for me to come in, and when I entered his cabin, I saw him seated at a wooden picnic table in the middle of the main room. He was focused on a computer monitor, pressing keys and taking notes.

I brought him up to speed on my interviews with Marcus Wellborn and Beryl McEntyre.

"I don't like being played," I told him at the end of the briefing.

"Who do you think is playing you?" He took his eyes off the screen and stared at me.

"Briscoe, for sure. Maybe Beryl McEntyre. Maybe Momma L. Maybe Slim Atwell. Maybe people as yet unidentified."

Red nodded. "In that category, I have a few new discoveries for you."

"I'm all ears."

"Except for your mid-drift."

Red laughed, and I laughed with him. It was better than crying.

"Let's begin with Caddo Panola," he said as he grabbed a yellow legal pad and flipped through several pages of hand-written notes. "What Momma L told you about her early life matches the record. She graduated from KHS by the skin of her teeth, worked odd jobs, had a few minor brushes with the law. Her employment record fades to black a couple of years after Carmel is born."

"What do you make of that?"

72

"She went off the grid. Probably gave herself over to prostitution and other jobs for which a person does not receive a W-2 or 1099. I found a handful of other minor charges at various jurisdictions mostly between here and LA. A few nights in jail, short periods of probation. I tracked down a misdemeanor probation officer in Phoenix who supervised her for six months. She said Caddo was a striking beauty but was showing wear around the edges. She got her a job in housekeeping at a La Quinta, but Caddo skipped town after nine days on the clock. The last hit I got on her was a bust for solicitation in Compton seven years ago."

"You think she's still in LA?"

"No way to know without more digging. She may be there or anywhere else in the country. The most I can say right now is that she doesn't show to be in the system presently, so I doubt she's in the penitentiary."

"She could be dead," I said.

Red shrugged.

He licked his thumb and turned a couple of pages on the legal pad. I knew that meant he had more to tell.

He slid a copy of Carmel's birth certificate in front of me. "Carmel was born at Laird Memorial Hospital in Kilgore. If you check the bottom of the birth certificate, you'll see the name of the nurse who gathered the birth information."

"Wanda Pruitt."

"Right. She works at Longview Regional Hospital in Longview now. When I showed her that document, she studied it for a second and the light came on. She said she talked to Caddo and thought the whole deal was hinky. Caddo was evasive when she spoke of the baby's father. 'Let's call him Hobo Sideout,' she said. Wanda asked her what she meant, and Caddo said, 'He's a piece of shit. He don't want this baby messing up his career.'"

"Hmmm," I said. "You reckon that means the father was married?"

"Could be. Or, he may just be a straight-running asshole."

"Momma L said the guy wasn't in the picture and the name Hobo Sideout was Caddo's code talk for someone who was passing through town."

"Doesn't sound like it. I think the daddy was local, and he wasn't going anywhere."

"And maybe that's why Caddo hit the road a couple of years after Carmel was born. She was tired of playing the guy's game and watching him go about his business, no strings attached. For whatever reason, she decided not to blow the whistle on him."

"The heart has reasons reason cannot know," Red said, quoting Blaise Pascal.

Red swiveled his monitor, so I could see it.

"As a follow up to your interview of Ms. McEntyre, I have a bonus feature for you."

"I just interviewed her this morning. You're working fast."

"I try to keep up," Red said.

"Does the name Marcie Brumbaugh ring a bell?"

"She's the twenty-something who's McEntyre's secretary."

Red tapped a few keys. In a second, a Facebook post popped up. It was a selfie of Marcie Brumbaugh, time-stamped two days earlier on Sunday afternoon. She wore a baseball cap and a college baseball jersey and sat among a crowd in the bleachers.

"Privacy is a thing of the past, counselor. Give a young person a phone, sit back and watch. They can't stand not using it."

Red panned out the picture.

"You recognize the guy next to her?"

I leaned toward the monitor to get a good look. "I'd say that was Merlin Hostetler. He's an assistant coach at KHS and Marcie's main squeeze."

"Right you are." Red panned out a few more feet. "How about the third guy? Does he look familiar?"

I saw before me Marcie Brumbaugh in the middle, Merlin Hostetler on her right, Coach Jim Briscoe on her left. Briscoe had a corn dog stuffed halfway in his mouth, suds of concession-stand beer still wet on his T-shirt.

"Looks really tore up about things, don't he?" Red hit a button, and I heard his color printer come to life.

I drove to the bookstore and checked in with May Ellen. Then I retreated to my office and pieced together what I knew about the school shooting. As Jim Thompson, the great pulp fiction writer of yesteryear, had said: Nothing is as it appears. A mother deserts her son and lies to her own mother about her reasons. A school principal brings a gun to school with good intentions. A student writes an inflammatory one-act play hoping to solve school violence. The shooter goes about his life without a worry in the world.

I still had some blanks to fill in, but my sense of the deal was that Jim Briscoe was rotten to the core.

About eight-fifteen, just as the light of a long summer day was fading, and fireflies blinked outside my window, May Ellen opened the door. I could tell from her face that something was up.

"What is it, baby? I thought you'd have gone home by now."

"I just heard it on the news," she said.

"Heard what?"

"KETK in Tyler is reporting that Levi Cohen was found dead a few minutes ago at his shop downtown."

"Oh, no," I said as I hugged her.

Through her tears, she added, "Apparent suicide by hanging."

Chapter Seventeen

1968.

That's what I was thinking about as May Ellen and I dressed to attend Levi Cohen's memorial service.

Nineteen days before my sixteenth birthday, Dr. King's assassination changed the world. In faraway Vietnam, young men were dying. In June, Robert Kennedy joined his brother in death. Cities were on fire, hatred was in charge. In rural East Texas, the white male ruling class held closed meetings in the back rooms of power, fearing a cultural coup, the overthrow of their privileges. A sense of doom hung in the air, while ordinary people sleepwalked through their occupations and avocations.

And young people, primarily students, took to the streets in protest.

Fast forward fifty years. Already, in a year only half-spent, students had died in Florida and Texas. In answer to those atrocities, we had retreated to the old ways, resorted to patently ineffective methods to address the violence. Politicians split into camps and did nothing. School officials wrung their hands and pleaded in vain for help. Meanwhile, kids died, and the students left behind stepped up to lead the charge.

We had seen up close and personal the human cost of young lives snuffed out. Those costs included the inestimable horror endured by the survivors, both those who were witnesses to the gunfire and those who buried the dead or joined them in death when they could not find a way out of the pain of loss, or when they succumbed to hopelessness.

Red drove us to the service, and on the way home each of us struggled to find words. I finally broke the silence.

"All we can do is play the hand that's been dealt us. We can't change the world, but we can do our best to address the facts of this one situation. Maybe if we get to the bottom of what happened at KHS, we will save a kid somewhere from a similar fate." It was thin soup, but it was all we had the power to do.

Three days passed before Abby Cohen, Levi's wife and Benjamin's mother, knocked on my door.

She stood barely five-feet tall, but seemed smaller, as if the events of the last six weeks had diminished her. Dressed in a short-sleeved black dress, a black headpiece and sheer black veil, she never looked directly at me. She tucked her chin on her chest, slanted her head to my left. Her voice was no more than a whisper when she spoke.

"Benjamin was our only child, Mr. Danielson. Levi adored the boy, loved him more than life itself. He felt that as president of the school board he was uniquely positioned to bring safety to our school. The shooting and Benjamin's death were, to him, a dagger through his heart. He believed he had failed the kids, the school, the parents and the community."

"He did the best he could do, the best anyone could have done, Mrs. Cohen," I said. "I sat at the table with him at board meetings, and I know the kids' best interests were all that mattered to him."

She waved her hand to silence me, nodded her head. "I know. I know. But it doesn't change anything." She moved a half step closer to me. "My husband had the deepest respect for you, Mr. Danielson. That's why he came to see you, and why he gave you a copy of Benjamin's play. He wanted you to make sense of what he couldn't. Please do that in honor of him. That's all I ask."

With those words she was gone.

In any criminal case, a prosecutor must follow a process. First comes the investigation, next the indictment, then pretrial wrangling, and finally a trial if the defendant has not agreed to a plea bargain.

The Jim Briscoe case was stuck in the first stage.

With the facts we had uncovered thus far in the investigation, I had a gut feeling of a deadly plot that involved Briscoe, but I couldn't connect the dots. And without proof of the fundamental elements of murder, such as intent and premeditation, my suspicions weren't enough to take the case to a grand jury.

Despite the remarkable assignment Abby Cohen gave me, I knew her husband's suicide was a tragedy susceptible to more than one interpretation. Its obvious meaning to most people, in my estimation, was that Levi had in fact failed to carry out his responsibilities as president of the school board. In that regard, the board had been lacking in its oversight of enforcement of the SPA, allowing Briscoe to operate above the law for months. Likewise, if what Marcus Wellborn told me was true, the board dragged its feet and did not embrace Carmel's crew when Beryl McEntyre pitched to it the formation of a student organization focused on school violence. On another level, some people would draw the conclusion that if Levi Cohen knew of his son's one-act play, he should have intervened and determined just how far Carmel's crew had gone in its preparation to bring the play to life.

The missing piece that bothered me most, however, was motive. Why would Briscoe concoct a scheme to murder Carmel, Maria and Benjamin? The law didn't require me to prove motive, but I damned sure wanted to know the answer to the question.

Red called the day after my meeting with Abby Cohen.

"I got a hit," he said.

"Could you give me a little context?"

"Beryl's desk drawer."

"What did you find?"

"I was able to lift some prints."

"The suspense is killing me, Red."

"Of course, I found Beryl's."

"We expected you would."

"This is where the plot thickens."

"Thicken it for me, please."

"You don't want to guess?"

"How about Marcie Brumbaugh?"

"Nope."

"I thought Marcie's prints would be all over McEntyre's desk."

"Me, too. But I didn't find them. Maybe we've underestimated her."

"How so?"

"The lack of evidence is evidence, too."

"You'll have to explain that one to me," I said.

"In all likelihood, Marcie sanitized the scene before I got there."

"If she wiped her prints, why wouldn't she have wiped everyone's?"

"For one thing, the scene would have looked too clean. For another thing, she wanted to be sure I found the other person's prints."

"Whose prints did you find?"

"According to the national database they belong to one V. T. Poteet of Laird Hill, Texas. He's worked as a maintenance man and custodian for the school for over thirty years."

"Mr. Poteet?"

"You betcha," Red said.

"His prints could be innocent. His duties may require him to clean Beryl's office, make repairs or whatever."

"Not according to Ms. McEntyre. She says he has no business being in her office."

"Have you talked to Poteet?"

"I'm on my way to the high school right now to see him."

"Keep me posted," I said, but Red was gone again.

I thought of my chance encounter with Mr. Poteet at the high school and replayed our conversation in my head. I wondered if he had been trying to tip me off, or if he had only wanted to throw me off track, to direct my attention elsewhere.

That's the thing about investigations. The more you learn, the less you understand.

Chapter Eighteen

While I was waiting for Red's report about his meeting with Mr. Poteet, I called Beryl McEntyre.

"Yes, sir," she said when she answered.

"Marcus Wellborn told me Benjamin gave you a copy of his one-act play?"

"That's right. He did."

"Where is it?"

"It's in my filing cabinet with my other important documents."

"Is it still there?"

I heard a thud when she placed her cell on the desk. Her chair creaked and, in a minute, I heard the sound of a metal file cabinet drawer opening, the rustling of file folders as Beryl searched. She came back on the line.

"I've got it," she said.

I sensed worry in her voice.

"Is there a 'but' you need tell me?"

She exhaled into the phone. "It was misfiled."

"Meaning?"

"Someone must have taken it out of the filing cabinet and replaced it in a different spot."

"Can you tell if anyone made a copy of it?"

I heard her flipping pages.

"I can't tell if it's been copied, but it is different than it was."

"Different?"

"When I received it from Benjamin, it was stapled in the top left corner. The staple is gone, and the pages are paper-clipped together."

I ended the call with her and hit Red's number on speed dial.

"Are you at the school?"

"Just pulling in the parking lot."

"While you are there do you think you could pay a pretext visit to Ms. Brumbaugh?"

"Any particular pretext?"

"Wing it. I'm sure one will come to you."

"I'll fly away," he sang before he hung up.

It was about eleven-fifteen on a Friday morning, so I left my man cave and wandered into the coffee shop ahead of the noon rush. My daughter, E. J., had steadfastly refused to train me how to make specialty drinks, a sign to me that she thought even though I could handle complex litigation, I couldn't master espresso. On the sly, however, I had watched some YouTube videos of baristas plying their trade and picked up enough know-how to make a decent americano. I fired up the two-station La Marzocco espresso machine, filled a twelve-ounce paper coffee cup with water hot enough to scald the fire out of someone at McDonald's, pulled two shots and dumped them in the cup. E. J. watched my performance with skepticism and hip-bumped me out of the coffee shop before any paying customers caught me desecrating her domain.

I scalded a few thousand taste buds off my tongue while I watched May Ellen shelving books in the main fiction room.

"Does le Carré go under L or C?" she asked.

"Beats the hell out of me," I said.

"L," one of the patrons said. She had a Kilgore Public Library name tag pinned on her shirt.

"L," I said to May Ellen.

She rolled her eyes.

I sensed my work in the book section was done and retreated to the back room again.

Before I could drain the rest of my americano, Red called.

"I was oh for two on my main assignments, but I had a serendipitous encounter that made up for it."

"Serendipity is good. Let's have it."

"First, I discovered that Mr. Poteet had taken a few days of vacation, sort of sudden like, according to the maintenance supervisor."

"Imagine that."

"Having struck out with Poteet, I went by the principal's office. Ms. McEntyre informed me that Marcie Brumbaugh was absent because her mother in Oklahoma had taken ill, and she needed to nurse her through her illness."

"Which is bullshit."

"Bullshit it is, indeed, counselor. Marcie posted another selfie this morning from Louisiana, which is not in Oklahoma unless they've moved it."

"You think the rats are jumping a sinking ship?"

"Their actions could be interpreted in that manner."

"How about the serendipity?"

"I bumped into Merlin Hostetler."

"How was he?"

"Sunburned, or more accurately, recovering. The skin was peeling off his face."

"Something like that'll happen when you sit through a baseball doubleheader in the bleachers in mid-June. Did you engage him in conversation?"

"We chitchatted. I asked him how Coach Briscoe was doing. He said he had talked with him a couple of times on the phone, and Coach was still taking it hard, said he'd been to some meetings of a PTSD support group, and it was helping him learn to cope."

"I don't suppose he mentioned visiting Briscoe, did he?"

"The lying little son of a bitch did not say anything about it. I found it odd."

"Odd my ass. A better word is incriminating."

"Sounds like a word a special prosecutor might use."

About four o'clock that afternoon, a call from a number I didn't recognize popped up on my cell. I often ignore those calls, but this time I picked up.

"Daniel Danielson," I said.

"Mr. Danielson, this is Sarah Gorsky. I'm an attorney in Dallas."

"I won't hold that against you, Ms. Gorsky."

As a result of three decades of practicing law in the sticks, I had come to understand that the common wisdom in East Texas was if you wanted a really good lawyer, you went to Dallas to find one. To her credit, Ms. Gorsky took my remark in stride.

"I hope not," she said.

"What can I do for you?"

"It may be the other way around, Mr. Danielson. As special prosecutor in the Jim Briscoe case, you may want to explore what my client can do for you."

"Who is your client, Ms. Gorsky?"

"Marcie Brumbaugh. She has some things she'd like to get off her chest, assuming we can reach a mutually beneficial agreement."

"It always gives me great pleasure to lighten a person's load, Ms. Gorsky. But before we can reach any agreement, I will need to get a sense of what your client has to offer. I'm sure you understand."

"I understand very well, Mr. Danielson. I would prefer to discuss the details in person if that is acceptable to you. How about we have a sit down tomorrow?"

"I'll have to juggle my schedule a little, but I can make it happen. Since you're coming from Dallas, why don't we split the difference and meet in Canton?"

"The Dairy Palace?"

"You're reading my mind, Ms. Gorsky. I'll have my investigator with me if he can get free. Will Ms. Brumbaugh be joining us?"

"I thought we might discuss the ground rules first. I'll have enough information with me to whet your appetite."

"See you at noon tomorrow at the Dairy Palace, Ms. Gorsky."

"Oh, and how shall we recognize each other?" she asked.

"I will be the old guy with another old guy wearing a Stetson."

She couldn't hold back a laugh. "Cool," she said. "We ought to be a good match. I'll be the Jewish chick who was hot stuff in Oak Cliff forty years ago."

As soon as the call ended, I Googled 'Sarah Gorsky Dallas attorney.' I selected 'Gorsky and Associates' from the list of hits and read her bio. Her firm held itself out as the go-to legal boutique in the Dallas area for criminal defense in state and federal court. Sarah was the name partner, and she managed seven other attorneys who varied in experience from recent law school graduate associates to seasoned partners. Her list of notable cases was impressive.

I figured an attorney with Sarah Gorsky's credentials and experience wouldn't jump into a case in Longview and drive to Canton to meet me at noon on a Saturday for a preliminary chin wag for less than a 45K retainer. I imagined those funds came from a second mortgage on her parents' or grandparents' homes and I was also pretty sure that meant we had Marcie Brumbaugh's attention, and she coveted the privileged position of first co-conspirator to flip.

I called Red.

"What you got on your calendar tomorrow?"

"Brunch with the Queen of England at ten a.m., golf at Augusta National later in the afternoon," he said. "You got a better offer?"

"How about we meet with Marcie Brumbaugh's high-powered Dallas lawyer in Canton for lunch?"

"Marcie's got a high-powered Dallas lawyer?"

"Not only that. Her high-powered Dallas lawyer wants to work out the ground rules, so Marcie can spill her guts."

"Does the high-powered Dallas lawyer have a name?"

"Sarah Gorsky."

"No shit?"

"You know her?"

"She and I go back a long way. When I was working homicide with Dallas P.D. in the '90s, she was a young felony prosecutor with the Dallas County District Attorney's office. We worked some cases together. She's topnotch. You can be sure she'll know what she's doing."

"Sounds like fun."

"I'm in, if I get to drive."

"Pick me up at the bookstore about a quarter to eleven."

"I'll let the Queen down easy," Red said as he ended the call.

Chapter Nineteen

Red picked me up at the shop in a '93 Crown Vic he'd named Pearline in honor of the custom pearl white paint job he'd given her about ten years earlier. Pearline tipped the scales just shy of a Sherman tank and wallowed down the highway like a freight train about to jump the tracks. For Red, the rules of the road were only suggestions, and his average cruising speed ranged from 92 to 95 miles per hour. If he spotted a state trooper set up in a speed trap, he honked his horn as he blew past him, stuck his left arm out the window and shot him the bird. If the trooper recognized Pearline, he would give chase, and Red would pull over on the shoulder and wait for him. What followed was twenty minutes when Red would regale the trooper with war stories, ask him about his family and sign an autograph if requested.

That's why he always wanted to drive.

"Let's talk about what to expect at this meeting," I said after our second trooper meeting. We were half-way to Canton, thirty miles or so out, which made our ETA about seventeen minutes.

"Sarah must have the goods on several people or she wouldn't have approached you this early in the game." Red said.

"And she must believe we were closing in on Marcie."

"She knows Marcie is a small fish, or she'll position herself as if that's the case."

"For us, a home run is evidence that Briscoe knew what was coming before Carmel discovered the gun. If Sarah can deliver that, she'll believe that evidence or testimony is worth immunity."

"Yeah, but I doubt she will have the whole thing wrapped up in a bow. More than likely, she'll have penultimate bits and pieces." Red changed lanes and streaked by a Porsche like it was standing still. "Can you believe a guy would drive a car like that below the speed limit?" He watched the Porsche recede from view in his rear-view mirror and shook his head.

"Did you say 'penultimate'?"

"The Greeks had the best words," Red said. He hit his brakes, slowed to eighty miles per hour and skidded up the exit at Highway 19 in Canton. He turned left at the light, floored the accelerator and drove flat out a half block before he shut Pearline down and coasted into a pull-through parking space on the east side of the Dairy Palace.

We walked into the hamburger joint and saw a lady wave at us who was sitting alone in a booth big enough for four people. I recognized Sarah Gorsky from the picture on her web page, and Red and I strolled over to meet her. She stood when she saw us coming and gave Red a big hug when he got to her booth.

"Long time no see, Sarah," Red said.

"Too long, Red." Sarah turned to me and extended her hand. "Sarah Gorsky, Mr. Danielson. It's a pleasure to meet you."

"Likewise, Ms. Gorsky."

She was already working on a double cheeseburger and tater tots, so Red and I placed our orders at the counter, returned to the booth and sat down across the table from her. Even though it was noon on a June Saturday in Canton, Texas, Sarah wore a brown business suit, her jacket buttoned down the front. She had one-inch heels, eyes the color of cured leather, and a mass of black hair that reminded me of Koko the gorilla. She held her burger in her right hand between bites and never loosened her grip on the Acme rollerball pen in her left.

"You called this meeting, Ms. Gorsky. So, the floor is yours," I said.

She was ready. "You want Jim Briscoe. You want him bad. What if I could give you indisputable evidence that he orchestrated the tragic shooting at Kilgore High School?"

"Orchestrated?" I asked.

"Planned it and executed his plan," she said.

Red jumped in. "Are you talking about physical evidence, witness testimony, or what, Sarah?"

"What if it was Briscoe himself talking about it? I am speaking hypothetically, of course," she replied.

"Do you mean Marcie testifying about a conversation or conversations she had with Briscoe?" I asked.

"That's not exactly what I mean, Mr. Danielson."

"She wore a wire?" Red asked.

Sarah didn't reply.

A sixteen-year-old boy brought out our food, a chili cheese dog with double onions for Red, a Frito pie, no jalapenos, for me. I shoveled a couple of bites into my mouth before I asked my next question.

"Do these hypothetical recordings incriminate people other than Jim Briscoe? Your client excluded, of course."

"Some of them do, and Marcie can give you a full run down on all the players in those situations where recordings perhaps do not yet exist."

Red pushed her. "You know how this thing works, Sarah. We need a taste of what you've got to let us know what we're dealing with here."

"For one thing, if someone told you about a pistol hidden in a drawer, don't buy it. Never happened."

Red and I looked at each other when she dropped that bomb.

"It's a made-up story?" I asked.

"I'm just saying," Sarah said.

I cut to the chase. "What does your client want in exchange for her cooperation?"

"How about total immunity from prosecution?" Ms. Gorsky asked.

"In your dreams, Ms. Gorsky." I replied. "We have three students who were murdered. No one involved in the crime can expect just to walk away scot-free. Besides, with Red working the case with me, we will probably fill in the gaps in due time without Marcie's help."

"'Probably' is the operative word in that sentence, Mr. Danielson. I'm talking about providing definitive proof that will nail Briscoe."

"Marcie would still have to do time in the slammer. The amount would be negotiable based on the quantum of proof, if you catch my drift, Ms. Gorsky."

"I will discuss that with her."

"Good. We'd like to set up a meeting with you and Ms. Brumbaugh as soon as possible to explore the evidence she can provide," I said.

"I plan to see her tomorrow. I'll touch base with you Monday."

On the way home, Red and I unpacked what we had learned.

"She's saying Beryl is lying to us about the gun to throw us off the trail," I said.

"When you think about it, it makes sense. Ms. McEntyre's story is impossible to verify. It's based strictly on her word," Red said.

"And the absence of Marcie's fingerprints on the drawer is consistent with what Sarah said."

"If Marcie is in Louisiana to obtain more furtive recordings of Briscoe, she's playing a dangerous game," I said.

"Furtive?" Red asked.

"It's not as good a word as 'penultimate,' but it's more literary than 'secret'," I said.

Chapter Twenty

The next call came in at seven-thirty Sunday morning.

"Etch, sorry to bother you so early on a Sunday. This is Dave Schmerz."

His voice had lost the edge it had during our standoff in Slim Atwell's office a lifetime ago.

"No worries, Dave. What can I do for you?"

"First, I want to apologize for the way I acted. I was out of line."

"Emotions run high in case like this. Consider our argument a thing of the past."

"I appreciate it, Etch. More than you know." He shifted gears. "Something came up about Jim Briscoe in a conversation I had with my mom, and I wanted to run it by you. It may be nothing."

"Let me hear it," I said.

He told me the story. "My dad was a state trooper. About thirty years ago, he was transferred to the Lufkin station."

"Red Roper told me what happened to your father, Dave. I'm sorry for your loss."

"Red's been a friend for a long time."

"So, what came up in conversation with your mom?"

"She still lives in Lufkin. I visited her yesterday. I mentioned the Briscoe matter, and she bristled. She said anyone who considered Jim Briscoe a hero didn't know the man. Just so you know, Etch, my mom never speaks ill of anyone. That's why I asked her what she meant. She laid it out for me.

"When she and dad came to Lufkin, she took a job as a secretary in the athletic department at Lufkin ISD. Shortly after she went to work there, Lufkin hired Briscoe straight out of Stephen F. as an assistant football coach. Briscoe hadn't been on board ten minutes when he started romancing the ladies. Teachers, district employees, girls still in high school. You name it. In those days, my mom was quite a looker, and Briscoe zeroed in on her. He dropped by the office all the time to chat her up, made off-color remarks, came up behind her and put his hand on her shoulders. You know the drill."

"He Weinsteined her," I said.

"Exactly."

"How'd your mom handle it? It was a different climate for women in those days."

"She sicced dad on him. Dad confronted him and told him to keep his hands off mom. He said if Briscoe got near her again, he'd whip his ass first, then see to it that he never coached anywhere in the state of Texas again."

"Did Briscoe behave himself after that?"

"He took the low road. He kept his distance from my mom, but he attacked her reputation by making up stories about her sleeping around on my dad and spreading them to anyone who would listen. Stuff like that."

"How did it turn out?"

"Mom ignored the rumors, held her head high. She was naive and didn't understand how gossip and innuendo infect whatever they touch. Over time, the stories caused tension between mom and dad. They had even talked about splitting up. Before they could work things out, or go their separate ways, my dad was killed. His widow never married again or dated another man.

"And the irony of it is that Briscoe never even slowed down. He chased women, white, yellow, red, brown, black, young, old, single or married, the whole time he was in Lufkin. Then he got a better job in Mt. Pleasant and did the same thing there. And on and on it went with him. He never paid the price for what he did to my mom."

"And, finally he landed in Kilgore," I said.

"Twenty years at KISD and counting," Dave said. "Etch, I don't know if that story has any bearing on your case. But I thought it was one of those odd reference points you might factor into the Briscoe equation. And, if you ever need an adverse character witness for the prosecution, I know a woman in Lufkin who would volunteer for the job."

"Thanks for the call, Dave. It sure sheds a new light on our man Jim."

As I thought about what Dave told me, I wondered how a man like Briscoe could spend all those years navigating the waters of sexual harassment and never suffer for it. How he could hold a job acting as a role model for impressionable kids. How he could slink through the system. The irony, as Dave said, was that Briscoe kept right on after it while his victims either shut their mouths, or distanced themselves from him as best they could, or picked up and went elsewhere, leaving Briscoe free to work the crowd. And now, in the wake of the shootings, the world was totally upside down. The man who long ago should have been thrown out the school house door had become the hero of the moment, maybe even the poster boy in the battle against school violence.

And I wondered if Levi Cohen had carried the burden of these thoughts inside him. Did part of his bottomless sorrow stem from reports about Briscoe's antics to which he had turned a deaf ear?

Unanswerable questions.

As I slotted the new information from Dave into Briscoe's time line, something I hadn't realized before emerged.

Another hunch.

I had spent most of the day what-iffing various scenarios about the Briscoe case when a call came in I hadn't expected.

It was Sarah Gorsky.

"I thought I wouldn't hear from you until tomorrow, Ms. Gorsky," I said when I answered her call.

She wasted no time getting to the point. "I met with Marcie Brumbaugh today, and she is anxious to put this chapter in her life behind her."

"How anxious is she?"

"She wants to meet tomorrow. I have already contacted a friend of mine who is a solo practitioner in Canton. He says we can use his conference room to ensure our privacy while we talk details." She gave me the address and phone number for the attorney's office. "I told him to expect us about nine in the morning."

"Ms. Brumbaugh is indeed anxious," I said.

I switched gears. "There's one thing I meant to cover with you at our first meeting, but it slipped my mind. That happens a lot at my advanced age."

"You and me both," she said. "What's the other thing?"

"Merlin Hostetler. The last report I received from Marcie was that she and Merlin were an item, promised to be promised, or some such."

"Love is fickle," Ms. Gorsky said.

"Perhaps the ficklest thing of all, Ms. Gorsky. My question about Hostetler was whether he was on board with Marcie's cooperation with the prosecution in the investigation. I had wondered if, given his close working relationship with Coach Briscoe, he might join us when we met with your client. However, I take it from your remark that he and Marcie have split the sheet and gone their separate ways. In your estimation of the situation, do you believe Hostetler wants to come to the table, or is he at loggerheads with us?"

"I can only speak for Marcie Brumbaugh. I don't represent Merlin Hostetler."

"Fair enough, Ms. Gorsky. Do you happen to know if Merlin has hired his own lawyer?"

"All I know is that Marcie said Hostetler was exploring his options."

"OK. I will cross the Hostetler bridge when I get to it. I'll see you in the morning, Ms. Gorsky."

I ended the call from Sarah Gorsky about eight-forty-five in the evening, just as the last light of day faded. I went outside and scanned the heavens, watching as the stars came out of hiding. I hadn't gazed at the constellations long when my cell buzzed, displaying, once again, a number I didn't recognize.

That didn't take long, I thought.

"Etch, this is Ron Braxton. You got a minute?"

Braxton was a local boy, a thirty-five-ish lawyer from Longview who handled any type of case he could get his hands on. He'd grown up in Gilmer, a small berg twenty miles north of Kilgore. His voice had the nasal, high-pitched timbre of a perpetual whiner or the class tattletale.

"Sure, Ron. What's up?"

"I just met with a guy named Merlin Hostetler."

"You don't say? How's Coach Hostetler doing these days?"

"He's a little concerned about his girlfriend, Marcie Brumbaugh. You know her?"

"I've met her, Ron. As a matter of fact, I believe I will soon get to know her much better. However, she might disagree with your characterization of her relationship with Merlin. I think they may no longer be an item."

Ron cleared his throat. "Now that you mention it, Etch, I believe he may have said she was a lying bitch. Pardon my language."

"Is there a reason you're calling to share this delightful information with me, Ron?"

"Yeah. Hostetler wants to come clean."

"And I assume he wants to do that before Marcie fingers him."

"Of course."

"He'd better work fast, Ron."

"How fast?"

"Tomorrow evening is the first time I could meet with y'all."

"He and I will be at your office at six."

"See you then, Ron."

Chapter Twenty-One

Red had charmed three state troopers, dodged a deer that ran across Interstate 20 in front of us, and explained the facts of an investigation to an Assistant United States Attorney from the southern district of New York in a conference call by the time we made it to Canton Monday morning. We pulled into the parking lot of Richard Hammaker's law office at eight-fifty-nine.

I was glad Sarah had contacted Richard about using his place for our meeting because he was one of the only lawyers still practicing in East Texas who made me feel like a youngster. Dick Hammaker was part of a dying breed. He was an old warhorse who saw the courthouse as a battle field, and in it he led one pitched battle after another. He was approaching ninety, the survivor of at least half a dozen heart attacks, a chain smoker of Camels, and a semi-recovering alcoholic. His clients were as loyal to him as he was to them, win, lose or draw.

Hammaker's office was a white frame house about his age on the outskirts of Canton. The rooms were packed with old files, the office equipment vintage 1960, his secretary worn around the edges from forty years of managing her boss.

When we walked in the front door, three clients sat in a minuscule waiting area, their heads hung, while they awaited an audience with Dick.

Miriam, Dick's secretary, greeted us. "Hey, Etch. Dick's waiting for you in the back." She resumed work on a pleading in a divorce case.

We snaked our way through boxes of dead files until we came to a room on the north end of the building. The door was open, and Dick and Sarah were drinking coffee while Dick smoked.

Marcie Brumbaugh was absent.

"Morning, Etch. Morning, Red," Dick said. He put both hands on the conference table and forced himself to his feet, shook hands with Red and me. He was bald as a cue ball, stood maybe five-eight, weighed 265, had age spots on his hands and wrists. He had a twinkle in his eye like he knew your dirty secrets, and he wheezed between comments.

"Thanks for letting us use your space, Dick," I said. "I see you've already met Sarah."

"Shit, yeah, Etch. She and I have battled it out a time or two, but both of us lived to fight another day."

"Barely," Sarah said. "Dick almost did me in the last time we squared off." She was grinning.

Red and I took our seats at the table.

"We seem to be missing someone," Red said.

Sarah checked her watch. "I'm sure she's just running a little late."

At nine-thirty, when our guest of honor still had not made her appearance, Sarah got up from the table. "I'll see if I can reach her." She left the room, her cell in hand. Fifteen minutes later, she returned.

"Her cell is going to voice mail. I don't get it," she said.

"Where did you meet with her yesterday?" I asked.

"She had a room at one of the casinos in Shreveport. After our meeting, I drove over here and checked in the Holiday Inn Select. I guess I should have had her follow me."

"Maybe she had to swing by Oklahoma and check on her sick mother," I said. I wanted Sarah to know we had kept tabs on her client. "Why don't you give us a summary of what she told you about Coach Briscoe while we're waiting, Ms. Gorsky?"

"That's my cue to take my leave," Dick said. "Y'all let me know if there's anything you need." The old lawyer excused himself and shut the conference room door behind him on his way out.

Red and I stared at Sarah. She checked her phone again. "Until we find out what's going on with Marcie, I am not at liberty to discuss her testimony, Mr. Danielson."

"Reminds me of my first date with Ramona Valdez," Red said. "I'd asked her three times to go out with me before she said yes. I showed up at her house to pick her up right on time. I had two tickets to see the Rolling Stones in my pocket, cost me fifty bucks. Her dad came out on the porch to give me the news."

"And?" I asked, playing the straight man.

"Her old man told me I must not have gotten the memo. Ramona had run off with Harry Boswell mid-afternoon. I asked her dad if he wanted to go see the Stones with me, and he said he wasn't a Mick Jagger fan."

At ten o'clock, I called time on the deal. I looked at Sarah. "We've got things to do, Ms. Gorsky. If this is any indication of Marcie's commitment to cooperate with the prosecution, I am not impressed with her sincerity."

"I don't like having egg on my face either, Mr. Danielson. I hope there is an innocent explanation for Ms. Brumbaugh's absence. I'll run it to ground and let you know something one way or another."

"The clock's ticking, Ms. Gorsky," I said. "As other people come forward to work with us, Marcie may lose her bargaining power."

"I know how the game is played, Mr. Danielson. How much time does Ms. Brumbaugh have before she becomes second in line?"

"Not long, Ms. Danielson."

We gathered up our files and were about to adjourn when we heard a knock on the conference room door.

"Come in," Red yelled toward the door.

The door swung open and Marcie Brumbaugh entered. She was wearing dark sunglasses, a velour hot pink jump suit and Paw Patrol flip flops. "Sorry I'm late. There was a long line at the Starbucks in Lindale." She took her seat next to Sarah, who ran the fingers of her right hand through her hair.

"Are you ready to begin, Ms. Gorsky?" I asked.

Sarah nodded. "Ms. Brumbaugh, the people sitting across the table from you are Daniel Danielson and Red Roper. Mr. Danielson is the special prosecutor in Coach Briscoe's case and Mr. Roper is his investigator."

"Sure. I know Etch, and I've heard all about Red," Marcie smiled a slight giggle.

Sarah continued. "We are here to provide information to them that can assist the prosecution. In return for your cooperation, Mr.

Danielson will consider favorable treatment for you if your testimony exposes you to potential criminal prosecution. Do you understand, Ms. Brumbaugh?"

"Sure. I'm cool with it."

"Go ahead, Mr. Danielson," Sarah said.

I cast the net as wide as I could. "Ms. Brumbaugh, why don't you just tell us what you know about any conspiracy involving Coach Briscoe and his role in the shootings at KHS. Also tell us how you came to know these facts."

Marcie took off her sunglasses, placed them on the table, settled into her chair and dropped the smile. "Jim Briscoe is the devil, Mr. Danielson. He had it out for Carmel. Maria and Benjamin were collateral damage, but killing them was part of the plan, too."

I felt certain she had rehearsed that line with Ms. Gorsky. But the matter of fact way she delivered the words *collateral damage* to describe the murders of Maria and Benjamin still sent a chill through my spine.

We listened as she laid it out her story for us.

"Ms. McEntyre's long-time secretary retired the end of December, and I went to work for her in January. She and I hit it off from the start. In early February, she asked me if I'd like to go on a double date with her and Jim. She said Jim's assistant coach on the basketball team, Merlin Hostetler, wanted to ask me out and double-dating would be a good way for the two of us to get to know each other."

"Ms. McEntyre was dating Jim Briscoe?" I asked.

"For sure. I think for a year or so," Marcie said. "So, Merlin and I did the double date thing with them and after that our relationship blossomed."

"Until recently, I understand," I said.

"Yeah, we broke up a few days ago."

"OK, Ms. Brumbaugh. I'm sorry I interrupted you," I said.

"After the Florida shooting, Benjamin Cohen came to see Ms. McEntyre at the office and explained to her that he'd written a play about school violence and wanted some of the kids to perform it for the high school at an assembly. He gave her the script. A few days later, Ms. McEntyre called him to the office and told him she thought the play was too much for the kids to process so soon after the Florida shootings. She said she would think about the best time to perform the play. Benjamin accepted her decision but told her he really wanted to do the play before the end of the school year. He also asked her about how to get permission for one of the actors to display a gun in the performance."

I jumped in again. "How is that you know all this?"

"She kept her door open. I could hear all her conversations."

"And, I guess anyone who came in your office could hear Ms. McEntyre's conversations, too?"

"Sure."

"Continue, please. You were about to tell us about Benjamin trying to find out how to get permission to have one of the actors display a gun."

"Yeah. She told him a toy gun would be best. Benjamin said he knew a student who had a fake gun that looked real. Ms. McEntyre got the kid's name, contacted him, went by his house and picked up the gun."

"What did she do with it?" I asked.

"She gave it to Merlin."

"Merlin Hostetler?" Red asked.

"Yeah."

"How do you know she gave it to Merlin?" I asked.

"He showed it to me at his house."

"It is your testimony, Ms. Brumbaugh, that Ms. McEntyre never brought the gun to school and never stored it in her desk?"

"That would've been pretty dumb," Marcie said.

"Why would she tell someone she had stored it in her desk?" I asked.

"Beats me."

"OK. So, why did Ms. McEntyre give the gun to Merlin?" I asked.

"Merlin told me Briscoe wanted him to have the gun, so he could plant it on Carmel when the time came," Marcie said.

I glanced at Ms. Gorsky. She had her head down, jotting notes on her legal pad, not making eye-contact with me.

Chapter Twenty-Two

By the time I finished grilling Marcie Brumbaugh and discussing her future with Sarah Gorsky, it was a little after 4 p.m. We adjourned the meeting, and Red and I headed back to Kilgore.

"First thing is that I didn't hear any recordings of conversations between Marcie and anyone. Did you?" I asked Red.

"Sarah may have over-sold us on that one. Or Marcie could have lied to her about it. It's hard to tell anything for sure about the Brumbaugh chick. She's a piece of work."

"Marcie connected a lot of the dots for us," I said. "But not all of them."

"I assume you mean the why," Red said. He was a pro at cutting to the heart of a case.

"Exactly. As she explained the deal, Briscoe had it out for Carmel, wanted to teach him a lesson. But, it's one thing to bring a kid down a notch or two, it's an entirely different matter to murder him in cold blood."

"And kill two of his friends."

"So far, we know Briscoe is a piece of shit, an expert manipulator. He's always working an angle."

"You know the hardest part of solving a case when a guy like Briscoe is in it?" Red asked.

"Tell me."

"Getting in his head. Most crimes are committed by dumbasses who don't think three minutes ahead. They act in the moment, snatch and grab what they need, worry about the consequences if they get caught. A guy like Briscoe is different. He's got an agenda, something gnawing at him, maybe for a long time. Guys like us have trouble figuring him because we can't put ourselves in that dark place where he lives. Or, really, it's not that we can't do it. We just don't want to take the train to that destination. Once you go there, it's hard to come home."

Red's remarks reminded me of my latest hunch. "Speaking of which, something came to me last night as I was stewing on what Dave Schmerz told me about his mom and Briscoe."

"Another assignment for me?"

"Yeah. I need you to focus on Briscoe and work your way through his time line."

"Anything in particular, or do I just start from his birth and cover each day?"

"I'll narrow it down for you. Start when he came to KHS twenty years ago and see what you can dig up about his girlfriends."

"I'm on it, counselor."

Merlin Hostetler was what you would expect. Six-feet-two-inches of muscle, brown hair cropped to one-inch, clean shaved, blue eyes. He presented himself with Ron Braxton wearing a sleeveless football practice jersey that accented the musculature of his shaved arms, gym shorts and ASICS running shoes. If you had seen him in a team picture of a Division One college football team, you would have pegged him for a middle linebacker.

Ron Braxton, however, was the polar opposite of his client. He was wispy and nerdish, a toothpick of a man, with taped-together metal-framed glasses askew on the bridge of his nose, his shirttail half tucked in his black nylon trousers, scuffed brown penny loafers that slipped loosely on his heels when he walked.

I motioned for them to take their seats across from me.

Braxton spoke almost before his butt hit the seat of his chair. "Etch, Mr. Hostetler and I appreciate you taking the time to meet with us. You'll be glad you did. Tell him what you told me," he said to Merlin.

I stopped them. "Hold on a minute, Mr. Hostetler. We need to discuss the ground rules. Do you understand that whatever you tell me in this room is not covered by the attorney-client privilege? I'm not your lawyer. I am the special prosecutor in Coach Briscoe's case. If you tell me things that incriminate you, I can, and will, use that information against you."

"I understand, Mr. Danielson. Ron explained to me why we're here. I want to set the record straight."

"Have at it," I said.

"Coach Briscoe made some mistakes, sir."

"Mistakes like killing three students?" I asked.

"That was a setup, Mr. Danielson. He thought he was under attack, and he did what he had to do."

I had expected something like this from Merlin, but I played out the hand. "Who set him up, Mr. Hostetler?"

"Marcie Brumbaugh. She was the mastermind."

"The mastermind of what?"

"She and Ms. McEntyre thought Benjamin was a dangerous guy who had persuaded Maria and Carmel to act out a play about a school shooting. Beryl and Marcie were afraid Benjamin and his crew were about to spring the play during class."

"Why would Carmel, Maria and Benjamin do such a thing?" I asked.

"They wanted the attention. They'd seen the media make heroes of the kids in Florida, and they thought the play would put them in the national spotlight. They had it figured as their springboard to stardom."

I looked at Ron Braxton. He was hanging on Hostetler's words, buying every syllable of his version of the facts. "What were the details of the plan Marcie masterminded?" I asked.

"Ms. McEntyre wanted Benjamin to believe she was on his side, so she got a gun from Marcus Wellborn and hid it in her desk drawer. Marcie was in charge of putting the gun in Carmel's backpack. She was to give Mr. Poteet, the school custodian, the heads up."

I interrupted him. "She who? Ms. McEntyre or Marcie?"

"Marcie. On the day of the shooting, she gained access to Carmel's locker and planted the gun. She was supposed to tell Mr. Poteet when the game was on, and his job was to bust Carmel, Maria and Benjamin in the hall outside Coach Briscoe's class. The deal would have blown up in the faces of all three kids, and they would have been suspended or expelled."

"How did it go wrong, Merlin?" I asked.

"Marcie didn't give Mr. Poteet word that all systems were go. So, he didn't bust them in the hall, and they ended up in Coach's class with the gun. Carmel happened on the pistol, pulled it out and all hell broke loose."

"And, you're saying that Marcie intended for Carmel to find the gun when he did? To 'happen on it' I believe were your words?"

"That's what she told me. She thought Coach would take control of the situation and disarm Carmel. When that had happened, Carmel and his crew would have been expelled for sure and maybe gone to jail."

"You said Coach Briscoe made some mistakes. What mistakes?" I asked.

"Like I said. He should have disarmed Carmel, not opened fire on him. He overreacted. I don't fault him for it. I might have done the same thing if I had been in his shoes. But Marcie is really the person responsible for the shooting. She set everything in motion."

Ron spoke up. "Merlin did anyone tell Coach Briscoe about the plan to bust the kids in the hall outside his classroom or about the fact that Carmel would have a gun on him?"

"No. Since the kids weren't ever supposed to make it into the classroom before Mr. Poteet uncovered their plot, no one thought there was any reason to tell Coach Briscoe about the plan. When Marcie changed things on the fly, she dropped Coach Briscoe in the middle of it."

I had been taking notes while Hostetler spoke. I put my pen down. "Merlin, I have to admit I am a little confused about your role in this plot. So far, I haven't heard you say anything about what you were supposed to do."

"I wasn't supposed to do anything, Mr. Danielson. I just wanted you to know what really happened."

"You're just being a good citizen?"

"Yes, sir. Marcie is behind the whole thing. She's the one who should do down for it."

"And you know all this because you and Marcie were close, she confided in you and confessed her involvement to you?"

"Yes, sir. That's how I learned about it."

"And now you and Marcie are on the outs?"

"We broke up. If that's what you mean, Mr. Danielson."

"She dumped you?"

Merlin sat up straighter in his chair, his face turning red with anger, not embarrassment, I thought.

"If you want to put it that way, sir," he replied, spitting out the *sir* like a sliver of bit-off fingernail.

"How would you put it, Mr. Hostetler?"

"I wanted to get away from her. She hatched this stupid plan and put Coach Briscoe in the cross hairs. I was through with her."

I started to point out to him the irony of his use of the cross hairs metaphor, but I let it slide, considering it casting pearls before swine.

After Braxton and Hostetler left my office, I recounted the events of the day, the two meetings and their evidentiary contradictions. I pieced together the stories I'd heard, giving each of them whatever measure of credibility I could. At the end of that exercise, I found myself short of proof beyond a reasonable doubt that Jim Briscoe had committed the heinous crime which my gut told me he had. But I did see a vague form taking shape in the fog, as if the lies of Marcie Brumbaugh and Merlin Hostetler had revealed the opposites of their substance and had given me insight into the essential missing piece of the puzzle.

I opened the box of documents Slim Atwell provided me and went to the file folder tabbed "Carmel Sideout." I flipped through the pages until I came to the inventory of items found in Carmel's backpack. And there, hiding in plain sight, I found it, the trigger which set death in motion.

Chapter Twenty-Three

Tuesday morning, I arrived at the shop an hour before opening time and ran through my typical routine for a day at the bookstore. I had found that my adherence to a mundane schedule calmed me and allowed my mind to work on submerged problems.

I unlocked the front door, disarmed the security system, turned on the lights, fired up the computers, checked the Internet connection and public wi-fi. I took the money bags, one for the front desk, the other for the coffee shop, and transferred the daily operating cash into the cash registers, signed in to the point of sale system and the software program we used to manage our inventory. I climbed the stairs and made sure the rooms on the second floor were clean and ready for our customers.

When I was satisfied that things were in order in the store, I walked outside, unlocked the door to the back room, turned on the light, adjusted the shutters so I could see outside. I reviewed the mail from the day before, paid a few bills and put the stamped envelopes in the front seat of my truck so I could drop them by the post office later in the day.

I had completed my opening checklist by a quarter to ten when E. J. arrived and went through her start-of-day ritual, preparing the coffee shop for her regulars.

I removed the insert from the sign on the front door, reversed it so that it displayed the word "Open" instead of "Closed," took my seat behind the front desk and checked our Facebook page for any messages left overnight.

By the time the phone rang at ten-fifteen, a trickle of coffee drinkers had converged on E. J.

"Bookstore," I said when I picked up the handset.

"Hold for Ms. Thompson, please," the female voice on the other end of the line said.

In my experience when a call began like that it always meant one thing. I was about to be granted an audience with a person convinced of his own importance, a person whose time was too precious to perform low-level activities and who delegated such things to his assistant. And in my sphere of activity that meant the person for whom I was holding was a hot-shot attorney from a big firm in a large city somewhere other than the rural southern United States. More than likely, that call emanated from the east coast, the west coast or the third coast, from a law firm ensconced on the forty-something floor of a downtown skyscraper at a posh address. Those of us who practiced law in the sticks lovingly referred to attorneys of that ilk as "tall building lawyers."

After I held for exactly one minute, the important person came on the line. "Etch, this is Jesmyn Thompson. I'm a partner in the Los Angeles office of Brimmer Mumford."

I cut her off. "Hold for a minute, please, Ms. Thompson. I have to change phones." I hit the hold button and checked my watch. I got up from my desk in the front room of the store, walked through the coffee shop and told E.J. I had a call to take, strolled through the store, went outside and entered my man cave. I arranged my legal pad on my desk, jotted down the date, time and Ms. Thompson's name and checked my watch again. I Googled Ms. Thompson's name, followed the link to her firm's web page and scanned her bio. Exactly two minutes after I pushed the hold button, I picked up the call. "Sorry about that, Jesmyn. What can I do for you?"

"We represent Coach Jim Briscoe. I was hoping I could discuss his case with you and see if there is a way we can resolve any issues amicably. The man has suffered a great deal, as I'm sure you are aware."

"I'm always in favor of resolving matters amicably, Jesmyn. But, I'm trying to catch up with you. I'm not aware of a pending case against Jim Briscoe. As special prosecutor, I am still investigating the matter. We haven't filed any charges against your client." I paused before I added, "Yet."

"Which is at it should be, Etch. We see no legal basis for an indictment. Coach Briscoe reacted legally to a threat to the students in his classroom. Even though his reaction was sudden and forceful, it fell within the provisions of the law. Briscoe is overwhelmed with emotion toward the families of the decedents. He demonstrated that by attending the funerals of those who died that terrible day. His life is a shamble, and he's attempting to pick up the pieces. A criminal prosecution would serve no purpose."

"I guess I missed the part where you discussed what you would consider an amicable disposition of the matter," I said.

"You're in an enviable position, Etch."

"How so?"

"Since no indictment exists, you can conduct your investigation and make a short official pronouncement that you found no basis for any criminal charges. Then you fold your tent and close the investigation for good. That approach will satisfy the citizenry and assist the healing process for your bereaved community and for Coach Briscoe."

"Except for one thing, Jesmyn."

"What's that, Etch?"

"My job as special prosecutor is to see that justice is done. From what my investigation has already uncovered, I believe justice requires more than you suggest. However, if Coach Briscoe is prepared to accept criminal responsibility for the murder of three innocent kids, we may be able to work out an amicable resolution, Jesmyn."

"You will be making a big mistake if you go down that road, Etch. You shouldn't trust the bitter babble of a spurned lover."

"Nor should you trust the self-serving statement of a mass murderer, Jesmyn."

"I guess we are at an impasse, Etch."

"Nice talking to you, Jesmyn."

Nothing about the call surprised me. I had often conducted preliminary conferences with opposing counsel in serious cases. The tone of such calls was predictable. Each side laid out its strongest case and felt out its adversary. My review of Jesmyn Thompson's vita showed she was smart, experienced and well-connected. That meant she had received her marching orders from above and would not vary from them. Coach Briscoe to her was simply a means to a larger end.

It also came as no surprise to me when I read the list of Brimmer Mumford's clients and noticed number one on that list: the American Gun Association.

Slim Atwell's prediction had proved to be right on the money.

Chapter Twenty-Four

I called Red after I hung up with Jesmyn Thompson and briefed him on our conversation and on my meeting with Ron Braxton and Merlin Hostetler.

A little before noon, Red parked Pearline in a staff-only slot and came in the bookstore. He ordered a large brewed coffee, black, paid for it and left E.J. a five-dollar tip. He gave May Ellen a hug and joked with some college kids for a few minutes, grabbed a copy of *Catcher in the Rye* off the shelf and settled into an arm chair across from me in the front room. I watched him as he turned the pages in J. D. Salinger's one-off masterpiece and waited for him to share his thoughts about life.

"A day or a lifetime," he said as he closed the book.

"Can you unpack that one for me?"

"That's what Tolstoy said a novel should be about. A day or a lifetime."

"I suppose Solzhenitsyn took his advice when he wrote *One Day in the Life of Ivan Denisovitch*."

"Yeah. Think what a day in a person's life tells you about who he is, Etch. It allows you to see where he is, where he's been, where he's headed."

"And seldom is anything about that moment obvious to a casual observer," I added.

"That's why you have to peel off the layers and drill to the core to understand what makes a person tick. And even after you've done the best you can to plumb the depths of a person's psyche, you know you can never exhaust it. There's always something else you don't or can't know about him."

Three people came in the front door, and I greeted them, explained the layout of the store and pointed them toward the coffee shop. I waved at May Ellen, and Red and I took our leave and reconvened in the back room.

"Let's begin with Coach Briscoe," Red said.

"Let's."

Red spoke from memory without consulting notes. "I spent several hours yesterday with Solon Prince. Do you remember him?"

"Years ago he was athletic director and head football coach at KHS."

"That's right. He retired sixteen years ago after nearly forty years in the public-school system. He spent the last twenty-three of those years at KHS. Everyone considered him a saint, and I have no reason to dispute that characterization of him. Except, of course, for one slight *faux pas*."

"What was that?"

"He hired Jim Briscoe away from Mt. Pleasant ISD."

"Does Solon consider the hiring of Jim Briscoe the one blemish on his otherwise spotless career?" I asked.

"He does. According to Coach Prince, Briscoe hit the ground running when he came to Kilgore. I'm not referring to his coaching duties, by the way."

"I assume you mean that Briscoe continued his antics with women."

"He did. According to Solon, Briscoe always had something going on with someone. He courted teachers and dropped them, he flirted with the cheerleaders, he occasionally disappeared for a few days at a time. Solon believes those disappearances were out of town trysts, although he admitted that was just speculation on his part. When he called Briscoe on the carpet about going AWOL for a day or two, Briscoe always played it off as a trip to visit his sick mom, or some such. Solon never had enough on Briscoe to can him, but he kept his eye on him and warned him about mixing his personal life with his school duties."

"It's the same old story, Red. Turn a blind eye to a guy's exploits as long as the football team is winning."

Red nodded. "There was one thing though that Solon said that stuck in my head. He said a year or so into Briscoe's tenure at KHS, Briscoe curtailed his extracurricular activities for a brief period. He withdrew and became more tight-lipped than usual. Solon asked him if everything was OK with him, and Briscoe shrugged him off, wouldn't come out with it. After a few months, Briscoe returned to his old ways."

"Did Solon have a theory about what made Briscoe act differently during those months?"

"He laughed about it. His guess was that Briscoe had met a woman who was his match, someone who turned the tables on him and gave him a dose of his own medicine."

"You're saying Briscoe fell in love and the object of his affection didn't reciprocate?"

"That's usually what takes a guy down a notch or two, isn't it?"

"Did Solon venture a guess about the identity of Briscoe's love interest?" I asked.

"He didn't have a clue," Red said.

"OK. It's my turn," I said, moving to another topic.

"Fire away."

I pulled two sheets of paper out of a file I had marked "inventory," and slid them in front of Red.

"Look at Exhibit G."

Red glanced at the sheet a second. "I've already seen this. It's the list of items found in Carmel's locker after the shooting."

"Now look at Exhibit H."

He switched the bottom page to the top of the stack and reviewed it. "I've seen this, too. It's a list of the contents of Carmel's backpack."

"Do you notice anything funny about it?"

Red scanned it again, moved his eyes slowly up and down the page.

"Give me a hint."

"Think cell phone," I said.

Red laid the two sheets side by side and compared them. "I see it now. They found a cell phone in his locker and a different one in his backpack."

"What kind of phones?"

"The one in his locker was an iPhone. The one in his backpack was a cheap burner."

"Can your phone guy pull the data off those phones?"

"Probably in a heartbeat."

"That's what I thought. And it makes me wonder why no one involved with the investigation hasn't already done it."

Red offered an explanation. "It's probably because everyone thought it was cut and dried. Carmel pulls a gun and Briscoe opens fire. In a deal like that investigations often are just down and dirty. You go with the obvious chain of events and don't sweat the small stuff. Especially when the perpetrator is dead, and you aren't preparing the case for trial."

"That's the way I see it, too. But our working hypothesis is that Briscoe was the perpetrator, not Carmel. And, according to Marcie, other people were in the loop. Plus, I think it's really strange that Carmel would own the latest and greatest cell phone, leave it in his locker and tote a cheap burner."

"It is an odd fact, for sure."

"Let's take it one step further," I said. "The issue I can't figure is the timing of Carmel's discovery of the gun. If we take Marcie's story at face value, we know that Merlin Hostetler had the assignment of planting the gun on Carmel. Let's say he did that in the short window of opportunity after Carmel got back to school from his field trip to the museum and the start of Briscoe's class."

"OK. I'm with you."

I continued. "No one intercepts Carmel along the way, and he makes it into Briscoe's room with the gun. Briscoe is primed for action."

"I see where you're going, Etch. For Briscoe to execute his plan, Carmel had to discover the gun and wield it at just the right moment."

I picked up my cell and hit a number on speed dial. Four seconds later, Red's phone buzzed. He fumbled around for a second before he pulled it out of his back pocket.

Red looked at his phone and then at mine. "So that's how they did it," Red said.

I nodded.

Chapter Twenty-Five

My next stop was Laird Hill, Texas, a crossroads without a town connected to it, a post office the size of a milk carton, five miles south of Kilgore. I turned off State Highway 135 onto a red clay series of potholes masquerading as a road and drove two miles into a pine forest before I came to a mud driveway the size of a biking trail. The mailbox, smashed by a baseball bat or a tire iron, bore the faded black-block letters POTEET. I parked in the road behind a rusted Chevy truck which had been new when Lee Harvey Oswald shot President Kennedy, and which displayed a KHS Employee sticker on the back window of the cab. I got out of my Ford F-150 and walked through low-hanging crimson-flowered mimosa branches to a shaded house.

In another life, Vesuvius Poteet and I had played little league baseball together, attended kiddie shows at the Texan theater in Kilgore on Saturday mornings, learned reading, writing and arithmetic under the tutelage of stern female teachers who instilled fear and admiration in our young heads.

As I approached his decrepit shack, he sat on the front porch wearing faded denim overhauls over a Beatles T-shirt smoking a corncob pipe. He had a ten-gallon plastic bucket turned upside down next to him as a stand and on it a leather-bound King James Bible, its cover frayed, finger tabs with letters of the alphabet indented in the gold-embossed pages.

I sat down in a rocking chair on the other side of the plastic bucket from him and swayed back and forth, listening to the wood of the chair and the weathered timbers of the porch creak to each other.

"I wondered how long it would be before you came to see me, Danny," he said, looking off into the woods not at me.

I saw no reason to dance around it. "Your name keeps coming up in the investigation, Ves. I figured the best thing to do was to ask you straight up if you had anything to do with what happened the day of the shootings."

"You should consider your sources, Danny. From what I can tell, we've had an outbreak of lying since those kids got killed."

"Maybe. Or maybe where there's smoke, there's fire. I'll keep digging until I find out which way it is."

He leaned down and set his pipe on the floor, placed his left hand on the Bible and raised his right. "This is what they'll make me do at the courthouse, right?"

"That's right, Ves. They'll make you swear to tell the truth, the whole truth and nothing but the truth. So help you God."

"When they do that, here's what I'll say. I didn't have nothing to do with Jim Briscoe killing those kids. But I made a bad mistake, and I'll regret it to my dying day."

"What was the bad mistake?"

"Briscoe and I were chewing the fat after school one day. It was probably mid-March or so, just before Spring break, I imagine. We got to talking about the seniors and the kind of people they'd make after they graduated. That's when I mentioned Benjamin Cohen. Beryl had told me about the play he'd written, and I didn't know it was a secret or anything. I let it slip to Briscoe. 'You're kidding,' he said, all surprised. 'Does Ms. McEntyre know about his play?' he asked. I figured I'd messed up, so I told him I didn't know if she'd heard about it. Briscoe didn't say anything else, but I could tell the wheels were turning in his head."

I pushed him. "Briscoe never discussed Benjamin's play with you again?"

"No, Danny. I swear." He still had his hand on the Bible.

"Did you mention your conversation with Briscoe to Beryl?"

"I figured he'd bring it up to her. I suppose you know they're tight."

"Still? Or is that a thing of the past?"

113

"Still. They talk 'most every day, even though he's out of town."

"How do you know that?"

"I've caught bits and pieces of their conversations when I've come by her office. She leaves her door open."

"I'm still having trouble putting two and two together here, Ves. You've told me you let the deal about Benjamin's play slip, but then you say that's all there was to it on your end. Briscoe never asked you to do anything before the day of the shootings? He never discussed a plan with you ahead of time, a plan that involved doing something bad to Carmel or the other kids?"

"Swear to God, Danny. It was really the other way around."

"What do you mean?"

"After the day I told him about the play, Briscoe kept his distance from me. It's like he was going out of his way to avoid me. He'd always shot the breeze with me before that, but not anymore."

"Did Beryl or Marcie or Merlin Hostetler say anything to you about Briscoe having a plan to take some sort of action against Carmel or Maria or Benjamin?"

"Nothing, Danny."

"Then why do you consider telling Briscoe about Benjamin's play a mistake that will follow you the rest of your life, Ves?"

"When I told Briscoe about the play, something clicked in his head. I'm sure of it. I don't know why or how, but those words of mine set him on fire, and that fire burned those kids up, as sure as I'm talking to you today. If I'd just kept my damned mouth shut about it, Carmel and Maria and Benjamin would still be alive." He lowered his right hand, withdrew his left hand from the Bible.

I had to tack down one more detail. "Ves before the shootings had you ever seen the gun Carmel had in his backpack that day?"

"I've never seen it before or since that day, Danny. Who would ever have thought a toy gun could cause all that killing?" He retrieved his pipe, reached in the top pocket of his overhauls and pulled out a box of wooden matches. He picked one match out of the box and struck it, lit the pipe again and puffed on it.

As I drove away from Laird Hill, I replayed my childhood friend's words in my head. As I did so, I came to an incontrovertible conclusion, one which gave me no pleasure.

Ves Poteet, despite his heart-rending story, told with his hand on God's holy word, had looked me straight in the eye and lied to me.

Chapter Twenty-Six

It came as no surprise to me that the day after my meetings with Beryl McEntyre and Ves Poteet I had another visitor.

Brigitte Malcolm had served as superintendent of schools at Kilgore ISD for the last four years. She was the first woman to hold the job, and, at thirty-five years of age, the youngest super in school history.

She found me doing some catch-up work for the bookstore in the back room at 7:45 a.m. She was a local girl who had graduated from KHS before she did her undergraduate and graduate degrees at Texas Women's University in Denton. Her rise in the insular world of school administration had been meteoric, a year as an assistant high school principal, two years as a high school principal, two years as an assistant superintendent, all at Highland Park ISD, a wealthy district in north Dallas.

Although I had not been on the school board when Ms. Malcolm was hired as superintendent, I had heard the scuttlebutt. She was friends with one of the sitting board members and had let it drop to her that she might entertain an offer of the job if Aurelius Simpkins ever stepped down from the position. When Simpkins announced his retirement after fifteen years at the helm, Malcolm's friend floated the idea of hiring Malcolm as his replacement, and the board courted her with a passion, never seriously considering any other candidate. My sense of it was that the board knew KISD would be only an interim stop for Malcolm, a stepping stone for the superintendent job at Highland Park. In spite of that, they saw having Malcolm at KISD as too good a deal to pass up. To their way of thinking, Malcolm would bring pizazz to the district, a young vibe that would draw parents with school-age children to the community.

And, for the most part, the school board's strategy had worked like a charm for the last three years and ten months. Brigitte Malcolm was not short on pizazz. The woman who had entered was my office stood five-feet-ten inches tall, her platinum shoulder-length hair immaculately styled, a black pants suit displaying her fashion-model physique, her slender build tending toward emaciated. She inhabited a bachelorette world of limitless expectations, until her career opportunities evaporated into five rounds fired from a Colt .45-caliber semi-automatic pistol.

She removed her Versace sunglasses, balanced them in her right hand as she spoke to me.

"Hasn't the school endured enough already, Etch?"

"I'm not sure I catch your drift, Ms. Malcolm."

"How about I put it in legalese for you. It's time for you to cease and desist this witch hunt." Her eyes were wide, with a slight tint of what I took as a well-rehearsed outburst of lunacy.

"My job is to get to the bottom of the shootings and see that justice is done. No more, no less."

"That's bullshit, Etch. You're chasing the almighty dollar, plain and simple."

There it was, the perennial criticism of lawyers.

"I assume you think I am planning to bring a lawsuit against the school district to collect money damages for the families of the kids who died."

"Well, isn't that exactly what you plan to do?"

"Let me clarify the situation for you, Ms. Malcolm. I have been appointed special prosecutor in the case against Jim Briscoe. As special prosecutor, I will receive the same level of pay as a criminal defense attorney appointed to represent an indigent defendant charged with a felony offense. My pay will be an hourly rate set by the county commissioners. I will submit an application for my fee to the presiding judge, he or she will review it and decide what amount the county should pay me. In the end, my rate of pay will be less than your hourly rate as superintendent.

"Also, I do not represent any client in connection with the shootings. Although Momma L came to me and expressed her desire

117

to clear Carmel Sideout's name, I do not have any employment contract with her and never will have one. If she plans to bring suit against the school, she will need to find her own private attorney to do so. That will be up to her, just as the same decision will be up to the other family members of the survivors.

"And, as you know, the school board adopted the Student Protection Act before the shootings occurred. That law provides the school a shield against civil liability. The only potential avenue around the SPA for anyone seeking damages against the school would, in my opinion, be to test whether the school not having Briscoe's right to carry permit on file before the shootings was a significant enough violation of the act to create liability on the district. It is my legal opinion that the failure to have the permit on file does not invalidate the shield of liability, although a court would have to answer that question. The civil ramifications of my investigation just are what they are. The chips will fall where they may. Does that clear things up for you, Ms. Malcolm?"

She switched her sunglasses from her right hand to her left, crossed her legs and leaned against the back of the chair.

"That's just legal mumbo-jumbo, Etch. If you tag Coach Briscoe with a felony conviction, lawyers will come out of the woodwork to sue the district. They'll have us over a barrel and we'll have to dip into our fund balance to settle the lawsuits. That money should be used to make our school safer, not to line the pockets of your brethren in the law."

I jotted a few notes on a legal pad while I waited her out.

The longer our standoff lasted, the redder her face turned.

"Well? What do you have to say to that, lawyer Danielson?"

"I say that I have just heard the top person in administration at KHS rant about legal fees when three of her students were executed in cold blood on her watch. It makes me wonder about your priorities, Ms. Malcolm. Are you more concerned about Coach Briscoe or those dead students?"

"How dare you?" she said. She stood up and pointed her finger at me. "Listen to me, Mr. Danielson. From this moment on, you are banned from coming on any campus of Kilgore ISD. You will not speak with any district employee without my prior approval, and the district will have its lawyer present at any interviews of school personnel. Is that clear?"

I remained seated. "What's clear, Ms. Malcolm, is that you intend to interfere with my criminal investigation any way you can. In legalese, as you put it, that's what we call obstruction of justice. It is also clear that you don't have a clue how the legal system works. Three of your employees already have attorneys who reached out to me. Those lawyers' jobs are to represent their clients, not the school district. The real question, as I see it, is: What are you afraid of, Ms. Malcolm? If Coach Briscoe has done nothing wrong, you should be working with me, not against me."

"Keep the hell off Kilgore ISD property, Mr. Danielson. And stay away from my people."

She turned and stormed out of my office.

Chapter Twenty-Seven

"Sounds like she won't invite you to her next block party," Red said when I reported my conversation with Brigitte Malcolm.

"Yeah, I may be off her list permanently."

"It's an interesting tactic on her part, though," the old investigator said. "Over the last fifty years or so snooping around in people's business, I've come to the conclusion that it's the guilty dog who barks the loudest." He paused. "Not that I'm calling Brigitte a dog, mind you."

"No, she's not a dog, and she's not a dummy. She spent six years working at Highland Park ISD before she came back to Kilgore. You can't throw a rock in Highland Park without hitting at least three lawyers. I'm sure she knows the legal system and has talked to some of her attorney friends in Dallas."

"Which means she was running a bluff."

"She is buying some time. Delay our case, throw up a roadblock or two and see if we cave," I said.

"And she's signaling you that she understands the playbook. People hate lawyers and lawsuits. If she can paint the investigation as a witch hunt and a money grab, she knows she can undermine it. She was firing a shot over your bow."

I thought about Red's reference to the playbook. "If we take Brigitte's tirade at face value and suppose for a minute that she has the district's interests in mind, then it makes sense she would line up with Briscoe. If his actions were authorized under the SPA, KISD has no civil liability. It also means that it probably wasn't her Dallas lawyer buddies that she consulted about strategy. Rather, the likely person who is calling the shots for Ms. Malcolm is Jesmyn Thompson."

"The battle lines are drawn, counselor."

"And we need more ammunition, Red."

Forty-five minutes later, I met Red in the parking lot of Kilgore Public Library. We went inside and setup in the research room of the Austin stone fortress which housed the local collection of books, a 1930s throwback to the era when the discovery of the East Texas oilfield brought fabulous wealth to the sleepy farming community of Kilgore.

To pursue our assignment, we retrieved from the library's archives editions of the KHS yearbooks spanning the last twenty years. Red and I divided the stack of books between us, started with the most recent annual, which ended with the junior year of the students killed in the shootings, and worked backwards in time. Each of our persons of interest grew younger as we searched, their hair styles reflecting the times, their faces less worn, in some cases their eyeglasses missing. We saw pictures of community leaders, many of them now deceased, others now in the prime of their adulthood.

Seventeen volumes into our search, Coach Briscoe made his first appearance. In his late twenties, he wore his hair in a burr cut. We found shots of him coaching football and basketball practice, teaching health in the same classroom where the recent tragedy occurred.

However, it was when I saw the shot of Briscoe with the girls from the tennis team that I poked Red in the arm.

"Take a gander at this," I said. I shoved the annual in front of him.

He adjusted his reading glasses, picked up the book, held it six inches from his face.

"Do you recognize the young lady standing next to Coach Briscoe?"

"The one who has his arm draped around her neck?"

"That very one."

"Looks like a younger version of Brigitte Malcolm to me." He flipped to the section of the yearbook that included an array of the graduating seniors, located Brigitte's individual picture. "That's her all right."

"What's the writing in the margin?" I asked as I pointed at it.

Red squinted at the hand-written, cursive note as he read it aloud. "Bridge, let's keep in touch. Go out there and knock 'em dead, baby."

"Can you make out the name of the kid who signed it?"

Red pulled the book a couple of inches closer and read the signature scribbled at the end of the inscription, "Jimmy B." He wet his thumb and turned the pages, searching for possible student matches for the name Jimmy B. After he had gone through all the boys whose pictures appeared in the annual, freshmen through seniors, he looked at me.

"I don't see any student names that match Jimmy B."

"As I remember the ritual, once the annual comes out, kids go around and ask their friends to sign their copy. That happens while they're at school."

"That's the way we did it."

"Which means Jimmy B was most likely someone Brigitte knew at school. If it wasn't a classmate, who does that leave?" I asked.

"How about a hot new coach on campus named James Briscoe, perhaps nicknamed Jimmy?"

"That'd be my guess," I said.

Red took the annual in his hands and motioned with his head for me to follow him. He led the way to the front counter where a teenage girl manned the checkout desk. She had a stick-on temporary name tag pasted on her blouse with the word "Cyndy" written in longhand with a blue Magic Marker.

"Cyndy," Red said. "We found this KHS annual in the archive stacks and I'm wondering how the library acquires old annuals like this one."

Cyndy looked at him like he was a person speaking a foreign language. "I'm not sure, sir. But I can find out for you."

She disappeared into a backroom, and, in a minute, a middle-aged woman emerged. Her name tag was permanent, as was the scowl on her face.

"Can I help you?" she said, speaking to the space between Red and me.

I moved slightly to my left into her line of sight and called her by her name badge name. "Yes, Ms. Wigglesworth. We have been researching some old high school annuals, and we're wondering how the library comes to have such an extensive collection of them."

She took her name badge off. "I only wear this name tag during children's reading hour. I forgot to remove it." She allowed a slight giggle, perhaps the first in a generation, I thought.

Red and I smiled at her while she regained her glum disposition.

"The yearbook staff provides the library a complimentary copy of the annual every year."

Red handed her the book with the note in the margin. "I thought that might be the case, Ms. Wigglesworth."

She giggled again, apparently unable to restrain herself.

Red continued. "But, as you can see this copy of the annual has a marginal notation in it. I take that to mean that at one time it belonged to the person to whom the inscription was made. In this case, that person would be Superintendent Malcolm."

The faux Ms. Wigglesworth examined the yearbook. "That's odd." She paused for a second before she finished her thought. "But, now that I think about it, Ms. Malcolm was in here two or three weeks ago. She looked at some old yearbooks, too. I thought, in light of the shootings, she might have been reviewing the annuals of the children who died, maybe putting together a tribute or something." She flipped to the front page of the yearbook, turned it over and checked the inside back cover. "Yes, it is odd, indeed."

"How so, Ms. Wigglesworth?" Red asked, smiling.

She giggled again before she answered. "This isn't the library's copy." She pointed at the one containing the inscription. "We always mark our complimentary copy with a stamp that says 'Property of Kilgore Public Library.' The copy you found in the archives doesn't bear the stamp."

"Any thoughts about how this copy may have ended up in your archive stacks, Ms. Wigglesworth?" Red asked.

She giggled twice this time.

"It's only a guess, you understand, but I would think it's in our stacks because Ms. Malcolm may have inadvertently swapped hers for ours while she was doing her research."

"Thank you, Ms. Wigglesworth," Red said.

"No trouble at all, Mister..."

"Roper. Red Roper," Red said.

"No trouble at all, Mr. Red Roper," she said as she giggled and wiggled her way to the back room and out of our sight.

Red and I walked back to where we had twenty yearbooks strewn on the massive oak library table. We sat down.

"It wasn't inadvertent," Red said.

"What wasn't inadvertent?"

"Brigitte Malcolm wouldn't bring her yearbook in here knowing it contained that inscription and then misplace it or lose it in the stacks."

"I agree, Red. She planted it here, hoping someone would find it."

Red shook his head. "Not someone, Etch. She left her annual here for you to find, Mr. Special Prosecutor."

"So that performance she gave at my office was all for show?"

"She wanted to come down hard on you, so you would be sure to investigate her along with the other people potentially caught up in this deal."

I pointed at the yearbook with the Jimmy B inscription. "You're saying this is a cry for help?"

Red nodded.

Chapter Twenty-Eight

That evening, May Ellen and I ate supper at Panda Express and then rode around town for a while as the summer sky turned softer, darkness falling gently on the only world we knew well. While we toured the familiar homes and yards, I laid out the case against Jim Briscoe for her, my sounding board whose insight into the human condition was unparalleled.

After I had summarized the key points of the investigation for her, I stopped talking and gave her time to mull the information.

"Why would Coach Briscoe do such a thing?" she asked.

"That's the part I haven't quite figured out."

"What's your best guess?"

"He had to be motivated by powerful forces, the sorts of things that make people willing to risk their lives."

"There aren't many of those, Etch. Love, hate, and revenge come to mind."

As always, May Ellen saw the human situation in its most profound essence. She could boil it down.

"The only person Jim Briscoe loves is himself. I am confident of that. Since that is the starting point, then he hates everyone who doesn't love him as he believes they should."

"Which brings us to revenge," May Ellen said.

"Yeah. The thing is that I don't know why those kids would be the object of his revenge. They hadn't spurned him, for God's sake."

"It'll come to you, Etch. You're getting close. Just keep digging."

And that was all she had to say on the subject, except for one last recommendation.

"Start at the top."

I had a blank look on my face.

"Brigitte Malcolm. There's no time like the present."

The old Malcolm place sat on five wooded acres of centuries-old live oaks, tucked away on the far corner of the oldest residential section of Kilgore. The structure was vintage farmhouse, a covered porch wrapped around the entirety of the one-story white frame building. The dog run that originally split the house into two sections had long been enclosed to form an interior hallway. The roof rose high on top of the house, gradually steepening from its edges to a point in the middle.

It was almost pitch-black outside when May Ellen and I pulled into the driveway. Clarence Malcolm, Brigitte's father, was still outside, on his knees, pulling weeds from his rose garden. He pushed himself up and walked over to my car. I rolled my window down.

"Good evening, Etch," Clarence said as he stuck his hand in the car window and shook mine. He leaned so he could see May Ellen in the passenger seat. "Good evening to you, too, May Ellen."

"Good evening, Clarence. Your roses are beautiful."

"There's no beauty without thorns," he said to her.

"Ain't that the truth, Clarence," May Ellen said.

Clarence looked at me. "Bridge is in the house, Etch. She's been expecting you to pay her a visit."

"I think I'll help Clarence pull a few weeds while you and Brigitte talk," May Ellen said.

"I'd appreciate that, May Ellen," Clarence said. "I've got an extra pair of gloves here somewhere." He smiled at May Ellen.

I parked near the house and May Ellen joined Clarence in the roses. When my foot hit the top step of the porch, the front door opened, and Brigitte Malcolm stepped outside. She was wearing faded blue jeans, her hair pulled back in a ponytail, red clay stains on a long-sleeved old denim work shirt. She removed her gardening gloves and shook my hand.

"You banned me from KISD property," I said. "But you didn't say the ban extended to your house, Ms. Malcolm."

"In this house, I'm known as 'Bridge,' Etch."

"I saw that name in your yearbook and wondered about it."

"I hoped you would."

She motioned for me to sit in a white wicker rocker, and she sat opposite me on an oak stool.

"Bridge, I take it that you have insight into the Jim Briscoe case, which you haven't shared with anyone yet."

"I do, Etch. It's a long story."

"I've got time."

For the next forty-five minutes, Brigitte Malcolm peeled the layers off the mystery for me. By the time she finished, I knew I could make the case against Briscoe, and I knew that she would be the star witness for the prosecution, one who had no need for a deal for immunity from prosecution in exchange for her testimony.

On the way home, I had a question for May Ellen. "When we arrived at the Malcolm place this evening, Clarence said Bridge was expecting me. Am I that predictable?"

May Ellen's eyes sparkled. "Maybe."

"Is there something else you'd like to add to that observation, baby?"

"Well, I may have forgotten to tell you one thing."

I braced myself for a litany of revelations about the weaknesses in my character. "What's that?"

"While you and Red were at the library doing your thing this afternoon, Clarence called me."

"And?"

"He said Bridge would like to visit with you this evening and wondered if we could stop by his place."

"You old manipulator, you."

May Ellen smiled. "But, you are pretty predictable, Etch." She patted my arm and winked at me.

Chapter Twenty-Nine

In Texas state court, a grand jury consists of twelve qualified persons whose duty it is to determine if probable cause exists to charge a person with a crime. If at least nine of those persons vote to return a 'true bill,' an indictment issues and the game is on.

I had served as an assistant district attorney in my early years as a lawyer and had often presented cases to grand juries. That experience taught me a couple of lessons. First, the prosecutor is completely in charge of the grand jury proceedings and can present the evidence however he wants. There is no defense attorney present to argue the other side of the case. This means the state's attorney can present only evidence favorable to the prosecution, or he can include exculpatory material, things that may suggest the possible innocence of the accused. The second lesson follows on the first. I had found that the best approach in the grand jury room, especially in a case which could go either way, was to give the grand jury enough evidence so that jurors must deliberate on the facts and not just act as a rubber stamp for the prosecution.

The case of the *State of Texas versus Jim Briscoe*, however, was a horse of a different color. It presented issues new to Texas jurisprudence and was premised on a patchwork quilt of assumptions and conflicting witness statements. I knew those twelve jurors would bring with them their gut feelings that were unreliable indicators of guilt or innocence, their viewings of media coverage of other episodes of school violence, their fears, and a pervasive frustration at our society's inability to stop the killings of our children.

I knew going in that the only way to prevail in the case was to depoliticize it, to lay it out not as a school shooting, but rather as an act of murder which Briscoe committed on a school campus. It was a crime that could have occurred elsewhere. In other words, my challenge was to deemphasize the school aspect and focus on the underlying reasons for the crime, the same vile motivations that had produced murders from the beginning of human history to the present day.

The more I thought about the uniqueness of the Briscoe case, the more I realized it was not one for a nuanced presentation before the grand jury. So, I took the chicken's way out. I gave those twelve citizens the Cliffs Notes version of the facts, cajoled them about the important message they must send to the entire country, about the role they played right here, right now.

I also built in an escape hatch for the jurors, a middle ground. It was what we in the trade referred to as a "lesser included." A lesser included was a crime with some of the elements of the highest possible charge supported by the evidence, but not necessarily all of them. In the Briscoe case, this meant that the jurors could compromise and decide not to charge him with capital murder, a crime that carried the possibility of the death penalty, but rather could vote to charge him with simple murder, a first-degree felony but not a capital one. It was my way of signaling them that if they felt capital murder was a bridge too far, they could still do their duty and charge him with an offense that would ensure he spent the rest of his life in the penitentiary.

And that's what they did. After an hour of deliberations, the grand jurors voted nine to three to indict Jim Briscoe for the murders of Carmel Sideout, Maria Juarez, and Benjamin Cohen.

In a case where the defendant has not been arrested for the crime for which he is charged, the law provides that the indictment be "sealed." This means the existence of the indictment is kept secret until the accused is taken into custody. However, in a case such as Briscoe's where the defendant has an attorney, the custom is for the prosecutor to contact the defense attorney once the grand jury returns an indictment so that the attorney can make arrangements for the defendant to turn himself in and post bail.

So, at 3:30 p.m. on the day the grand jury voted to indict her client, I called Jesmyn Thompson to give her the news.

"Etch Danielson for Jesmyn Thompson," I said to the receptionist who answered the call.

"Is she expecting your call, Mr. Davidson?"

"It's Danielson. I don't know what she expects."

"Please hold, Mr. Davidson."

Before I could correct her again about my name, she was gone. I listened to an LA news feed for a minute and a half.

"Ms. Thompson's office," the next voice said when Jesmyn's assistant answered.

"Etch Danielson for Ms. Thompson."

"What case are you calling about, Mr. Daniels?"

"It's Danielson. Tell her it's about Coach Jim Briscoe."

"Is Mr. Briscoe a current client?"

"Just deliver the message." My patience was wearing thin.

Ninety seconds later, Jesmyn came on the line. "Etch, this is Jesmyn Thompson. Sorry to keep you waiting. I was in a meeting."

An important person like Jesmyn Thompson was always in a meeting.

"The grand jury just indicted Coach Briscoe for murder. This is a courtesy call to see if you plan to turn him in."

"I'll have to check my schedule."

"You seem to have misconstrued my call, Jesmyn. Let me be slightly more blunt. A warrant has issued for Coach Briscoe's arrest. It is not subject to your appointment calendar. Either he turns himself in now or we will bring him in."

"Etch, I'm in LA. I can't be in Longview in ten minutes."

"Do they have phones in LA?" I asked. "If so, I assume you can call your client and tell him to turn his ass in. I am also confident that you already have local counsel on board who can meet your client in Longview and accompany him to the jail for processing."

"My, aren't we pissy today?"

"The clock is ticking, Jesmyn. Will you turn Briscoe in or not?"

"Let me call you back." The phone clicked dead.

Twelve minutes later she called me. "I can't reach him right now, Etch. My calls are going to voice mail. I'll keep trying and let you know when I get through to him."

"Are you telling me your client is on the lam, Jesmyn?"

"I'm telling you I can't reach him right now, Etch."

"You represent a guy facing murder charges in one of the most high-profile cases in the country and you expect me to believe he won't take your calls?"

"You can believe whatever you please, Etch. I will call you back when I reach him. Until then, I am in a holding pattern. I'm sure you have found yourself in similar circumstances at some point in your long career."

"If you're asking me if I've had clients who ran, you're right. I have. Bad on them," I said. "We'll see you at the arraignment, Jesmyn. Oh, and in light of Coach Briscoe's failure to turn himself in, I will inform the judge at the bail hearing that he's a flight risk who should be denied bond. Nice talking to you, Jesmyn." I ended the call.

I speed-dialed Red.

"At your service, counselor."

"Where are you?"

"Just outside Alexandria, Louisiana, across the street from the Waffle House."

"You wouldn't happen to have a visual on some guy named Jimmy B, would you?"

"Him and a friend. They're drinking coffee and eating scrambled eggs. Jimmy B just took a short call from someone on his cell. It didn't seem to faze him."

"Really? Who's he hanging with these days? Inquiring minds want to know."

"The wizard himself."

"Not Merlin the Great?"

"The one and only. You want me to bring in both of them? I could make hindering apprehension stick against Hostetler if we want him to catch a ride with me back to Texas."

"I like the way you think, Red. But, let's give Merlin a pass on this one. I'd prefer he had some time to reflect on his choices in life."

"And perhaps have a heart to heart with his attorney about the importance of cooperating with a murder investigation?"

"Perhaps."

Four minutes later, a text from Red hit my cell. '1 Under' was all it said. I knew that was cop-speak for one person under arrest.

I thought about calling Jesmyn to tell her that her client was in custody and on his way to the Gregg County jail in Longview, Texas. But, I didn't think it would be nice of me to interrupt her important meeting again.

Chapter Thirty

With the arrest of Jim Briscoe the fat was in the fire. The news that the coach had been charged with three counts of murder for the KHS shootings spread like wildfire, and reporters from the major news outlets descended on East Texas, clamoring for sound bites and scraps of information. The coverage was relentless and merciless, each new broadcast or article or social media post reigniting the horror of the killings and ripping the scab off the community's six-week-old wound.

On the third day following Briscoe's arrest, Jesmyn Thompson and I stood at our battle stations in front of the honorable Arrick Merrell, visiting judge in the Jim Briscoe case.

Briscoe had spent the last three days in the crossbar Hilton, unable to make the two-million-dollar bond Judge Merrell set when Red delivered the coach into custody. When a deputy brought Briscoe in handcuffs to the courtroom for the hearing and led him to his chair next to his attorney, I saw him for the first time since the day of Carmel Sideout's funeral. He was dressed in an orange jumpsuit with Gregg County Jail stenciled on the front and back, his belly bulging against the front zipper, a three-day growth of salt and pepper beard on his face, his tufts of brown hair jutting north, south, east and west.

The judge's oak bench was elevated four-feet above the floor level of the courtroom. I stood at the counsel table nearest the jury box and defense counsel stood to my left at an identical table. Beyond the railing that separated the attorneys and judge from the gallery, a middle aisle cut the room into halves, each section containing ten pews capable of seating a dozen people.

Reporters, concerned citizens and gawkers filled every available seat.

Red stood at the back of the room, keeping an eye on the double glass doors which constituted the public entrance to the courtroom, while Ron Braxton sat on the end of the last pew adjusting his eyeglasses and biting his fingernails.

Ms. Thompson had entered the courtroom two minutes before Judge Merrell took the bench. She was a Black woman in her mid-fifties, five-six, maybe one hundred and fifty pounds, her black hair straight and hanging just above her shoulders. She wore a tailored brown jacket, a brown skirt, a white blouse with a dark blue scarf threaded through her collar to simulate a necktie. With her was her local counsel, Harold Fleming, a Longview attorney who had served twenty-four years as a federal judge before retiring from the bench two years before to spend the remainder of his career in private practice. Fleming was my age and height, silver-haired, tanned, a little shy of two hundred pounds, his trademark half-glasses anchored by his ears and resting on the top of his head at a forty-five-degree angle to his face. He wore a window-pane navy three-piece suit, a green tie with a gold Baylor Law School logo embossed on it. Both he and Jesmyn gave me a perfunctory handshake before they assumed their positions at the defense table.

Judge Merrell studied the papers in the court file while we waited for her to address us. She had been elected to three four-year terms as a criminal district court judge in a neighboring county before her retirement from the trial bench ten years earlier. She occasionally sat as a visiting judge when the supervising judge of the judicial district requested her to take an assignment. Her hair, once jet black now pure white, hung down her back to her waist. Her silver-framed glasses had circular lenses, which barely covered her blue eyes and magnified them into a Doctor Magoo look. Several surgical interventions had tightened the white, translucent skin of her face so that it displayed the chiseled architecture of her facial bones and gave her the fine features of Queen Nefertiti.

"The Court calls The State of Texas versus James Briscoe," Judge Merrell said. "What says the state?"

"Etch Danielson, special prosecutor for the state of Texas, Your Honor. We are ready to proceed on the arraignment and Motion to Reduce Bail."

"What says the defendant?" the judge asked.

"Jesmyn Thompson and Harold Fleming for the defendant, James Briscoe, Your Honor. We are ready to proceed. We have received a copy of the indictment and would waive formal arraignment and enter a plea of not guilty, Your Honor," Jesmyn said.

"Very well then," Judge Merrell said. "The defendant having waived formal arraignment and entered his plea of not guilty to the indictment, we will turn our attention to the Motion to Reduce Bail. It's your motion, Ms. Thompson. Everyone else may take their seats."

A rustling of clothes and papers filled the room and the old wooden pews creaked as the people in the gallery shoe-horned themselves into their seats.

Jesmyn remained standing and spoke from her place at the counsel table. "I'll be brief, Your Honor. Coach Briscoe is a pillar of the community. He's been an employee at Kilgore ISD for twenty years, owns a home in Kilgore, and has no prior arrests. A generation of citizens of this county have entrusted their children into his care. He is not a flight risk and not a danger to the community. As a career teacher and coach, he has limited resources, and a two-million-dollar bail for him amounts to an unconstitutional denial of bond. For these reasons, Your Honor, we ask that you reduce his bail to an amount he can post."

"Response, Mr. Danielson?" the judge asked.

"Several things, Your Honor. First, the defendant was apprehended out of state, and he has exhibited efforts to conceal his whereabouts. That makes him a flight risk."

Judge Merrell interrupted me. "How did you find him so quickly, Mr. Danielson?"

"I have a good investigator, Your Honor."

The judge raised her head and scanned the courtroom. When she saw Red at the back of the room, she smiled. "I think he's talking about you, Mr. Roper."

Red saluted her.

"OK. Continue your response, Mr. Danielson."

"The second thing is the nature of the offense, Your Honor. Three students are dead. I can think of no greater danger to the community."

"As you know, Mr. Danielson, an indictment is no evidence of guilt. Mr. Briscoe is presumed innocent of the charges," Judge Merrell said.

"Finally, Your Honor, is the question of the defendant's resources. He was able to retain two preeminent attorneys. We have seen no evidence that he lacks the ability to make the current bond."

"Maybe the lawyers drained him dry, Mr. Danielson," the judge said. Laughter skittered through the gallery.

The judge spoke to Jesmyn, who stood again. "Ms. Thompson is there a specific bond amount you are requesting?"

"One hundred and fifty thousand dollars, Your Honor."

"What do you say to that, Mr. Danielson?" Judge Merrell asked.

"We would not oppose bond in the amount of five hundred thousand, Your Honor."

The judge considered the numbers for a second. "I agree with the prosecution on this one, Ms. Thompson. I hereby reduce bail to half a million."

"Thank you, Your Honor," Jesmyn said.

The judge addressed both sides. "I will issue a scheduling order in the case before the end of the day. It is my intention to move with all deliberate speed, and I do not take kindly to unnecessary delays. Does everyone catch my drift?" She stood up, descended the steps to floor level and exited the courtroom through a side door.

An hour later, Jim Briscoe posted the half-million-dollar bond.

Chapter Thirty-One

With the case on the fast track thanks to Judge Merrell's scheduling order, I fought the tendency to lose myself in the details of trial preparation. I had found that even though a trial may turn on a seemingly insignificant fact, for the most part, jurors were concerned with the big picture.

I had to focus on the things that mattered, the submerged mass of the iceberg, not the small sliver that jutted through the surface of the icy water.

That's why shortly after sunup the day following the preliminary hearing, I walked among the graves at Kilgore Cemetery. While the grounds crew manicured the burial plots, emptied dried flowers from garbage containers, set up a tent for a mid-morning grave side service, I paid my respects, first to my mother and father, then to my maternal grandparents, their final resting places clustered near each other. A hundred yards or so to the east, I could make out four splotches of red clay, silent markers of bodies recently offered back to the earth from which they came.

I watched as Pearline lumbered next to the new graves in the southeast corner of the burial ground, and Red got out, removed his Stetson and stood near the array, his head bowed.

When I reached the spot where Red stood, I noticed for the first time the white marble border that outlined the perimeter of the plot, the word COHEN chiseled in the stretch of stone nearest the drive.

"I had forgotten that Levi Cohen donated the plots for Maria and Carmel," I said to Red.

Red took a white handkerchief from his back pocket, dried his eyes. "He wanted the kids to be together in death as they had been in life."

We stood in the shade of a pecan tree, its trunk six-feet in diameter, and watched the sun as it climbed away from the eastern horizon, its fire shrouded by wispy cirrus clouds.

"I wonder if even then Levi knew he would soon join them here," I said.

"It's a helluva thing, Etch." He looked at Levi Cohen's grave, the mound of dirt on it fresher than the others.

I stepped inside the border and walked next to each grave, reading the hand-written temporary markers that identified them, Benjamin closest to his father, Maria between her two friends. When I came to Carmel's grave, I noticed a bouquet of summer flowers still fresh. Attached to the makeshift wreath was a card containing a note to the fallen young man. I leaned closer and read the words aloud, "I will always love you, baby boy, Momma."

"Momma L has always been true," Red said when he heard me read the inscription.

I studied the note a few seconds before I straightened up. "She has. But, she didn't write this note, Red. I saw her handwriting the other day when she gave me her cell phone number. This isn't a match."

Red knelt and studied the card. "The cemetery work crew makes a sweep at least once a week and removes dried flowers. That means someone placed this wreath on Carmel's grave in the last few days."

"Someone who identified herself as 'Momma.'"

"Caddo Panola?" Red asked.

"It must be her. She's come home."

"Momma L told you she hadn't heard from Caddo in ten years, that she didn't even show for Carmel's funeral. What's changed in the last six weeks to bring her home?" Red asked.

"Beats the hell out of me. But I'd sure like to know."

"She's close, Etch. I figure she'll come forward soon enough, when whatever brought her this far brings her all the way back."

We both glanced around the cemetery grounds, as if we expected to see Caddo Panola pop out from behind a tree.

But she remained hidden.

I pulled into the covered parking at my office about a quarter before eight in the morning and saw a maroon Mustang waiting for me in the main parking lot. I got out and stood next to my truck until Marcus Wellborn came next to me.

He had a friend with him. I took her to be a high school classmate, her dark hair long down her back, the bright glow of youth in her brown eyes and radiating from her tanned arms.

"Mr. Danielson, this is Eugenia Dacus. She and Maria Juarez were best friends."

I shook her hand. "It's a pleasure to meet you, Eugenia. I'm sorry for your loss."

"She needs to talk to you, sir. I can wait in the car," Marcus said.

"That's all right, Marcus. Y'all come in."

I unlocked the door to the back room, left it open for them and stepped inside to turn on the lights. Marcus and Eugenia sat down in the high-backed chairs in front of my desk and waited for me to sit opposite them.

"What would you like to tell me, Eugenia?" She was staring at me like a puppy that had just received a spanking for wetting the floor.

Marcus took her hand. "Just tell him like you told me, Gennie. He wants to help."

She held his hand while she spoke. "Maria and I did everything together, Mr. Danielson. When she wasn't with Carmel, she was with me."

I nodded.

"Tell him about the Back Porch, Gennie," Marcus said.

"I'm getting there, Marcus." The glow in her eyes had turned to fire as she snapped at him and dropped his hand.

"What happened at the Back Porch, Eugenia?" The Back Porch was a local fixture, a restaurant that served hamburgers and fries, sandwiches and salads. The rear of the place was a bar with a dance floor where bands played three nights a week, and the diner hosted karaoke on the off nights.

Eugenia came out with it. "During Spring break, Maria and I went to the Back Porch. I don't know the exact day, but it was a week night, probably Tuesday or Wednesday, a karaoke night. It was crowded when we got there, so we looked around for a place to sit and couldn't find a table. We saw Ms. McEntyre and Coach Briscoe in one of the booths and they motioned for us to join them."

"I take it that Ms. McEntyre and Coach Briscoe were there together?"

"Sure. Everybody knows they're a couple," she said. "They were sitting next to each other on one side of the booth. Coach was on the inside. Maria slid in first, so she was sitting across from Coach, and I sat on the outside across from Ms. McEntyre."

"What happened next?"

"We sat there a few minutes just visiting. Ms. McEntyre said she needed to go to the ladies' room, and I went with her. That left Maria and Coach in the booth together. We were probably gone ten minutes or so taking a powder. When we got back to the booth, I could tell from the expression on Maria's face that something was up."

"What kind of expression?"

"It was a mixture of scared and mad. Before I could sit down, Maria slid to the edge of the booth and motioned for me to come with her to the ladies' room again. I played it off to Coach and Ms. McEntyre like it was a typical girls' thing, and they laughed about it."

"Neither of them, Coach Briscoe or Ms. McEntyre, seemed concerned about anything that might have happened while you were gone the first time?"

"No. They were oblivious. Just laughing and eating their burgers, you know."

"So, what happened when you and Maria got to the ladies' room?"

"Maria was so mad her hands were shaking. She said Coach came on to her as soon as Ms. McEntyre and I were out of sight. He took her hand, told her how beautiful she looked, all that stuff. We were used to that treatment from Coach. He was always pushing it, getting close to the line with the girls."

"But this time was different somehow?"

"Yeah. Maria said Coach told her a girl like her could do a lot better than ..." She paused.

"Than what, Eugenia?"

"I don't want to say it, Mr. Danielson." She looked away from me.

"He needs to know, Gennie," Marcus said. "Please tell him."

Eugenia took a deep breath. "OK. He said a girl like her could do a lot better than that N-word she was with. Except he didn't say 'N-word.'"

"How did Maria handle the situation, Eugenia?"

"Like I said. She was so mad she was shaking. She texted Carmel and asked him to come get her as soon as he could. She said in the text that Coach Briscoe was giving her a hard time at the Back Porch."

"Did Carmel come to the Back Porch?"

"He and Benjamin showed up about fifteen minutes later."

"Benjamin came with him?"

"Carmel was working a shift at Starbucks in Longview and didn't have a car at the time. So Benjamin carried him to work and picked him up when he got off. Carmel bought him a tank of gas every time he got paid. Carmel received Maria's text just as he was clocking out, and he and Benjamin came straight to the Back Porch."

"What happened when the boys arrived?"

"As soon as Maria saw Carmel come in, she elbowed me and we slid out of the booth and stood up. Carmel came up to Maria and asked her if everything was OK. He wasn't a guy to show his temper, Mr. Danielson, but he wasn't taking his eyes off Coach Briscoe. Maria played it down and said things were fine, that she wasn't feeling that well and needed to get some air. Maria, Carmel, Benjamin and I walked outside, but we looked around and Ms. McEntyre and Coach were coming out right behind us. Carmel wheeled around and got in Coach's face, told him to keep his hands off Maria. Benjamin stepped between them and told them to break it up."

"What was Ms. McEntyre doing all this time?"

"Nothing. She was just standing there taking it all in."

"How did y'all leave it, Eugenia?"

"We went our separate ways. Maria and I met the boys over at Benjamin's house, and we didn't see Coach and Ms. McEntyre until school began after Spring break."

"Did you or Maria ever have a meeting with Ms. McEntyre and tell her what Coach said about Carmel?"

"No, sir. We left it alone."

"Eugenia, do you know if Maria ever told Carmel what Coach Briscoe said to her that night at the Back Porch?"

She leaned forward in her chair, cupped her face in her hands, wrinkled her brow. "I've thought about it a lot, Mr. Danielson. Maria didn't tell me that she told Carmel about the N-word. But that's not the sort of thing she would have shared with me. She would have kept it private, just between Carmel and her. Part of me says she would have told him. But the other part says she would have spared him that insult. I mean they were planning to leave Kilgore behind as soon as we graduated and Coach Briscoe would have been a thing of the past."

"Did Carmel and Coach have any other run-ins after that night at the Back Porch, Eugenia?"

"Not until the day Coach killed him, Mr. Danielson."

Chapter Thirty-Two

An hour later, Red sat across from me in the back room and listened as I gave him Eugenia's report about the incident at the Back Porch.

"It cuts both ways," he said after he heard the story.

"Yeah. On the one hand it gives Coach motive to strike out at Carmel, Benjamin and Maria. On the other hand, Jesmyn Thompson will say the standoff at the Back Porch may have been what spurred Carmel to go after Briscoe."

"The part I don't get is Beryl McEntyre. She's right in the middle of this deal, but she's acting like a disinterested observer."

I looked at my notes, processed the pieces. "All we really know about the Back Porch is what Eugenia said. Under her version of the facts, Beryl wasn't present when the conversation took place between Maria and Briscoe. When things escalated between Carmel and Coach, she may have thought it was typical Briscoe bullshit. She had to know he was always coming on to the girls, and she may have chalked up the confrontation to a case of teenage drama."

"Maybe. But, it happened during Spring break and within just a few days she learned about Benjamin's one-act play. She had to make a connection. Plus, I can't imagine that she didn't grill Briscoe about what went on between him and Maria while she was in the ladies' room."

"I don't know, Red. My guess is that Beryl knew anything Briscoe told her about his interactions with women was a lie."

"But she stayed with him anyway. Go figure."

Red laid a folder on my desk and opened it. "What you got there?" I asked.

"My guy's report on the cell phone issue. We're trying to track down the source of the call to the burner phone in Carmel's backpack."

"And?"

"He's come up empty so far. None of the likely suspects made a call from their cells that triggered Carmel's burner phone the day of the shootings. So the call either came from another burner one of them had or from someone we haven't identified yet."

"Any update on the missing phone at the DPS lab in Austin?"

"Nothing."

"Can you expand on that 'someone we haven't identified yet' comment?"

Red flipped the file folder closed. "That means there may be someone else in the loop who was helping Briscoe. If we're right about the plan, Briscoe couldn't act until the burner phone in Carmel's backpack buzzed. Whoever made the call to set things in motion was cold-blooded. That person knew things would come unhinged right after he hit send, and he did it anyway."

"Any thoughts about how we can identify the mystery person?"

"Not yet. But I do know one thing."

I waited.

"It wasn't some sort of game for whoever placed the call. It was personal."

"Personal against whom? Carmel or Maria or Benjamin?"

"Maybe one of them, maybe some combination of a couple of them, maybe all three of them."

"We need to keep rattling cages, Red. Someone's gonna break."

"Let's just hope they break before a jury cuts Briscoe loose," Red said.

"Amen to that."

We were about to adjourn our sit-down when I heard the fax line on my copy machine shriek. I got up and walked over to the machine. It spit out fifteen pages before it shut off. I grabbed the sheaf of documents, made a quick read-through, and sat down at my desk again.

"Love notes from Jesmyn?" Red asked.

"Most of it is standard stuff. Requests for copies of witness statements, police reports, criminal history searches. I already have that stuff ready to send to her."

"What's not standard?"

"This one." I held up a copy of a three-page motion. "It's a request for a speedy trial."

"I thought defense attorneys filed speedy trial requests all the time."

"They do. Usually that happens when the defendant is in jail awaiting trial. They file for a speedy trial to keep a guy from spending a lot of time incarcerated before his case is heard. This deal is different. Briscoe has made bail. He's on the street. In that situation, the thing defense attorneys want the least is a speedy trial. The passage of time works to their advantage. Maybe witnesses go missing or die. Maybe someone flips on somebody else and their guy walks. The longer they can keep their guy away from the courthouse the better. Criminal Law 101 is that a defendant out on bond won't go to the penitentiary until he's had his day in court."

"So why would Jesmyn want a speedy trial for Coach Briscoe, counselor? Enlighten me."

I read through the motion again just to buy a little time before I answered Red. "Only two reasons come to mind. First, Jesmyn believes she's got a winner in Jim Briscoe. Her marching orders are to make this trial a national referendum on the importance of arming teachers in public schools."

"What's the other reason?"

"Because she wants the case to go to trial before we put all the pieces together. She thinks we're closing in on figuring out Briscoe's plan and his motive. The faster she moves the case to trial, the more pressure she puts on us. It's a smart play on her part. She can paint Briscoe as God's gift to Kilgore High School, to the whole country, while we wallow around trying to find out who else is in on the deal. The good guys are dead and the bad guys are only interested in protecting themselves."

Red stood up. "Let's make sure the good guys don't get the shaft, Etch."

"Where are you headed next?" I asked him.

"I've got some cages to rattle." He let himself out. In less than a minute, I heard Pearline roar, her tires screeching as Red charged out of the parking lot.

I rifled through the files in the Briscoe case until I found my notes from the conversation I had with one of the witnesses.

I picked up my cell and entered a number.

On the third ring, the voice of a woman came on the line, a person who had been less than candid with me in our first meeting.

Chapter Thirty-Three

Mid-afternoon, I was working the front desk at the bookstore, answering questions about some of our new books, inquiring of customers about their genres of choice, accepting books in trade, entering them into inventory, when the woman I had spoken to earlier that day entered.

This time, Patty Douglas was in her sloppy copy, jogging pants, an over-sized Texas A&M sweatshirt, her hair pulled back in a ponytail. A man I took to be her husband kept his distance from me and scampered out of the lobby and around the corner toward the coffee shop without introducing himself.

"You wanted to talk to me about the case, Mr. Danielson?" Ms. Douglas asked.

"That's right, Ms. Douglas. I would prefer we do that in private. Would your husband care to join us?"

"No. He's good," she said glancing down the hall where the man with her was last seen. "He'll catch up to us if he wants to."

I escorted her outside, and we entered the back room. I closed the plantation shutters to ensure our privacy.

I cut to the chase. "I have received information about an incident at the Back Porch involving Maria, Carmel, and Coach Briscoe. It happened during Spring break this year. Do you know anything about it, Ms. Douglas?"

She crossed her legs, folded her hands and rested them on her knee. "Maria mentioned it to me."

"What did she tell you?"

"She said Coach Briscoe made advances toward her and she called Carmel and he came to the Back Porch and rescued her."

"How did he rescue her?"

"He got her away from Briscoe, told him to keep his hands off her or he'd make him pay."

Eugenia hadn't mentioned that part of the confrontation. "Did Carmel say what he meant by making Briscoe pay?"

"Maria didn't break it down for me, Mr. Danielson."

"How did you interpret what Carmel said?"

"I assumed he planned to report Coach Briscoe if he acted like that toward Maria again."

"Report Briscoe to whom?"

Ms. Douglas shifted in her chair while she thought about it. "Principal McEntyre, I assume."

"You know Briscoe and Ms. McEntyre are together, don't you, Ms. Douglas?"

"That's what I've heard."

"Do you think it would have done much good for Carmel to report Coach Briscoe to Ms. McEntyre? She was there at the Back Porch when it happened."

"Well, then, maybe he would have made the report to the superintendent."

"Did Maria report the incident to the superintendent? She was Briscoe's target. There was no reason she had to wait for him to be inappropriate with her again."

"If she reported it to Ms. Malcolm, Maria didn't tell me about it."

I had to raise the other issue, the one that lay just beneath the surface. "Did Maria mention a racial remark Coach Briscoe made about Carmel to Maria?"

She leaned forward. "What sort of racial remark?"

"Any sort."

"No. She never said anything to me about Briscoe talking like that about Carmel. What did Gennie say Briscoe said?"

"I didn't mention my source, Ms. Douglas."

Patty Douglas stiffened in her chair. "I know Gennie and Maria went to the Back Porch together that evening. Obviously, Maria couldn't have been your source, so that means the report had to come from Gennie." I noticed irritation in her voice.

"Does something about Gennie reporting the incident to me upset you, Ms. Douglas?"

"She needs to keep her nose out of Maria's business, that's all. Gennie has been known to exaggerate if it suits her purpose."

"Are you saying you don't believe her report of what happened that night?" I needed to know if Gennie could be trusted to tell the truth when the time came.

Ms. Douglas slumped in the chair. "I don't know what to believe any more, Mr. Danielson. Since the shootings, I've felt that the whole world is out of focus. Nothing makes sense." She paused for a couple of beats. "I shouldn't have said what I did about Gennie. I just hadn't heard before the business about the racial remark. I lived with a man who said such things. You let yourself be around a person like that, then you grow to resent him, then you beat yourself up from putting up with it, then you wonder how it has affected your children, then you leave him, then you swear not to make that mistake again. Then you learn your child had to face the same shit from a guy like Briscoe and you want to strike out at him, but you realize it's too late. The harm's done, and there's no taking it back, no making it right, ever again."

She was crying by the time she finished.

Something clicked in my head as I thought back on my first conversation with Patty Douglas. "Did learning today about Coach Briscoe's racial remark to Maria upset you because it reminded you of the sort of thing Maria's father might have said?"

She nodded. "I knew from the get-go he was a bigot, Mr. Danielson, and I stayed with him anyway."

"Maria knew the way he was, didn't she?"

"Sure. We talked about it a lot of times."

"And she still took Carmel to meet him?"

"She thought that when Raul met Carmel, he would see the error of his ways, that we would turn the corner on his bigotry."

"But that's not how it played out, is it?"

"No. Raul threw them out of his house. He told Maria she wasn't welcome there so long as she was with Carmel." She raised her head to look at me. "I suppose those were the last words her father ever said to her."

Something was still nagging at me. "Ms. Douglas, can you help me understand the time line? The confrontation at the Back Porch was the week of Spring break. When did Maria and Carmel go to Houston to see your ex?"

She thought about it. "I think it was mid-April." She took out her phone and studied a calendar on it. "I remember now. It was on the Easter break. They left on Good Friday and planned to come home Sunday. But the blowout between Maria and her dad happened the day they arrived, so she and Carmel cut their visit short and came home Friday evening."

"Maria's dad didn't come to Kilgore after that to patch things up with her?"

She shook her head.

Chapter Thirty-Four

By my calculation, right at thirty years had passed since I had been to Momma L's house. As I drove up the red dirt drive to her home, I entered a time warp, the same wind blowing through the pine trees, the same rusted screens blocking the breeze before it could billow the white cotton curtains which hung still against the window sills. On my last visit, I sat in the front room, which she called 'the parlor,' and informed her and her seventeen-year-old daughter, Caddo Panola, about the plea deal I had cut in Caddo's misdemeanor possession of marijuana case. They were pleased that under the terms of the deal Caddo's arrest record would be expunged, wiped clean, if she complied with the terms of a six-month probation.

An old bird dog, its splotched brown and white coat grayed with the weight of time, lay under the porch when I stepped out of my truck. It raised its head to greet me before it dropped back into its slumber. I rapped my knuckles on the door, and as I waited for Momma L the incongruity of my presence struck me as it had so many times when I played my role as small town lawyer to small town people. It was my otherness, my imagined access to the halls of justice, that they welcomed in me, and which guaranteed us a permanent status as acquaintances. Because they bared their souls to me, they kept their distance from me. For I was a perpetual reminder of their worst failures, their one moment of terrible, unforgivable rage, of a night of drunken stupor, of first love lost forever, of business deals between brothers gone bad.

"Come on in, Etch," Momma L said as she unlatched the screen door for me.

In the parlor I sat in a caned-back rocker and she sat across from me on a yellow Naugahyde sofa.

"I have a couple of things to talk with you about, Momma L."

"Let me have it, then."

"Did you know about a fight Carmel and Coach Briscoe had at the Back Porch during Spring break this year?"

"It wasn't a fight. Carmel was just standing up for Maria."

"Says who?"

"Carmel and Benjamin told me about it the next morning. I guess they figured it would be all over town and they wanted me to know about it before I heard it on the street."

"Why is it that we are almost to trial in a murder case, the case in which you want me to clear Carmel's name, and I am just now hearing about it? Don't you see that the defense will make that fight the center piece of its argument? They will say Carmel had a bone to pick with Coach Briscoe about an affair of the heart, perhaps the deadliest thing known to man."

She put both her hands on the couch and shifted her position. "I should have told you about it, Etch. But nothing came of it."

"Nothing came of it that night, but how do you know Carmel wasn't trying to finish the fight in Coach Briscoe's class the day of the shootings?"

She didn't answer.

"Did you know Coach Briscoe made a racial slur about Carmel to Maria that evening?"

"What kind of slur?"

"You didn't hear about it?"

"Not 'til right now."

I let it drop.

"There's another thing you need to know. Red and I were at the cemetery this morning visiting the kids' graves. We saw a bouquet of fresh flowers on Carmel's grave that had a hand-written card attached to it."

"I know. I saw it, too. I go out there every day, Etch."

"Then I guess you know Caddo is back in town."

"Sure looks that way."

"She hasn't contacted you?"

"She's been in the wind for ten years, Etch. She's good at it."

"Why would she bother to visit his grave when she didn't even attend his funeral?"

"I long ago gave up on trying to figure what makes her tick. Maybe she was locked up and just got out, maybe she wants to be here for the trial, maybe a thousand other things I can't imagine."

"She hasn't contacted you?"

"Not a peep."

I stood up. "You and I have to make a deal, Momma L."

"What deal?"

"No more surprises."

She stood up and shook my hand. "I promise, Etch. I'm sorry I let you down on this one. I didn't mean to hide it from you. I thought it didn't amount to anything. Now I see how Briscoe's lawyers could latch onto it."

"Just keep me in the loop, Momma L. That's all I'm asking."

She walked out on the porch with me, watched while I got in my truck.

I was half-way to the office from Momma L's house when Red called.

"What's up, Red?"

"I've been rattling a few of those cages we talked about."

"Update me."

"When an investigation hits a brick wall, one of the best things is a do-over."

"Such as?"

"I called Quasi, and he and I met at Kilgore PD and went through the file again from start to finish. I examined the gun, checked it for prints."

"The report says the only prints on the pistol belonged to Carmel."

"Like I said. Sometimes you start from scratch and re-do things you've already done."

"So, are you telling me you found other prints on the gun?" I thought Red was about to make the big reveal.

"No. The only sure prints are Carmel's although there was a partial I couldn't be definitive about."

"You're calling me to tell me you don't have anything new?"

"Just hold on. I'm leading up to it."

"Lead on up, please."

"Another thing you can do if an investigation stalls is to manufacture the evidence you need."

"Ordinarily the law frowns on that, but I'm sure there are exceptions you can clue me in on."

"I went out to Poteet's house and told him I'd used a new technique and had been able to lift a set of his prints off the gun in Carmel's back pack."

"That technique would be called lying."

"That's not against the law, counselor. It's a well-known interrogation tactic."

"How did Ves Poteet handle the news?"

"Let's see. His face turned white as a sheet, and he lost his lunch right in front of me. Fortunately, he missed my boots. Then he asked me if I was arresting him or if he could have a day to get his affairs in order. I told him to check in with you first thing in the morning at your office, and you'd tell him how things would go down for him."

"Is he expecting a deal for his testimony?"

"I believe it would be more accurate to say he is praying for one."

"Good work, old friend."

"That's not all."

"Tell me more."

"Quasi and I checked the log on the burner phone that the PD sent to the lab in Austin."

"And?"

"And I have the guy's name who supposedly checked it in when it arrived at the lab. I'm on my way to Austin now to meet with the lab tech and search every nook and cranny in the building until we find that phone. It has to be there somewhere."

"Yeah, and when you find it you can manufacture some more evidence."

"My thoughts exactly, counselor." Red was gone again.

Chapter Thirty-Five

By noon the next day, I had seen neither hide nor hair of Vesuvius Poteet, but I had experienced an epiphany. Red was running a scam, and he had given Poteet just enough rope to hang himself.

I called Red.

"You knew he would run, didn't you?" I asked when he came on the line.

"It was an educated guess. You'd already given him the chance to come clean, and he failed the test. I thought the odds were good that if he knew we had solid evidence on him, he'd make a few contacts on his way out of town."

"He'd let the rest of the gang know the score."

"Well put, counselor."

"So how are you managing to keep tabs on him while you're in Austin?"

"One old school technique, one new school."

"Explain, please."

"Quasi is the lead investigator on the case for the PD. He set up in an unmarked vehicle and waited for Poteet to hit the road. He's already followed him to two stops."

"What's the new school method?"

"I stuck a tracker inside the front passenger-side wheel well of his old truck. It's beaming a signal to my IT guy, giving us a digital real-time play by play."

It was in moments like this that I thanked my lucky stars Red was on my side, not zeroing in on me.

"What two stops has Poteet made so far?"

"Care to venture a guess?"

"My money is on Merlin Hostetler and Coach Briscoe."

"Bingo, counselor. Whatever he told them didn't take long. He was in and out of their places in less than ten minutes each."

"Just long enough to deliver the message that they might need to adapt to a new set of facts."

"I suppose. But there's not a lot of wiggle room left for them."

"Except that we don't actually have Poteet's fingerprints on the gun."

"Yeah. But they don't know that. I reckon that about now Briscoe and Hostetler are drawn up tighter than Dick's hat band."

"I've always wondered who Dick was and why his hat band was so tight."

"Me, too," Red said.

"Do you have any idea where Poteet is now, or where he's going next?"

I heard a click on the line.

"What was that?"

"Another text from Quasi. Poteet is on the move again. He's headed south on Highway 259 and has already passed through Henderson."

"I wonder where he's going this time?"

"Let's just hide and watch, counselor. I'll keep you posted."

Before he could hang up on me, I had one more question for Red. "Have you made it to the DPS lab, yet?"

"I spent the night in Austin and called my contact at the lab first thing this morning. He told me to check in at the lab right after lunch. I'll be there in about fifteen minutes."

"Happy hunting."

Red had already ended the call.

With Poteet on the run and the pieces of the puzzle coming together, I decided it was time to fire a return shot over Jesmyn Thompson's bow.

Every trial is a chess match, and each side has a strategy. Jesmyn had tipped her hand with the speedy trial motion, and I knew she expected me to counter her move with one of my own. Most likely, she thought I would push back and tell Judge Merrell that the prosecution was still investigating the case and needed additional time to prepare. I mean, it was a murder case only a couple of months old with three victims and novel legal issues to brief, for God's sake. The lawyers could argue the fine points of the law for months, perhaps file motions to transfer venue based on the widespread publicity surrounding the case. Either way it went on the venue motion, if the judge moved the case to another county or left it where it was, the losing side on the venue issue could bring an interlocutory appeal, and the case would be on hold until the appellate court ruled on proper venue. It could take the appeals court months to hand down its decision while we twiddled our thumbs.

Yes, that was the obvious move, the one Jesmyn almost certainly expected I would make.

Alas, I would disappoint her.

I sat down at my computer and composed a response to her speedy trial motion.

My pleading was two pages long, most of it consisting of its heading, boilerplate language, and a signature block. Only one paragraph contained any operative words, and those were simple and direct.

"The prosecution joins defense counsel's request for a speedy trial and urges the Court to set the case for trial at the earliest available time."

I didn't file a motion for change of venue, and, because Jesmyn had not asked Judge Merrell to move the case elsewhere when she asked for a speedy trial, the venue issue was waived. In other words, the time had passed when either of us could request the trial of Jim Briscoe occur in another county. We would try him at home, and we would try him, as Judge Merrell had put it, with all deliberate speed.

I signed my response, scanned it to my computer and sent it as an email attachment to the district clerk's office for filing, to Judge Merrell, to Jesmyn Thompson, and to Harold Fleming.

Twelve minutes later, my phone rang, a California number displayed on my caller ID.

"Etch Danielson," I said.

"Hold for Ms. Thompson," the receptionist said.

This time I held for less than ten seconds before Ms. Thompson came on the line.

"I just saw your response, Etch."

"I thought you'd be pleased that you and I could agree on something, Jesmyn. We might as well get the show on the road."

"Or we could simply fold our tents and call it a wrap."

That was the way a lawyer from Los Angeles might inquire about what we could do to resolve the case short of trial.

"How so?"

"Jim Briscoe pleads no contest to misdemeanor reckless conduct, gets six months' probation. You garner a conviction, the community concentrates on healing its wounds and preventing the next shooting."

"And you are free to say Briscoe really did nothing wrong, except that he may have slightly over-reacted to the threat he perceived."

"Something like that, Etch. You know the only way to resolve a case is for both sides to get less than they hope for on their best day, and more than they'd suffer on their worst."

"Jim Briscoe should be glad he's not looking at the needle, Jesmyn."

"His worst day is life in the pen. Your worst day is that he skates."

"He won't skate, Jesmyn. But I'll make it easy for you. I'll offer him fifty years on murder. With good behavior, he could be out in twenty-five and still have a few years of freedom left in his pathetic life."

"I'll get back to you, Etch."

"See you in court, Jesmyn."

Chapter Thirty-Six

A little after three-thirty that afternoon, Red called again. The reception from his cell was poor, and his voice crackled, fading in and out.

"Can you hear me?" he asked.

"You're breaking up off and on."

"I'm still in the lab and can't get a good signal."

I heard a door open and Red's boots clacking against a concrete floor.

"Is that better?"

"Yeah, it's better. Still not great."

"I just sent you coordinates on Poteet. Google them and tell me what you find."

My phone beeped with an incoming text. I scribbled the address on a piece of scrap paper, went to my computer and entered the information.

"It pops up as a residence on the north side of Houston."

"Quasi is set up there. He says Poteet just went in the house."

"OK. Any luck in the search for the missing burner phone?"

"I don't know how they find anything at the lab. It's a total mess. On top of that, they just cleaned house because of some lost drug samples that caused the DA in San Antonio to have to dismiss a bunch of cases. In the process of reorganizing the drug lab, they misplaced a whole raft of other shit. We'll be lucky if we can find the phone in a week of searching, if ever."

"I guess that could be good or bad for us."

"It's your turn to explain."

"If neither we nor Jesmyn can access the data on the phone, then either side can tell its story without fear of contradiction about what the evidence from the phone would have shown us. We just have to develop enough facts from other sources that support an extrapolation about the missing information. It's a long shot, but Judge Merrell might allow it since the phone's absence is the lab's fault, not ours."

"So, do you want me to keep looking for it, or do we leave it alone?"

"Keep searching. It will make the judge's decision easier if we convince her we used due diligence in our attempt to locate it."

"10-4," Red said before he hung up.

I turned back to my monitor and looked at the Google Maps information about the Houston address where Poteet was. Then I made a couple of searches on sites that contained more specific information about Harris County, Texas, real estate. On my fourth try, I hit pay dirt.

I called Red back, but his phone went to voice mail. I left a message for him to call me as soon as he could.

The information I had discovered about the owner of the house where Ves Poteet was in Houston provided the answer to the biggest question we faced and confirmed just how sinister Coach Jim Briscoe really was and the extent of his premeditation in the murder of Carmel Sideout.

It was a few minutes after five o'clock that afternoon when Red called in.

"We just broke for the day. No luck with the search for the phone. The guys at the lab are under a lot of pressure to clean up their act, and they said they'd put a crew on it tomorrow. I'm on my way to Houston to relieve Quasi."

"Is Poteet still there?"

"Yeah. Quasi says he hasn't shown his face since he entered the house."

"You think he'll hole up there for a while?"

"Maybe. He might think he's safe."

"Did I tell you who his host is in Houston?"

"You forgot to mention it."

"The real estate records show the house belongs to one Raul Juarez."

"I don't remember hearing that name."

"Patty Douglas told me about him. He used to live in Kilgore."

"His daughter is Maria Juarez?"

"That's right, and now he's harboring one of the co-conspirators involved in the shooting that killed her." I heard a click on Red's phone.

"Quasi's calling in," Red said as he went off the line.

Less than a minute later, Red called again.

"Poteet and Juarez just came out of the house. They're in Raul's car headed east in a hurry."

"OK. Keep me posted."

The line was dead.

It was eleven-thirty that night before I heard from Red again.

"I caught up with Quasi a few minutes ago. We're in the parking lot of the Holiday Inn Select on I-45 in Lafayette and we can see a trio of our friends, new and old, in the lobby restaurant. The young woman in the group appears perturbed."

"Catch me up a minute. Who's the third member of the trio?"

"The lovely Marcie Brumbaugh."

"OK. Well, I suppose that makes some sort of weird sense in the bizarre universe of Jim Briscoe connections. Can you tell why she's perturbed?"

"We can't hear the conversation, but from her body language I would conclude, in my professional opinion as a highly-trained investigator, that she is telling them how the cow ate the cabbage."

"Which means that your revelation to Poteet about finding his fingerprints on the gun requires Marcie to revise her version of the story, the account she hoped would bring her immunity. She told us it was all on Merlin, and now she has to amend her statement to create an innocent explanation for Poteet's handling of the gun."

"Amend she must," Red said. "What I don't understand is Raul Juarez's part in the deal."

"From what you've seen of the trio's interactions, could you tell if Marcie knew Raul?"

"Poteet introduced Raul to Marcie first thing, and Raul hasn't had much to say. My take on it is that she knew he was involved, but she hadn't dealt with him before tonight."

"Which might be another reason she's upset. She doesn't appreciate Poteet hooking Raul up with her. Now their fortunes are inter-twined, and Raul has become a potential witness against her if the water gets too hot for him."

"You catch me up this time," Red said. "What role is it that we think Raul played in the deal? Surely, he wouldn't have been in on helping Briscoe kill his daughter."

"I have a working hypothesis about Raul's involvement, but it's too early to tell if I'm right about it. It might help clarify things if you could get your hands on his cell phone."

"You know me, counselor. I'm all about clarification."

Chapter Thirty-Seven

My cell rang at six-fifteen the next morning. This time it was Sarah Gorsky.

"Sarah, you just set a new record for the earliest request-for-immunity call I've ever received from counsel."

"The early bird catches the worm, Etch."

"So, to what do I owe the pleasure of this wake-up call?"

"Marcie Brumbaugh is burning up my phone, Etch. She wants me to set up another meet and greet. She says she's remembered something she failed to mention earlier, something that may have a major impact on the case." She paused. "And she really wants to know what you have to offer her in exchange for a game-changer."

"I'm not sure she is in a strong bargaining position, Sarah. Especially if she's having problems with selective memory. Let me hear what new tidbit she has, and we can discuss what it's worth after that."

"Fair enough," Sarah said. "It's Saturday, so can we squeeze in a meeting with you this afternoon or evening? We'd come to your place this time."

"Let's say six o'clock at my office. And you might want to impress on Marcie that trial is right around the corner, and I don't like my witnesses remembering things at the last minute."

"I'll deliver that message with emphasis, Etch."

Ten minutes 'til seven, I received my second Saturday morning wake-up call, this one from Red.

"I have his cell phone numbers."

"Numbers as in plural?"

"For some reason, Raul carries a burner phone."

"Do I want to know how you acquired those numbers?"

"It was pretty slick actually. Only cost you two-hundred bucks."

"OK, lay it out for me."

"I saw a hotel worker emptying the trash while Quasi and I were in the parking lot last night. The guy was a Cajun about a hundred and ten years old, humming *Jolie Blon* and taking his time on the garbage detail. I flashed my badge and asked him if he'd like to make a quick hundred dollars. His smile showed three gold teeth. I told him I needed the cell phone numbers of the three people talking in the lobby. 'I'll need a hundred for my grandbaby the waitress, too,' he said. We shook hands, and I gave him a hundred-dollar bill and told him he'd get the rest on delivery. He went inside, and in a minute, we saw the waitress approach the trio. She had a clipboard in her hand and some slips of paper, like coupons or something. She had all three of them laughing within thirty seconds. She wrote some numbers on a sheet of paper on the clipboard and passed out the coupons. Whole deal took her less than a minute.

"The old man came back outside and handed me the paper. It was a list of four cell phone numbers. 'She tell them de hotel had a deal going to comp they rooms if she collect they cell phone numbers. One guy ask if he get two coupons for two numbers. She say sure.' I gave him another C-note, and he went back to his trash detail."

"You're telling me Raul upped his personal cell number and the number for his burner?"

"Greed makes fools of us all."

"What's the situation with the surveillance?"

"I cut Quasi loose last night and caught a few Zs in Pearline. I saw the trio eating their continental breakfasts a few minutes ago. They're about to check out."

"Don't worry about Marcie. She's headed this way." I told him about Sarah Gorsky's call.

"OK. I'll stick with Poteet and Juarez. I'll send the cell numbers to my IT guy in a little while. He's not an early riser."

I was about to say something cute about not being an early riser on Saturdays either, but I was too late.

Red was gone again.

I was thankful it was Saturday, not because it was a weekend, but because summer Saturdays at the bookstore had a rhythm all their own. We had children's reading hour from ten-thirty to eleven-fifteen or so. On the heels of that mayhem, we hosted other activities such as a panel discussion of the plays in progress at the college summer theater across the street from us, or author signings or book club meetings. Each of these kept E. J. busy making specialty drinks for parents, or art aficionados, or plain old book nerds. They also kept May Ellen and me hopping, arranging chairs, looking up books in our inventory, handling special orders, gabbing with the regulars and introducing new comers to the stacks.

The day flew by, and as I was flipping the OPEN sign to CLOSED at 6 p.m., I noticed Sarah Gorsky pull into the parking lot. Marcie Brumbaugh got out of the passenger side, and she and Sarah walked toward the building. I met them outside and invited them into the back room.

"Nice place, Etch. You'll have to give me a tour of the store when we finish our business."

"Yeah, Mr. Danielson," Marcie said. "My brother owned a book once. He loaned it to me, but I lost it. Can I check out another one from you while we're here?"

Sarah looked at her client as if she were an alien visiting planet earth for the first time.

"We're not a library, Ms. Brumbaugh. We sell books."

"Cool beans," she said.

I had them sit across from me and opened the discussion with a statement directed to Marcie. "Your attorney tells me you're here to supplement your former statement, Ms. Brumbaugh." She was wearing flip flops with red crawfish painted on them, shorts that struggled to cover her rear end, and a pink halter top with the logo of Prejeans, a famous Cajun restaurant in Lafayette, printed on it. Her face was sunburned, and grains of sand flecked her scalp at the hairline.

"It was Mr. Poteet, not Merlin," she said.

Sarah Gorsky scratched a few words on her legal pad, inhaled deeply through her nose and didn't make eye-contact with me while Marcie spoke.

"Can you back up and give me the context, Ms. Brumbaugh? What was Mr. Poteet, not Merlin?"

"I told you the other day that Merlin told me Ms. McEntyre gave him the toy gun. I remembered later that what Merlin actually said was that Ms. McEntyre gave Mr. Poteet the gun and asked him to deliver it to Merlin for safekeeping. That's why Mr. Poteet's fingerprints were on it." She smiled like a kid who had successfully recited three lines of poetry a teacher required her to memorize.

"Ms. Brumbaugh, who told you Mr. Poteet's fingerprints were found on the fake Glock?"

She blurted out, "Mr. Poteet." She stopped and then added, "I ran into him the other day, and he told me the police said they got his prints off the gun."

"You ran into him the other day? Just out of the blue? I thought you weren't in Kilgore anymore."

Sarah placed her hand on Marcie's arm. "Ms. Brumbaugh, it is very important that you answer Mr. Danielson's questions truthfully. Please think carefully before you speak."

That was lawyer talk for 'keep your mouth shut.'

I pressed Marcie on her last statement. "You said you ran into Mr. Poteet the other day. Where did you happen to see him?"

Marcie didn't take her attorney's advice to heart. "I was at Six Flags and saw him on one of the rides. It was the double-loop roller coaster. Yeah, that was where it was."

"And he yelled this information to you as he was looping along?"

"That's mean, Mr. Danielson. You're making fun of me."

"No. I'm not making fun of you, Ms. Brumbaugh. I'm calling you a liar."

I looked at Sarah. "This conference is over, Ms. Gorsky. I can't use testimony from a witness who makes up the facts as she goes."

I stood up to signal it was time for them to leave.

"Can you give us a few minutes to confer, Mr. Danielson?" Sarah said.

Marcie was picking at her fingernails.

"I guess so, Ms. Gorsky." I checked my watch. "Ten minutes." I walked out of the back room and entered the store to give Sarah an opportunity to meet with her client in private.

Before my ten-minute deadline expired, I saw Sarah and Marcie walking out to Sarah's car. She started the car, left it running with

Marcie in the passenger seat, and came back to the front door of the store to say her goodbyes.

"I'm sorry about all this, Etch. It will take me a lot longer than ten minutes to get to the bottom of what's happening with Marcie. I still believe she may be of help to you in the case, although I understand your reticence." We shook hands. Before she walked away, she had a question. "Can you let me in on what just transpired in there?"

"I'll give you this much, Sarah. It isn't public knowledge that Poteet's fingerprints were on the gun. Her knowledge of that fact had to come straight from Poteet, and she could only have learned it in the last twenty-four hours. If she doesn't come clean, she's going down with the ship."

"You set a trap and she stepped right into it, didn't she?" Sarah asked.

I nodded.

Chapter Thirty-Eight

Not long after I watched Sarah Gorsky drive out of the parking lot, Red called. I could hear the weariness in his voice.

"They've reversed course and are back at Raul's house. How'd it go with Marcie Brumbaugh?"

I filled him in and included my last exchange with Sarah Gorsky. "She said she understood my reticence."

"She used the word 'reticence'?"

"Didn't I just say that?"

"Yeah. But I didn't know if it was her word or yours."

"Have you ever known me to say 'reticence'?"

"I've observed you being reticent, but I didn't tell anyone." He changed the subject. "Do you want me to bring Poteet in?"

"We don't have him charged with anything and the fingerprint thing was a feint. I think we still give him some rope and see if he leads us to anybody else. You've got the tracking device on his car, so why don't you head home and get some rest."

"I've tagged Raul's car, too. We'll be able to keep up with them."

"Good work, Red. Check in with me after you get some shut eye."

"By the way, my guy says we have a possible on Raul's burner."

"A possible?"

"He says Juarez made a call that matches the time line for the shootings at KHS. All he can tell so far is that the target number was also a burner phone."

"Since we know Poteet and Raul have a connection, we can probably get that call in evidence even if the lab doesn't find the burner from Carmel's backpack."

"Now all we have to do is figure out why Briscoe did it and how he was able to enlist Beryl, Marcie, Poteet, Merlin and Raul to help him," Red said.

"No hill for a stepper."

"I know that's right."

At ten o'clock that evening, I received an email notification on my phone. The attachment was Judge Merrell's revised scheduling order. In response to Jesmyn Thompson's speedy trial request and my response joining it, the judge had called our hands as only judges can do. She set the case for trial three weeks from Monday. Such an act on the judge's part was a clear message to the attorneys: Time to pay up or shut up.

As I thought about the impending trial, I wondered how Jesmyn Thompson had taken the news, how she planned to counter my every move with one of her own. I reminded myself how easy it would be in the hustle and bustle of the next three weeks and during trial to lose track of the things that mattered, that the lives of three bright young students had been snuffed out at the hands of a man who I believed had neither conscience, nor remorse for the suffering he had meted out.

The Jim Briscoe case, simply put, was good versus evil, justice versus randomness, a small vestige of hope in a world sinking into despair.

In such moments of sober reflection, late at night when the events of the day are quieted, I often find myself in my study, a book of great wisdom lying open in my lap as I flip through its worn pages. And in that setting, on this late evening when the battle loomed large on the horizon, I allowed my index finger to follow the words one by one: "Stand therefore, having your loins girt about with truth, and having on the breastplate of righteousness."

I closed the book, steeled myself.

And I decided win, lose, or draw, I would give Coach Briscoe hell.

Chapter Thirty-Nine

Ninety-three days after Jim Briscoe fired the shots that killed Maria Juarez, Benjamin Cohen, and Carmel Sideout, he went on trial for murder.

In the state of Texas, the first phase of a criminal trial is jury selection, a process known as *voir dire* and which Texas attorneys pronounce "voy dire." The process is cumbersome, and the attorneys approach it as a witch doctor does a cauldron filled with herbs, spices, eye of newt, chicken tongues and Tabasco sauce. It is the ultimate pseudo-science, practiced without regard to advances in psychology or other disciplines which focus on human decision making, bias or the processing of complex information. In other words, it is a matter of pure instinct and gut feelings.

Jury selection more accurately described is juror non-selection. The lawyers have a single goal in mind: keep anyone off the jury who will vote against them. To accomplish this goal in district court, each side has ten peremptory strikes, which it can use without providing any explanations.

A strike is exactly what it sounds like. The lawyer has a piece of paper with the names of the jurors listed in the order they are seated before him. To exercise a strike, he draws a line through the name. That's it.

In addition to the ten strikes each side may use without explanation, the attorneys may also challenge a potential juror for cause. For cause strikes come into play when a prospective juror gives answers to questions that reveal he cannot be impartial or follow the law. Common for cause issues which disqualify people from serving would be things such as a personal relationship with one of the victims, being a witness to the event that forms the basis of the alleged crime, and a religious belief that prevents the person from sitting in judgment on another person.

One unusual aspect of Texas law also comes into play during jury selection. In Texas, a criminal defendant has the option to allow the jury, the people who decide his guilt or innocence, to set his punishment. Because they may ultimately determine the defendant's sentence, they must be able to consider the full range of punishment the law provides for the crime the accused faces. In a murder case, a convicted killer may receive a punishment ranging from five years supervised probation up to life in the penitentiary. Any of the prospective jurors who cannot consider both ends of the range, and anything in between, are not able to follow the law, and should be disqualified from serving on the accused's jury.

The jury is made up of twelve jurors and two alternates. The alternates listen to the evidence at trial but are dismissed from service before the jury deliberates unless some event transpires that renders one of the original twelve jurors unable to perform his duties. For instance, if one of the twelve falls ill, he is replaced by an alternate.

If you do the math, you see that to select a jury of twelve persons, the attorneys must question a panel of at least thirty-two people. Those thirty-two are the twelve who will ultimately make up the jury plus twenty people who will be eliminated when the lawyers exercise their peremptory strikes. Because some of the first thirty-two people on the panel will almost certainly be struck for cause, most judges bring in a panel of at least forty people.

Judge Merrell requested a panel of one hundred and twenty people in the Jim Briscoe case. I knew the size of that panel reflected her belief that many of the people sitting in the courtroom that first day would disqualify themselves one way or another. Her instincts were correct, because by the time the jury and alternates were seated, we had gone eighty-five deep in the panel and spent a full day in *voir dire*.

Tuesday morning at nine o'clock, Judge Merrell called the case for trial, and the battle began in earnest.

Red sat with me at the counsel table closest to the jury, and I had also asked Dave Schmerz to join us as a representative of the DA's office. At defense's table were Jesmyn Thompson, Harold Fleming and Coach Briscoe. Briscoe was wearing a red sports coat with a KHS logo on the breast pocket, a white cotton shirt, a blue necktie with embroidered images of The Alamo sprinkled on it, and black slacks. He looked straight ahead and never made eye contact with me.

As the state's first witness, I called Marcus Wellborn. When I said Wellborn's name, Jesmyn Thompson stood and addressed Judge Merrell. "Your Honor, we invoke The Rule."

Under Texas law, 'The Rule' requires that witnesses in the case must remain outside the courtroom while other witnesses testify. The purpose of the requirement is to protect against parroting, to ensure that witnesses not shape their testimony to that of other witnesses. Since the attorneys on both sides of the case are the people who know who will testify, they have a duty to police the gallery and enforce The Rule.

"Ladies and Gentlemen, the defense has invoked The Rule," Judge Merrell said. "That means the witnesses must remain outside the courtroom while other witnesses testify. At this time, I ask that all witnesses in the case please stand."

About a dozen people stood up. Among them were Momma L, Patty Douglas, Abby Cohen, Marcie Brumbaugh, Beryl McEntyre, Brigitte Malcolm, Merlin Hostetler, Marcus Wellborn and Quasimodo. Red, as my investigator, was exempt from The Rule and remained seated.

"Please raise your right hand," Judge Merrell said to those standing. She administered the oath witnesses must take and had them lower their hands. "Please wait outside the courtroom until you are called to testify. You are not to discuss your testimony among yourselves and may only discuss it with the attorneys in the case. Mr. Wellborn, since you are the first witness, you may remain in the courtroom."

Those standing grabbed their things and filed slowly out of the courtroom through the back door. While the procession was underway, Red poked me and whispered, "The guy seated next to the wall on the back row is Raul Juarez. Would you like me to do my thing?"

I nodded at him and he made his way along the outside aisle to Raul. He motioned for him to get up, handed him a folded piece of paper, and escorted him out of the courtroom along with the other witnesses. The back door closed behind the last witness, and, within a minute, it opened again and Red made his way back to the counsel table and sat down next to me.

I knew Red had just served Raul Juarez with a subpoena. "How'd he take it?" I whispered to Red.

"I told him that since he was Maria's dad we might need to call him as a witness to testify about her. He said he understood and acted meek as a lamb."

"So, he doesn't know what's coming?"

"Not that I could tell."

When Judge Merrell was satisfied that the requirements of The Rule were met, she looked at me.

"You may proceed, Mr. Danielson."

I motioned at Marcus Wellborn, and he made his way to the witness stand and sat down. He had his hair pulled behind him in a ponytail and wore a white, long-sleeved dress shirt, a red tie, gray slacks and shined black penny loafers. He carried himself with the thoughtless ease, grace and muscularity of a teenage athlete, and he rested his right hand on the rail in front of him, his long fingers gripping the wood, his posture that of a lookout expecting the arrival of enemy forces.

"State your name for the Court, please," I said.

"Marcus Wellborn."

"How old are you, Marcus?"

"Eighteen, sir."

"Are you a student?"

"Yes, sir. I graduated from KHS in May, and I will be starting Kilgore College in the fall semester."

"What do you plan to study at KC, Marcus?"

"Criminal justice, sir. I come from a long line of police officers and plan to continue the family tradition."

I watched the jury as Marcus answered the preliminary questions. They were hanging on every word.

"Marcus, I know what I am about to discuss with you is difficult, but you understand I have to get into the details of what happened on May fifteenth of this year."

"Yes, sir. I understand."

"All right. Why don't you go through the events of that terrible day for us? Start from when you arrived at school and take us through it step by step."

Marcus swiveled his chair to face the jury, leaned forward toward them when he spoke.

"It was just a day like any other. The seniors were revved up because we only had a couple of weeks left until graduation, and we had the deal on a downhill slide. I went to my first three classes, then ate lunch in the cafeteria. Fourth period class started at twelve fifty and about twelve-thirty, I finished eating and was walking to my locker when I saw Carmel."

"By Carmel, you mean Carmel Sideout?"

"Yes, sir."

"Had you seen Carmel earlier that day?"

"No, sir. He'd been on a field trip to the Longview Art Museum and had just arrived at school."

"When you saw Carmel, did he have his backpack with him?"

"Yes, sir. He took it off and placed it in his locker, then headed for the lunch room to grab a sandwich before Coach Briscoe's fourth period class."

"You saw him put the backpack in his locker?"

"Yes, sir. His locker was close to mine."

"Did you accompany Carmel to the cafeteria?"

"No, sir. I'd already eaten, so I went outside in the courtyard and visited with my friends until the bell rang for us to go to class."

"Before you went outside to visit with your friends, did you notice anyone else in the hallway near Carmel's locker?"

"There were a few kids milling around in the hallway like always. And I saw Mr. Poteet, one of the school maintenance men."

"What was Mr. Poteet doing?"

"He had one of those large trash containers with wheels on it, and he was emptying trash into it from the trash cans in the hall."

"Did you have any conversation with Mr. Poteet?"

"No, sir. I may have said hi, or something like that, but we didn't talk about anything."

"OK. Marcus, you said your fourth period class was with Coach Briscoe. Do you see him in the courtroom today?"

Marcus glanced at the defense table for a second and turned his head to face the jury again. "Yes, sir. He's seated at the table over there next to Ms. Thompson."

"Your Honor, please let the record reflect that the witness has identified the defendant James Briscoe."

"The record will so reflect," Judge Merrell said.

I turned back to Marcus. "Let's continue with the events of that day, Marcus. You heard the bell ring and went to Coach Briscoe's class. Where was your seat in the classroom?"

"The seats were arranged four across. My seat was the one closest to the window on the third row from the front."

"Who sat in the other three seats in the third row?"

"They were all to my right. Next to me was Maria Juarez, then Carmel Sideout, and on the far side of Carmel was Benjamin Cohen."

"You knew all of the students you just named?"

"Yes, sir." For the first time while he was on the stand, I heard Marcus's voice crack. "They were friends of mine."

The jury, six men and six women, stared at Marcus, as if they were waiting for the shots to ring out in the courtroom.

"Did you see Carmel Sideout enter the classroom that day?"

"He came in a little before the second bell rang, put his backpack on the floor in front of him and sat down."

"Was there anything unusual about that?"

"No, sir. Nothing unusual. Most of us stash our backpacks at our feet like that, so we can reach them if we need to get something out."

"So, Marcus, by the time class began everyone was in their seats on the third row, and that would've been you next to the window, Maria to your immediate right, Carmel to her right, and Benjamin closest to the class room door?"

"Yes, sir."

"Where was Coach Briscoe?"

Marcus glanced at Briscoe again before he answered. "His desk was at the front of the room in the middle. Most of the time he taught class sitting down, reading from the text book or calling on some of us to read sections from our assigned pages. That day he was seated at his desk at the first of class."

"Did Coach Briscoe have a gun with him that day?"

"He always had his gun." Marcus had his eyes on Briscoe now. "Ever since the new law came into effect, he wore it in a holster on his right hip."

"The new law you're talking about was the one that allowed teachers to carry weapons?"

"Yes, sir." He was still watching Briscoe.

"Are you familiar with guns, Marcus?"

"Yes, sir. I've been around them all my life. Like I said earlier, we are a police family."

"What kind of gun did the defendant wear on his hip at school every day?"

"It was a Colt 1911 Government Model forty-five. My dad carried one just like it for years when he was a police officer. It's a gun designed to stop someone dead in his tracks."

Jesmyn Thompson stood up. "Your Honor, we object to Mr. Wellborn's last characterization of the weapon Coach Briscoe carried. He is not qualified to speak as an expert about it."

"I think he laid the groundwork for it, Ms. Thompson. He already testified he'd been around guns all his life and had personal knowledge of this type of gun. I overrule the objection," Judge Merrell said.

Jesmyn sat down.

"How did it make you feel to see the defendant walking around with that forty-five on his belt every day?"

"It scared the fire out of me. He carried that pistol like it was his baby. From February until the day we are talking about now, I always wondered when he would use it on one of us."

The jury members stared at Briscoe.

"OK, Marcus. I want you to focus on the shooting and tell us what you remember about that terrible day."

Marcus straightened in his chair, closed his eyes and tilted his head back while he gathered his thoughts. "About fifteen minutes into class, I noticed Carmel look at his backpack. He had a puzzled expression on his face like he heard something or saw something moving. He picked up his backpack, rested it on his lap and unzipped the top compartment."

"Was there anything unusual about a student doing that in class?"

"No, sir. We were always getting stuff out of our backpacks."

"What did you see Carmel do next?"

"He reached into his backpack and felt around. His hand contacted something, and I saw Carmel mouth some words like he was surprised."

"What words did he mouth?"

"Is it OK to say it in court, Mr. Danielson?"

"It's OK, Marcus. We need to know exactly what happened."

Marcus looked down while he gave us the report. "He mouthed the words 'What the fuck?'"

"What did that mean to you?"

"It meant whatever he had just found in his backpack was not something that he put in it. He didn't know what it was doing there."

"What happened after Carmel mouthed those words?"

"Right after that, I saw him pull a gun out of his backpack and stare at it for a split second like he was in shock."

"Could you tell anything about the gun?"

"It was a plastic BB gun designed to look like a scaled-down version of a Glock 17."

"What happened when Carmel drew out the gun?"

"All hell broke loose. Coach Briscoe had been watching Carmel fiddling around in his backpack."

"Why do you say that, Marcus?"

"You could see he had his eyes on him. He was watching him just like I had been."

"Go ahead."

"As soon as the gun came out, Coach Briscoe jumped up from his desk, pulled his forty-five."

"He didn't call out to Carmel, give him any warning, or try to take the gun away from him?"

"No, sir. None of that. He was moving around the room, getting an angle on them. BOOM! The first shot went high and struck the back wall." Marcus covered his ears with his hands.

When he yelled BOOM, several of the jurors jumped, all of them flinched, their eyes glued on the teenage witness.

"Benjamin dove at Carmel to knock him out of the line of fire, and Maria did the same thing from the other side. BOOM! The second shot hit Maria. BOOM! The third one hit Benjamin. BOOM! The fourth missed again and hit the door." Marcus still had his eyes closed. "Carmel was on the floor. Coach moved a step closer to him. BOOM!"

He was sobbing, bent over at the waist, his head almost hidden behind the rail of the witness stand.

"Your Honor, perhaps we should take a short break."

"I agree, Mr. Danielson," Judge Merrell said. "Court is in recess for fifteen minutes."

"All rise," the bailiff said. And we watched Judge Merrell leave the bench and retire to her chambers.

Chapter Forty

During the recess, while Marcus Wellborn's parents attempted to console their son's inconsolable loss, Red, Dave Schmerz, and I adjourned to a witness room to compare notes.

"I've sat in many a courtroom over the years and listened to witnesses in murder trials tell their stories. But I've never heard anything even close to the power of Marcus Wellborn's testimony," Red said.

"Me, either," I said.

Dave sat with his hands clasped, his eyes red, shaking his head.

I broke the mood. "We've got a long way to go. There are a lot of land mines out there, and Jesmyn Thompson will do her best to ensure that we step on them. I figure we will spend most of the rest of the day with Marcus on the stand. We know what he'll say on the big issues. Tomorrow and Thursday will be a different story. My sense of it is that Merlin, Marcie, Poteet and Beryl McEntyre will each spin a yarn to make themselves look good. I hope their lying ways don't throw the jury off track."

"You want me to bring in Poteet?" Red asked.

"Let's see how far we get by the end of the day. We may want to save him 'til Thursday."

"He's holed up at his cousin's house not far from here in Overton. Just give me the high sign and I can have him here in less than an hour."

I looked at Dave Schmerz. "Are you ready for your talking part?"

"I'm ready, Etch. Thanks for letting me be on the team."

The bailiff knocked on the door, and Red opened it. "The Judge is coming back on the bench, gentleman."

I continued my direct examination of Marcus Wellborn. "Are you ready to proceed, Marcus?"

"Yes, sir. I'm sorry I broke down like that."

"There's nothing for you to be sorry about, son."

I took him back to the crime scene. "Marcus, after the shooting ended, where did you end up?"

"I was on the floor near the window. I really don't remember how I got there."

"Could you see Carmel's body?"

"Yes, sir."

"Did you see if he still had the gun in his hand?"

"Best I can remember, sir, the gun was next to his hand, but not in it."

"But you didn't see how or when it came out of his hand?"

"No, sir."

"Did Carmel ever brandish the gun? By that I mean, did he wave it around or point it at Coach Briscoe or any of the students?"

"No, sir. When he pulled it out of his backpack, he had it between his thumb and index finger, holding it away from him. The barrel was tilted toward the floor. Then the shooting began."

"OK, Marcus. I want us to change gears now. You've already said you were friends with Carmel, Benjamin, and Maria. Were you aware of their involvement in the movement to stop school violence?"

"Yes, sir. After the Florida shootings, they organized a local chapter against school violence. Benjamin was the spokesperson."

"And you attended some of their meetings?"

"Yes, sir. We all did what we could, passed out pamphlets and stuff like that."

"Did you also learn about a one-act play Benjamin had written about school violence?"

"He showed it to me. That was probably mid-March or so."

I addressed the court. "Your Honor, the parties have stipulated that the text of the play is admissible, and we have agreed that Mr. Schmerz from the DA's office can read it to the jury."

"Is that your agreement, Ms. Thompson?"

"Yes, Your Honor."

"Very well, then. Mr. Schmerz, please come around next to the witness stand and broadcast the play to the jury."

I thought about the irony of the use of the arcane legal term *broadcast* in this context, how the one-act play Benjamin Cohen had labored to create would have its debut in a courtroom where his killer was on trial for murders committed at school.

Dave Schmerz read the play, his calm, firm voice belying the horror of his text. At the end, when the gunman lashes out with deadly force then turns the weapon on himself, Schmerz's voice faded to a stage whisper. The members of the jury sat rigid throughout the presentation. As Schmerz turned and walked back to the counsel table, two of the women on the jury wrapped their arms around themselves as if to seek shelter from the words they had heard.

I spoke to Marcus. "Do you know why Benjamin Cohen wrote that one-act play?"

"I think I do, sir. He wanted to bring home to the kids, to everyone really, that school violence wasn't a game. That it wasn't something that happened off somewhere but would never come to visit us. He wanted people to wake up and realize it could happen here."

"Marcus, did you ever see Benjamin Cohen, or Carmel, or Maria engage in any acts of violence towards anyone?"

"No, sir. They were kind and gentle. We, their classmates and friends, looked up to them and admired them. Their hearts were pure. Maybe the best way to put it is that they had beautiful souls."

"Did Benjamin have plans to perform the play?"

"He wanted to present it to the student body before the end of the school year. He told me he went to Ms. McEntyre's office to discuss it with her."

"Ms. McEntyre is the high school principal at Kilgore?"

"Yes, sir."

"Did she schedule the play for a performance at school?"

"No, sir. She told Benjamin that because of the subject matter she needed to clear the performance with the school board. As far as I know she never took it to the board, and she let it drop."

"How do you know that, Marcus?"

"In the play the main character uses a pistol. Benjamin was worried about bringing any kind of gun on campus and he didn't want to do anything against school policy. He told Ms. McEntyre that I had a plastic pistol that looked like a Glock, and I had offered to let Benjamin use it in the play if Ms. McEntyre okayed it. Ms. McEntyre came to my house, and I gave her the gun for safekeeping until the play could be scheduled."

I went to the counter where the attorneys had laid out the exhibits to be used during the trial and picked up the gun Carmel had removed from his backpack.

"Permission to approach the witness, Your Honor?"

"Permission granted, Mr. Danielson."

I walked to a position in front of the witness stand and showed the gun to Marcus, its barrel pointed at the floor. "Is this the gun you gave Ms. McEntyre?"

He looked at it for a second. "Yes, sir. I received it as a birthday present from my parents when I turned thirteen. It's a BB gun, and I used to shoot paper targets with it in the backyard."

"After you gave it to Ms. McEntyre, did you ever see this BB gun again before Carmel pulled it out of his backpack on the day of the shooting?"

"No, sir. When I saw him take it out, I thought 'What the hell?'"

"Why?"

"Because Ms. McEntyre was supposed to keep it until the play was performed."

"Do you have any idea how this gun got from Ms. McEntyre's custody into Carmel's backpack?"

"No, sir."

"Was the play scheduled to be performed on the day of the shooting?"

"No, sir. Benjamin was waiting to hear from her about the schedule."

I returned the gun to the exhibit counter and walked to the counsel table. I changed the line of questioning. "You were around Carmel often, weren't you?"

"Yes, sir. I saw him every day at school."

"What kind of cell phone did he have?"

"He had a new iPhone. It was his pride and joy."

"Did you ever see him with a second phone, a burner?"

"No, sir. I don't see any reason why he would have had one."

There are fundamental tactical rules trial attorneys used to present evidence. You lead with the best stuff early in the day. I had done that when I had Marcus tell about the shooting. A second rule is that, if you have the chance, you bring out the bad stuff, get it on the table, before the other side has a chance to use it against you. That's why I introduced the one-act play before Jesmyn Thompson did. I had one more chance to steal her thunder with Marcus Wellborn.

"Marcus, I am almost finished with my questions for you. But I need to cover one more thing. You have already testified that Carmel was a kind and gentle person, 'a beautiful soul' is how you put it, I believe. Are you aware of an instance that occurred over Spring break when Coach Briscoe and Carmel had a confrontation?"

"Yes, sir. I wasn't present when it happened, but my girl friend told me about it."

Jesmyn Thompson stood. "Objection, hearsay, Your Honor. If Mr. Wellborn wasn't there, we need to hear about the incident from a person who was."

"Objection, sustained," Judge Merrell said. She looked at me. "You'll have to use a witness with personal knowledge on that issue, Mr. Danielson."

"Yes, Your Honor," I said. I knew Jesmyn might block me on that one, but I didn't care. I had planted the seed about the confrontation and sent the jury a message that I wasn't afraid of it.

I reviewed my notes for a second, making sure I had hit the points I needed to cover with Marcus. "Marcus, that's all the questions I have for you right now. Ms. Thompson will question you next."

"Yes, sir."

"I pass the witness, Your Honor."

Chapter Forty-One

"Mr. Wellborn, my name is Jesmyn Thompson. I am an attorney from Los Angeles, and I represent Coach Briscoe. Do you understand my role in these proceedings?"

"Yes, ma'am."

"First, let me say that I am sorry for your loss, and I regret that you and I must meet here today in this courtroom."

"Thank you, Ms. Thompson," Marcus said, his voice just above a whisper.

Jesmyn began her cross-examination. "The question I am sure the members of the jury have is how your gun got in Carmel Sideout's backpack. Can you shed any light on that for us?"

"All I know is that I gave it to Ms. McEntyre when she came to my house. After that, I never saw it again until the day of the shooting."

"And no one has given you any additional information about the gun's chain of custody? No one has filled in the gap for you about who may have handled the gun between the time you gave it to the high school principal and when Carmel pulled it out in class?"

"No, ma'am."

"For instance, Mr. Wellborn, you don't know whether at some point Ms. McEntyre may have delivered it to Carmel?"

"No, ma'am. I don't know if that happened. But I am pretty sure Carmel or Benjamin would have told me if it did. They knew she had come by and picked it up, and they were expecting her to keep it until the time Benjamin's play was performed."

"Fair enough, Mr. Wellborn. But the fact is that you don't know who may have had possession of the gun after it left your hands. Correct?"

"Correct."

"As we sit here today, do you believe Ms. McEntyre planted the gun in Carmel's backpack?"

"I don't know how it ended up there, Ms. Thompson. I believe it was planted, but I don't know who did it."

"But it is possible that Carmel got the gun from Ms. McEntyre or someone else before the shooting?"

"I guess, it's possible, Ms. Thompson. But if he knew it was there, he wouldn't have looked surprised when he found it that day."

"You don't know what Carmel was thinking right before the shooting do you? When you say he looked surprised, you're just giving us your interpretation of the situation aren't you? That's the way it looked to you, but you could be wrong about how Carmel felt at that moment?"

"Again, I would say that's possible. But Carmel and I were good friends, and he looked surprised."

"OK, Mr. Wellborn, let's talk about that burner phone Mr. Danielson asked you about. You said you never saw Carmel carrying a burner?"

"That's right."

"But that's sort of the point with a burner isn't it? It's a phone a person might keep to himself and only use for very limited purposes. Don't a lot of the kids at school have a second phone?"

"I wouldn't say a lot of them do. The only time I see someone with a burner is if they have lost their phone or it's broken. I've never seen anyone carrying one just for the heck of it. And I am sure I never saw Carmel with one."

"But he may have just been good at hiding it, right?"

Marcus didn't answer. Red splotches were popping up on his face.

"You'll need to answer my question, Mr. Wellborn."

"I guess so."

"Mr. Wellborn, do you know a teacher at school named Merlin Hostetler?"

"Yes, ma'am. He's the assistant basketball coach and I played on the team."

"Did you ever have any problems with him?"

"No, ma'am. We got along fine."

"He treated you and the other players on the team fairly?"

"Yes, ma'am."

"What about Marcie Brumbaugh? Do you know who she is?"

"She's Ms. McEntyre's assistant."

"Do you know if she and Merlin Hostetler were friends?"

"They went out together. Everybody at school knew that."

"Do you know if they still see each other?"

"I haven't seen either of them this summer, so I don't know what their status is."

"Would it surprise you to learn that they broke up?"

"I guess it wouldn't surprise me. Coach Hostetler had broken up with a couple of girls since he came to Kilgore two years ago. But I don't know one way or the other about him and Marcie Brumbaugh."

"When Mr. Danielson asked you about the day of the shootings, you said you saw Carmel when he arrived at school after a field trip?"

"Yes, ma'am."

"And in the hall near his locker you ran into Mr. Poteet, the maintenance man?"

"Yes, ma'am."

"You didn't see Mr. Poteet at Carmel's locker, did you?"

"No, ma'am. I saw him in the hall near his locker."

"Did Carmel have a lock on his locker?"

"Yes, ma'am."

"Did he give out the combination to his locker to anyone?"

"Probably. I didn't have it, but I imagine Maria did."

"Is there anyone else you suspect he gave his combination to?"

"I don't know for sure, but probably Benjamin."

"That morning you saw Mr. Poteet in the hall, did you happen to see Merlin Hostetler, or Marcie Brumbaugh, or Ms. McEntyre, or Coach Briscoe near Carmel's locker?"

"No, ma'am. I didn't see any of them in the hall near Carmel's locker."

Jesmyn looked down at her notes, made a few check marks. "Those are all the questions I have for you, Mr. Wellborn. And again, I am sorry for your loss." She took her yellow legal pad and returned to her seat.

"Any re-direct, Mr. Danielson?" Judge Merrell asked.

"No, Your Honor."

"All right. You may step down, Mr. Wellborn. Let me remind you that you are under The Rule and must remain outside the courtroom while other witnesses testify."

"Yes, ma'am," Marcus said.

"Please call your next witness, Mr. Danielson," Judge Merrell said.

"The state calls Jean Middleton, Your Honor."

The rear door of the courtroom opened, and a woman entered and walked down the center aisle. She was about five-two, early sixties, her gray hair in a bun. Her glasses dangled around her neck and hung half-way down the front of her floral blouse. She carried a leather valise in her left hand. The bailiff motioned for her to take a seat on the witness stand.

"Were you present earlier, Ms. Middleton, when I administered the oath to the witnesses?" Judge Merrell asked her.

"Yes, Your Honor."

"Proceed, Mr. Danielson."

"State your name, please."

"Jean Marie Middleton."

"How are you employed?"

"I am the curator of the Longview Museum of Art." Her voice was nasal and flat, and she held her head back as she spoke like an actress projecting to the rear of a performance hall.

"We're here today to inquire about the museum's security protocol, Ms. Middleton. We have heard testimony that Carmel Sideout, a senior at Kilgore High School, attended a field trip to the museum on May fifteenth of this year. Have you reviewed your records to determine if students from KHS were at your facility that day?"

"Yes, sir. I checked the records. They arrived a few minutes after nine that morning and left to return to school shortly before noon."

"Do you have a list of the names of the people who were in the group that day?"

She pulled a piece of paper out of her valise. "Yes, sir. I have it."

"Is Carmel Sideout's name on that list?"

"Yes, sir."

"Please tell the jury what security measures were in effect at the museum the day of that field trip."

"We have a number of valuable items on display, so we take security very seriously. Each student enters through a metal detector and must empty the contents of any bags so that our staff can examine them."

"Did your staff follow that protocol that morning?"

"Yes, sir. I was there and witnessed it."

"Did your staff find any contraband when it searched the students' belongings?"

"No, sir. They were an exemplary group. It always does my heart good to see young people who are eager to learn about the arts."

"Do you specifically recall anything about Carmel Sideout?"

"At the time, I didn't make any mental notes about him. But after the shooting, when his picture was in the news, I remembered seeing him that morning."

"You described the security procedure when the students arrived. Did you have a similar process when they prepared to leave?"

"Yes, sir. Visitors go through the same process on their way out of the museum. We want to ensure that nothing dangerous comes in the door and nothing valuable goes out it."

"So, Ms. Middleton, you are confident that Carmel Sideout did not bring a gun into the museum, and did not have one on him when he left it?"

"Absolutely sure, Mr. Danielson."

"I pass the witness, Your Honor."

"Any questions for this witness, Ms. Thompson?" Judge Merrell asked.

"Just a couple, Your Honor."

"Ms. Middleton, your security personnel do not search school buses when they arrive at the museum?"

"No, ma'am. Our process begins when they enter the front door."

"Likewise, you don't search the buses when the students return to them?"

"No, ma'am."

"So, is it correct to say that you would have no way of knowing if Carmel Sideout hid a gun in the bus on the way to the museum and retrieved it and put it in his backpack on the way back to KHS?"

"That's right, Ms. Thompson. I would have no way of knowing about that. Is that what happened?"

Judge Merrell intervened. "Ms. Middleton, as a witness you are to answer the questions propounded you by the attorneys. They are not at liberty to answer your questions."

Ms. Middleton put her hand to her mouth. "Oh. I'm sorry, Your Honor. I won't do that again."

"It's OK, Ms. Middleton. I just didn't want you to think Ms. Thompson was ignoring your question." Judge Merrell looked at Jesmyn. "Any other questions for this witness?"

"No, Your Honor."

Jean Middleton stepped down from the witness stand and left the courtroom.

Judge Merrell checked the clock on the back wall. "Ladies and gentlemen of the jury, it is almost noon, so I am going to dismiss you for lunch. Please be back by one-fifteen, and we will resume testimony."

"All rise," the bailiff said.

Chapter Forty-Two

During the lunch break, Red, Dave Schmerz and I sat in the witness room and ate peanut butter and jelly sandwiches May Ellen had packed for us in a brown paper bag.

"No Twinkies?" Red asked when he finished scarfing down his sandwich.

I reached into the bag and tossed a package of Twinkies to him and another to Dave.

Dave looked at me. "How do you think it's going, Etch?"

"Jesmyn is doing her job. She's sowing seeds of reasonable doubt with every witness."

"Yeah, but that business about Carmel hiding the gun in the bus won't fly. She still has to explain how the gun got from McEntyre to Carmel," Dave said.

"No, she doesn't, and that's the point. It's our job to connect the dots. She can sit back and throw darts at us. One thing I've learned about criminal cases is that it only takes one off-hand remark to plant doubt in the head of a juror, and one juror can hang up the case, even if the idea in his head is a screwball one. That's why a good defense attorney does what Jesmyn is doing. You never know when you're scoring points. You throw everything at the wall and hope something sticks."

"Who's next up, Etch?" Red asked.

I flipped through the files I had piled on the table. "I had planned to put Quasi on this afternoon, but I've changed my mind. I'm calling

Beryl McEntyre to tack down her story on the gun. I need for you to bring in Poteet."

"You want to be sure he doesn't have a chance to hear what Beryl says about the gun before he testifies," Red said. "That's a good play. I'll keep him cooped up until you give me the high sign that it's time for him to take the stand."

"What's your bet on McEntyre's story about the gun?" Dave asked.

"There are several ways she could play it. My bet is she says what she believes is best for her."

"There are a lot of sharks in those waters," Red said. "I'll see you guys when I have Poteet in tow." He grabbed my pack of Twinkies and charged out of the room.

After the lunch break, I called Beryl McEntyre to the stand. She was dressed like she had come from her office on a regular day at school, her half-glasses balanced on her nose, sprigs of her salt and pepper hair askew.

"State your name and occupation for us."

"Beryl McEntyre. I've been the principal at Kilgore High School for the last eight years."

"How many people work in your office, Ms. McEntyre?"

"Just two. Me and my assistant, Marcie Brumbaugh. She came to work for me in January of this year when my former assistant retired."

"Is Ms. Brumbaugh currently on leave?"

"She is taking some time off following the shooting. I am not sure if she will be able to return to her position, but I'm holding her job open for now."

"You are working solo?"

"Yes, sir."

"Ms. McEntyre, let's focus first on the Student Protection Act, better known as the SPA. Can you give the jury a brief explanation of your duties under the SPA?"

"The SPA became effective in February of this year. It provides, among other things, that a Texas public school teacher can carry a firearm on campus and use it if he has sufficient certainty that a student is using or is about to use deadly force."

"What must a teacher do in order to comply with the SPA?"

"He must complete a one-day course in firearms training, receive a certificate of completion, and file the certificate in the principal's office before he begins carrying a firearm at school."

"Under the SPA was Coach Briscoe qualified to carry a firearm on the campus of Kilgore High School?"

"Yes, sir. He was."

I expected that Ms. McEntyre would throw some new twists at me, but I hadn't seen this one coming. "Perhaps I didn't make myself clear, Ms. McEntyre. Based on the statement you gave to the police, I was under the impression that there was a glitch in the filing of Coach Briscoe's certificate. Am I wrong about that?"

"My statement did say that, Mr. Danielson. But, I am revising it today based on new information I just discovered."

"How new?"

She didn't make eye contact with me or the jury when she answered. "Earlier today I discovered a document that had been missing since February. It was Coach Briscoe's right to carry permit he attempted to file in my office."

"Did you bring a copy of that certificate with you today?"

"In my haste to get to the courthouse I left it on my desk."

"I see. But you can provide it to us when you return to your office?"

"Yes, sir."

"OK, Ms. McEntyre, now that you've cleared up that issue for us, if I follow you, you're saying Coach Briscoe had complied with the SPA in February and was authorized to carry on campus."

"Yes, sir."

"How many other teachers are certified to carry on the KHS campus?"

"Coach Briscoe is the only one."

"You see him at school every day, or almost every day, don't you?"

"Yes, sir."

"Does he always wear a gun on his hip?"

She glanced at Briscoe, but he was looking straight ahead.

"He carries a weapon every day at school."

So far, she had varied one fact, but it was not a critical one. I already believed any appellate court in Texas would determine the small glitch in the filing of Briscoe's certificate did not disqualify him under the SPA. The civil lawyers would have to work through that issue. However, I wondered what big lies lay ahead courtesy of Beryl McEntyre.

"Ms. McEntyre, we've heard testimony today about a one-act play Benjamin Cohen wrote about school violence and wanted to have performed at KHS before the school year ended in May. You are familiar with that play, aren't you?"

"Yes, sir. He came to me and we discussed it. I told him I would speak to the school board about it because of its incendiary content, and I would let him know if we could schedule a date for the performance."

"Did you and Benjamin talk about a gun to be used in the play?"

"We did. He wanted to be careful about the gun thing, as you can imagine. He told me Marcus Wellborn had a toy gun that looked a lot like a real pistol, and that Marcus had told Benjamin he could use it as a prop in the play. I suggested to Benjamin that I pick up the gun from Marcus and hold onto it until we did the play."

"It was your suggestion?"

"Yes, sir. I wanted to be sure they didn't rush into the play and thought that having control over the gun gave me something of a veto over it."

"Did you believe the play would have served a useful purpose in helping to curtail school violence, Ms. McEntyre?"

She hesitated.

Yet another variance from her prior statements.

"I was torn about it actually. I thought Benjamin and his friends were well-intentioned, but the play was violent itself."

I interrupted her. "The jury has heard the one-act play, Ms. McEntyre."

"Well, then they know what I mean. I suppose part of me wanted to shield the students from any more exposure to violence, either in a drama or in real life. I've often regretted that Benjamin didn't see his play performed before he died." Her voice was clinical, analytical when she spoke about the play, not charged with emotion as Marcus Wellborn's testimony had been.

"Despite your ambivalence about the play, you did go to Marcus Wellborn's house and pick up the gun from him?"

"Yes, sir."

"What did you do with it, Ms. McEntyre?"

"I placed it in the middle drawer of my desk at the office."

"You brought the gun to school and stored it there?"

"I did. I know it may sound crazy, but I thought it was the safest place for it and having it at school would make it easy to use it as a prop in the play when the time came."

"Did you lock the gun up in your desk?"

"No, sir. No one knew it was there, and I had never had a problem with theft in my office."

"But you could have locked your desk, and you also could have locked the gun in one of your filing cabinets, couldn't you?"

"Yes, sir. But I checked the gun every day. It was right where I put it."

I could see where she was going with her story *du jour*, the account of the facts she would float to justify her deeds. Before I asked her the big question, the one the jury wanted to know, I decided to turn the heat up on Beryl McEntyre.

"Ms. McEntyre, I realize I have neglected to cover a couple of matters that will provide the jury some context for your actions. So, let's back up a minute."

"All right, Mr. Danielson."

"I am familiar with your background, but the jury may not be. Are you a married woman?"

She fidgeted on the stand, her face fell, and she focused her eyes on me for the first time during my direct examination. "I am a widow. My husband passed away suddenly with an aneurysm three years ago."

"You have remained single?"

"Yes, sir. I have no plans to marry again. I lost the love of my life. No one could ever take his place."

"But, you are not alone, are you, Ms. McEntyre?"

"I don't know what you mean, Mr. Danielson." She took her eyes off me and stared at Coach Briscoe, who did not return the look.

"I mean you are in a relationship and have been for quite some time. Isn't that right?"

Jesmyn Thompson stood. "Objection, Your Honor. The witness is not on trial here, and her personal life is none of this court's business."

Judge Merrell addressed me. "Mr. Danielson, I tend to agree with counsel for defense. Is there a reason I should allow you to continue this line of questioning?"

"I believe it will become clear in just a minute, Your Honor."

"Tread lightly, Mr. Danielson. Objection overruled."

I asked my question again. "You are in a relationship, aren't you, Ms. McEntyre?"

"I had been seeing someone, but we broke it off last year."

"I need to remind you that you are under oath, Ms. McEntyre. You are testifying in a murder trial and perjury can land you in jail. Please tell us the name of the person you 'had been seeing,' as you put it."

Jesmyn Thompson began to push herself out of her chair again, but before she reached her full height Beryl McEntyre answered the question.

"Him," she said, as she pointed at Coach Briscoe.

Jesmyn settled back into her seat. The members of the jury looked at Beryl and Briscoe, Briscoe and Beryl.

"Let the record reflect, Your Honor, that the witness pointed at the defendant when she said '*him*.'"

"The record will so reflect."

"And to clarify your answer, Ms. McEntyre, the truth of the matter is that you are still in a relationship with him, aren't you?"

She took her eyes off Briscoe who sat rigid as a stone, his head turned away from her.

"Yes, I am. God help me."

"Before we move forward, Ms. McEntyre, do you care to change or clarify or retract any of the answers you have given to my questions today?"

"Yes, sir."

"Please do so."

"I didn't find a certificate to carry from February as I testified earlier. Briscoe didn't file a certificate until after the shooting. My office messed up. I messed up. He wasn't authorized to carry a gun until a few days after the shooting when he brought a certificate by for filing."

"So, under the terms of the SPA Coach Briscoe should not have been allowed to carry a firearm on campus until after the shootings occurred?"

"Yes, sir. That's right."

"Thank you for clearing that up on the record, Ms. McEntyre." I checked my notes. "Also, isn't it true that today is the first time you have publicly reported the facts about having the gun in your possession prior to the shooting?"

"Yes, sir. I did not mention it when the police took my statement."

"Why not?"

"I was scared, Mr. Danielson, afraid that I might lose my job and afraid that the families of the victims and the community at large would blame me for the terrible tragedy that occurred at KHS on May fifteenth."

Seldom had I seen a witness change direction on the stand the way Beryl McEntyre had in the last few minutes. My gut told me that she wasn't finished with her truth-telling, so I put the ultimate question to her. "How did the gun end up in Carmel Sideout's backpack, Ms. McEntyre?"

She didn't hesitate. "I can only tell you what I know. I placed the gun in my desk drawer. That would have been probably sometime in early March. A few days later, Briscoe told me he had heard a rumor about Benjamin's one-act play and wanted to know if I had learned about it. He pressed me until I gave him the details, including the fact that I had Marcus Wellborn's gun. He said the kids wanted to use the play as a publicity stunt to put themselves in the national spotlight, not to prevent school violence.

"I didn't authorize the play. I sat on it hoping the kids would drop it. Then, one evening Briscoe was at my house and said he had worked out a prank to teach Benjamin and his crew a lesson."

"He used the word 'prank'?"

"Yes, sir."

"Who did he mean when he said, 'Benjamin and his crew'?"

"The kids at school called Benjamin, Maria and Carmel 'Benjamin's crew' because they were inseparable."

"So, the defendant told you he was planning a prank to teach them a lesson. Did he explain the prank to you?"

"No, sir. He told me it would be harmless but would embarrass them and shatter their hopes of becoming Internet celebrities."

"Did he ask you to help him carry out the prank?"

"Briscoe never asks for anything, Mr. Danielson. He demands it. It's his way or the highway."

"Then, why didn't you show him the road, Ms. McEntyre?"

"You have to understand. He wears a person down, doesn't let go until he gets his way. Like a fool, I went along with his plan."

"What did he ask you to do, Ms. McEntyre?"

"He asked me to give the gun to Mr. Poteet, and the next day I called Poteet into my office and handed him the pistol."

"Was Mr. Poteet surprised when you gave him the gun?"

"No, sir. He knew that's why I'd called him to the office."

"When did you do deliver the fake Glock to Mr. Poteet?"

"The day before the shootings." She looked at Briscoe. "Goddamn you, Jim Briscoe. How could you do such a thing?" Then she broke down and cried, her face in her hands, her wails ricocheting off the walls like stray bullets.

Chapter Forty-Three

Judge Merrell called a recess after Beryl McEntyre's outburst, and Dave Schmerz and I huddled up in the witness room again.

"Have you heard from Red? We need to put Poteet on right after Beryl for the one-two punch."

"He's got Poteet, and they're on the way here. ETA is about fifteen minutes."

I nodded.

"You OK, Etch? It looks like you may have drifted off somewhere."

"I can't get that class room off my mind, the bullets tearing those kids to pieces, Briscoe murdering them like they were rabid dogs." I inhaled a couple of times to calm the surge of adrenaline coursing through me. "Emotion is a powerful thing in a courtroom, Dave. But we can't allow it to make us sloppy. We must tack down every issue in the case beyond a reasonable doubt. And we have to provide an answer to the question that is in the minds of every member of the jury."

"Why did Briscoe do it?"

"Exactly. If we can't give the jury an explanation for murder, they may waffle on us. We can't let that happen."

There was a knock on the door, and Dave walked over and opened the door wide enough to see who it was. He let it swing open and Sarah Gorsky joined us. I'd seen her observing the trial from the front row of the gallery.

"I'm not sure you need Marcie Brumbaugh any more, Etch. The deal was between McEntyre, Briscoe and Poteet. Marcie may have been overzealous because of her recent disappointment in love, but I don't see any crime she has committed. Can you cut her loose?"

"Good try, Sarah. We're in the early innings, and Marcie may still have a role to play. Tell her to keep her powder dry."

"If you call what Beryl just said the early innings, you must be expecting a grand slam in the bottom of the ninth, Etch. There's no way Briscoe can come back from the blows McEntyre landed."

"You know as well as I that it's not over 'til it's over."

"OK. Marcie and I will cool our heels. But let us know when we're free to go." On her way out the door, she stuck her head in one more time. "The bailiff says the judge is coming back on the bench."

When we entered the courtroom, Beryl McEntyre was on the witness stand, her eyes still red from crying.

"You may proceed, Mr. Danielson."

"We pass the witness, Your Honor."

Jesmyn walked to the lectern without notes and started in on Ms. McEntyre. "First thing this morning, you lied to the jury about the last-minute discovery of Jim Briscoe's right to carry permit. Right, Ms. McEntyre?"

"I corrected that statement, Ms. Thompson."

"But not until Mr. Danielson threatened you with jail for committing perjury, right?"

Ms. McEntyre nodded.

"You have to answer aloud, Ms. McEntyre."

"Yes."

"Then you lied about your relationship with my client, saying it was a thing of the past. Right?"

"I was ashamed to admit it."

"Then you told us you brought the gun to school, the last place it belonged. That was a lie, too, wasn't it?"

"No. That was the truth. It was bad judgment on my part, but it's what I did."

"'Bad judgment' is what you call bringing a gun to school?"

"It was stupid. But I explained why I did it."

"You explained by saying you thought it was a way to ensure that Benjamin and his crew didn't stage the play. Isn't that what you said?"

"Yes, ma'am."

"Ms. McEntyre you are a trained school counselor, aren't you?"

"Yes, ma'am."

"You've often listened to students tell you about bad decisions they've made and counseled them about how to move forward to correct things. Right?"

"Yes, ma'am."

"You could have shut Benjamin down and told him the play was too inflammatory, that it would stir the pot of school violence and very possibly backfire on him. But you didn't do that, did you?"

"No, ma'am."

"Rather, you encouraged him, even gave him the impression that you were in favor of staging the play at school. Isn't that right?"

"I suppose, if you want to put it that way."

Ms. Thompson gauged the reaction of the jury to Ms. McEntyre's answers. She leaned on the lectern, as if to get in Beryl's face. "You want us to believe that you've come clean, don't you, Ms. McEntyre? But you haven't come clean, have you?"

"I don't know what you mean."

"I mean that you didn't bring the gun to school and then deliver it to Mr. Poteet on Coach Briscoe's command. In your mixed-up brain, you decided the best thing was to accelerate the staging of the one-act play."

"I still don't know what you're getting at, Ms. Thompson."

"You didn't give the gun to Mr. Poteet. You gave it to Carmel Sideout, didn't you?"

"No, ma'am. I didn't do that."

"You're still lying to us, aren't you?"

"I'm telling the truth. I gave the gun to Mr. Poteet."

"So he could help Coach Briscoe play a prank on Benjamin and his crew? Do you really expect this jury to believe that a high school principal in our current climate of school violence would assist a teacher in playing a prank that involved brandishing a gun in class?"

"He badgered me about it until I gave in. It's what he always does," Beryl said nodding toward Briscoe.

"Oh, that's right. Poor pitiful you. A highly trained and experienced educator was willing to toss her career out the window because of a romantic fling? Is that what you'd have us believe, Ms. McEntyre?"

"You don't understand how it was, Ms. Thompson. Briscoe is a monster."

"You've got it wrong, Ms. McEntyre. You created the tragedy in which three students died when Coach Briscoe reacted to a threat you created. You gave Carmel Sideout the gun. And you're still not able to tell us the truth because you can't accept responsibility for your actions. Isn't that the way it really is, Ms. McEntyre? My client's not the monster, you are. Aren't you?"

"I didn't give Carmel the gun," McEntyre said, her voice weak.

"I have no other questions for this witness, Your Honor," Jesmyn said. She left the lectern and returned to the defense table.

"Any re-direct, Mr. Danielson?"

"No, Your Honor."

"You may step down, Ms. McEntyre."

Beryl McEntyre walked toward the back of the courtroom, never taking her eyes off Coach Briscoe until she disappeared out the rear door.

"Call you next witness, Mr. Danielson."

"We call Vesuvius Poteet, Your Honor."

The bailiff opened the rear door. "Vesuvius Poteet," he said like a town crier.

In a minute, Poteet entered the courtroom, Red right behind him until they made it to the banister that separated the gallery from the pit where the battle raged. Red opened the swinging half door for him and motioned for him to take the stand.

"This witness has not been sworn, Your Honor."

Judge Merrell administered the oath to Poteet. While she did, I thought of the time on his porch when he placed his hand on the Bible and lied his ass off, and I wondered what he would tell the jury now that the day of judgment had arrived.

Red leaned over to me and whispered, "He was brush-hogging his cousin's back forty when I invited him to the party."

That explained why Poteet was wearing denim overhauls flecked with hay, lace-up boots, a ragged wife-beater undershirt, and a John

Deere baseball cap for his court appearance. I couldn't see the bottoms of his boots, but I suspected a close inspection might reveal cow-patty shards.

"Please remove your cap, sir," Judge Merrell said when Poteet sat down.

I went to the lectern. "I request permission to question him as an adverse witness, Your Honor." That was lawyer-speak for questioning Poteet using leading questions, a technique usually proper only on cross-examination.

"Permission granted, Mr. Danielson."

"Your name is Vesuvius Poteet, and you are employed as a maintenance man at Kilgore High School?"

Poteet snapped out of the haze he had exhibited when he entered court and focused on me. "That's right, Danny."

"You call me Danny because we have known each other since childhood?"

"Yes, sir."

"That was a long time ago, wasn't it, Ves?"

"Seems like ages."

"A minute ago, you took an oath to tell the truth?"

"Yes, sir."

"And you realize, don't you, Ves, that if you lie on the witness stand you can be charged with perjury?"

"I know, Danny. I plan to tell the truth, the whole truth and nothing but the truth." He crossed his legs and glanced at the jury.

"As a maintenance man at KHS you have access to students' lockers?"

"Yes, sir. I have a master key."

"And one of those lockers was the one Carmel Sideout used during the school year that ended in May of this year?"

"Yes, sir. But Carmel left his locker unlocked most of the time."

"We've already heard the testimony of Beryl McEntyre. You have had frequent contact with her haven't you?"

"Sure. She's the high school principal. I see her most every day."

"You understand we are here trying Coach Briscoe for the murders of Carmel Sideout, Maria Juarez, and Benjamin Cohen?"

"I do understand that." He looked at Briscoe for a second.

"And you've known Briscoe for years?"

"Ever since he came to Kilgore almost twenty-years ago. I knew the kids, too. Bless their hearts."

"About an hour ago, Ms. McEntyre sat where you are now and told us that in May of this year she called you to her office and delivered a gun to you. It was the gun Carmel Sideout had in his backpack on the day he died. Did Ms. McEntyre give you that gun?"

The members of the jury locked their eyes on Poteet. He fiddled with his cap in his hands, looked at Briscoe, fiddled with his cap, looked at the jury, fiddled with his cap.

"Could I get a glass of water, Danny?"

I filled a paper cup with ice water from the thermos on the counsel table. "May I approach the witness, Your Honor?"

"You may, Mr. Danielson."

I walked to the witness stand and set the paper cup on the railing. Poteet took it and drank all the water in a gulp. I went back to the lectern.

"Do I need to repeat the question, Ves?"

"No, Danny. I remember it. The answer is yes. I went to her office, and Beryl gave me the gun."

I cut my eyes at Jesmyn Thompson. She had her head down, not looking at the jury. I thought I heard the wind going out of her sails.

"And you took that gun and planted it in Carmel Sideout's backpack, didn't you, Ves?"

"No, you're wrong about that, Danny. I didn't plant the gun on Carmel. I carried it to Merlin. That's the last time I saw it."

"By Merlin, you mean Merlin Hostetler, an assistant coach at KHS?"

"Yes, sir."

"Why did you take the gun to him?"

"Coach Briscoe told me he was going to play a joke on some of the kids to make a point with them. He said Merlin was in on the deal and needed the gun for the skit, or whatever they had cooked up. He'd told Beryl about his plan, him and Beryl being tight and all. And he knew she'd picked up a toy gun from the Wellborn boy to use in the play Benjamin wrote."

"You knew about Benjamin's play?"

"Yes, sir. Beryl mentioned it to me."

"So, you're telling us that all you did was act as a delivery man? You carried the gun from Ms. McEntyre to Merlin Hostetler, and that was the extent of your involvement in Briscoe's plan?"

"That's it, Danny."

"Why didn't Ms. McEntyre deliver the gun to Merlin herself?"

"Beats me. I suppose it was because she knew I went by the athletic department every day as part of my maintenance duties and would see Merlin in his office." He paused for a second.

"Is there something else you were about to add to your answer?"

"Yes, sir. The thing is that I didn't think the gun was any big deal. It was a BB gun, not a real one, and it was part of a practical joke Coach Briscoe was playing. I never in my wildest dreams thought the whole deal would go south like it did." He turned and addressed the jury. "I want all of you to know how sorry I am about how things turned out."

My mind was racing as I thought back on the various versions of the story I had heard from Beryl, Marcie Brumbaugh, and Merlin Hostetler. "If someone testified that you were in on the joke, that you had a part to play in it more than just delivering the gun to Merlin, they would be lying?"

"Who said that, Danny?"

"I'm asking it as a hypothetical, Ves. If anyone took the stand and said you were in on the deal, would they be lying?"

"Yes, sir. They surely would be. All I did was carry the pistol to Coach Hostetler."

"But you knew someone planned to use the gun in some capacity, didn't you?"

"Like I said, Danny. All I knew was that Coach Briscoe had some kind of prank planned. I thought it was harmless."

"If that's true, Ves, then why'd you go see Raul Juarez?"

"Who?" He was juggling his cap, switching it from hand to hand.

"Are you telling the jury you don't know who Raul Juarez is? I thought you said you were here to tell the truth, the whole truth and nothing but the truth."

He picked up the paper cup and turned it upside down, draining the last drops into his mouth.

"Raul is Maria's dad. I went to see him to express my condolences."

"When you learned we were getting close to figuring out this whole scheme, you left your home in Laird Hill, went to see Coach Briscoe and Coach Hostetler, then drove to Houston to meet with Raul Juarez, and then Juarez and you drove together to Lafayette, Louisiana, and met with Marcie Brumbaugh. You didn't do any of that to express your condolences, did you, Mr. Poteet?"

He dropped his cap on the floor, bent over and picked it up. He looked at Judge Merrell. "I plead the Fifth, Your Honor. I'm not answering any more questions."

"It's your constitutional right to invoke your Fifth Amendment protection against self-incrimination, Mr. Poteet. Are you telling me that you will not answer any questions whether they are propounded by Mr. Danielson or Ms. Thompson, the attorney for Coach Briscoe?"

"Yes, ma'am. I plead the Fifth."

"Very well then. Please step down, Mr. Poteet." Judge Merrell addressed the bailiff. "Mr. Bailiff have a deputy escort Mr. Poteet to a holding cell where he shall remain until further order of the Court."

"Yes, Your Honor." The bailiff escorted Ves Poteet to the rear of the courtroom where he handed him off to a Gregg County deputy.

Chapter Forty-Four

After Poteet's testimony, Judge Merrell recessed the case for the day. I spent a few minutes in a strategy session with Red and Dave Schmerz about the order of presentation of our witnesses for the next day, and then, as is common while I am in trial, I retreated to the privacy of the back room at the office.

I mulled what we had heard from the witness stand and what might lie ahead, and I let my mind wander, not to the details of the Briscoe case, but to a small frame house on the outskirts of town.

It was not Momma L's family home that appeared before me. It was mine.

I had not learned much of the truth about my father until he was dead and enough years had passed to bring me into young adulthood and to give my mother a degree of separation from the spell the man cast on her.

He had come home from World War II a veteran of the Battle of the Bulge and a shell from which the tenderness and thoughtfulness of his youth had been removed and replaced with anger and madness. He slept with a pistol under his pillow at night, and during his waking hours, he radiated a mercurial vengeance, an unpredictable streak, which made us tread quietly through the house. On our few family outings, when my mom and my brother and sister and I were confined in a car with him, we would sing and joke, and do whatever might work to keep him away from one of his moods. For if he entered his other world, we knew our only hope was to ride it out in silence and fear and keep our distance from him as best we could.

Five years after we buried him in the same cemetery where Carmel, Maria, Benjamin and Levi Cohen now lay, I put the question to my mom.

"Why did you stay with him?"

"He told me if I ever left him, he would track me down and kill me."

For thirty-six years, my mother wondered when the other shoe would drop, when something would finally trigger my dad and he would snap and lash out at her, or one of her children, or all of us. And all those years she worked a job six days a week, went to church on Sunday, and kept her family afloat.

As I thought about life with my dad, Marcus Wellborn's testimony slipped into my head. It was what he had said about Coach Briscoe having a forty-five on his hip in class every day. "I always wondered when he would use it on one of us."

I knew that feeling too well, too intimately.

Jim Briscoe had not earned madness on the battlefield. Rather, he was an impostor, a person who possessed a disdain for the rules that constituted the moral fabric of society, a master manipulator who preyed on the fears and desires of others, who charmed them, and blustered at them, and bullied them, and wormed his way past their defenses until he got a stranglehold on them. And when he had them where he wanted them, he stuck the blade between their ribs and twisted it.

The State of Texas versus James Briscoe was not about a random act of violence at school. It was about Briscoe being Briscoe, about the ransom he exacted on those who let him into their lives, and the destruction they allowed or helped him commit in exchange for their own safety.

I took the picture of my father, the one I kept on my desk, the one that showed him dressed in his Army uniform, his hair in black ringlets, his face clean-shaved, his lips pressed tight for the portrait, and I placed it in a desk drawer out of sight.

I had grown weary of looking at it.

The next morning at nine o'clock, I called Quasi to the stand.

"State your name and occupation for us, please."

"Reginald Clark. I am the detective at Kilgore Police Department in charge of the investigation of the Jim Briscoe case."

Clark was a fire hydrant of a man, five-foot-two-inches tall, two hundred and sixty-five pounds, late fifties. His eyes sparkled as if he were in on a joke about you that involved details about your personal life you kept secret. He wore dress slacks, spit-shined black lace-up Oxfords, and a light-blue Kilgore Police Department long-sleeve dress shirt, a KPD logo above the pocket. He had his badge clipped on his belt.

"You prepared the official incident report about the May fifteenth shootings?"

"Yes, sir. I have a copy of it with me." He held it up so everyone could see it.

"Let's focus on the gun Carmel Sideout had on him that day. What can you tell me about it?"

He flipped through a few pages of the report. "I found the gun two feet and three inches from Carmel Sideout's body. It was a plastic facsimile of a Glock 17."

"Are you familiar with the functionality of such a gun?"

"It was a BB gun. Pistols like that are sold in department stores, Walmart, Target."

"You've often worked cases involving deadly weapons?"

"Many times."

"Would that BB gun be considered a deadly weapon under Texas criminal law?"

"No, sir. Not at all."

"I am going to give you a hypothetical, Detective Clark. If in your capacity as a law enforcement officer you were confronted with a situation in which someone had a gun you knew to be identical to the one Carmel Sideout had that day, how would you proceed?"

"I would disarm the person by asking them to drop the gun or order them to get down on the ground."

"Would you use deadly force?"

"No, sir. Deadly force is always a last resort. In your hypothetical, the law enforcement officer would not be in danger of serious bodily injury or death, and should only use force sufficient to subdue the potential assailant."

"Were you able to determine if Carmel shot the BB gun in the classroom?"

"It was not loaded, Mr. Danielson. No BBs were found at the scene."

"How many shots did James Briscoe fire with his forty-five?"

"Five. We found slugs in the back wall and the door frame. The other three shots were located in the bodies of the victims."

"Were you able to determine the range from which the defendant fired the shots?"

"The classroom was eighteen feet wide and twenty-six feet long. Briscoe's chair was four feet from the wall. The row of seats where the victims sat was fourteen feet from his chair. Based on the locations of the spent shell casings from Briscoe's forty-five, we concluded that he fired the first shot from near his desk. He moved closer to the victims with each shot until he was only five or six feet from Carmel when he fired the fifth round which struck him in the head and killed him instantly."

Clark's delivery was matter of fact, surgical, but I could see members of the jury watching Briscoe as Clark described him going in for the kill.

"Were any fingerprints found on the BB gun?"

"Carmel's and a set that were too smudged to allow a definitive match."

"Detective Clark, you took a statement from Coach Briscoe?"

"Yes, sir. The day after the shooting he came to my office at the police station. He had already prepared a hand-written statement, and he delivered it to me."

"In that statement, Coach Briscoe said he fired all five shots from a position near his desk, didn't he?"

"Yes, sir."

"Does that statement square with your findings?"

"No, sir. He was moving towards the victims as he fired."

"In connection with your investigation, Detective Clark, did you inventory the contents of Carmel Sideout's backpack?"

"Yes, sir."

"Did you find a burner phone in it?"

"Yes, sir. We found one. I have spoken with a number of people about that phone. All of them said Carmel had an iPhone. None of them had ever seen him with a burner phone like the one we found in his backpack."

"What steps did you take to analyze that burner phone?"

"We logged it into evidence. Under our protocol, we are required to send phones recovered at a crime scene to the DPS crime lab in

Austin for analysis. We followed the protocol and sent the phone to the lab. The lab shows that they received it, but presently they are unable to locate it."

"Have you asked the lab to continue searching for it?"

"Yes, sir. Your investigator Mr. Roper and I have requested they continue searching for it. Mr. Roper actually traveled to Austin to assist the lab in its search. But so far the phone is still missing."

"Detective Clark, in the course of your investigation were you able to identify the persons who died and to determine their cause of death?"

"Yes, sir. The victims were Maria Juarez, Benjamin Cohen and Carmel Sideout. Each of them died from a gunshot wound."

"I pass the witness, Your Honor."

Jesmyn Thompson had a short list of questions.

"Detective Clark, Mr. Danielson gave you a hypothetical in which a person was confronted with a gun he knew to be a toy. Let me change that and ask you a hypo of my own. If you were confronted with a person brandishing a gun you didn't know to be fake, one which you assumed was the real thing, that would change your answer wouldn't it?"

"I would still hope to be able to disarm the suspect without use of deadly force."

"But you would also resort to deadly force to contain the situation if necessary, correct?"

"Yes, ma'am. Sometimes we have to make a split-second decision."

"You mentioned Coach Briscoe's statement and the fact that he didn't say anything about moving toward the victims as he fired. Isn't it true that witness statements are often incomplete and do not contain every detail of an event?"

"Yes, ma'am. That can happen."

"Did you take Ms. McEntyre's statement?"

"I did."

"And she never mentioned anything to you about having custody of the BB gun used in the attack, did she?"

"No, ma'am. That information came out later."

"Finally, Detective Clark, if I understand your testimony, the burner phone you recovered at the crime scene has not been analyzed and is now missing. Is that correct?"

"Yes, ma'am."

"I pass the witness, Your Honor."

Chapter Forty-Five

Eugenia Dacus took the stand.

The young graduate wore her church clothes, a pink dress with a background of violets, purple flats, a gold cross around her neck, dangling twelve inches below her chin, a white handbag just large enough to hold a cell phone on a white strap around her left wrist. Her hair was freshly washed, its brown almost black waves subtle and curled against her. Her hazel eyes glowed with the fire I had first witnessed in my office when Marcus Wellborn brought her to see me.

"State your name, please."

"Eugenia Dacus."

"Ms. Dacus, I understand that you were close with Maria Juarez, one of the victims in the shooting. Tell us about your relationship with her."

"Maria and I were like glue since fifth grade. She was my best friend, and we were always together. We talked about life, boys, our dreams. We knew we'd always be together, if not physically at least in spirit." She paused. "I still talk to her, and sometimes I feel like she's in the room with me."

"Do you feel her here with you today?"

"Yes, sir. Absolutely." She wrapped her arms around her like she was hugging a teddy bear.

"Did Maria have plans after graduation?"

"She, Carmel, and Benjamin hoped to go off to college together. They were checking out schools, dreaming about sharing an apartment. She and Carmel weren't engaged yet, but I knew Maria loved him with all her heart and that they would marry when the time was right."

"How would you describe Carmel Sideout?"

"He was smart and funny. A total mess really. When he was with Maria you could see in his eyes the love he had for her. He treated her like a princess, opening doors for her, complementing her, joking with her. They were adorable together."

"Was he protective of her?"

"He admired her strength and was always there for her."

"Eugenia, I want you to tell us about an incident that occurred during Spring break when you and Maria were at the Back Porch restaurant in Kilgore."

She described the events, how Beryl and Coach Briscoe had invited Maria and her to sit with them, how Briscoe came on to Maria, the racial slur Briscoe made toward Carmel, the arrival of Carmel and Benjamin, the standoff between Carmel and Briscoe in the parking lot.

I saw members of the jury wince when Eugenia used the N-word.

"Ms. Dacus, after your group separated from Coach Briscoe and Ms. McEntyre that evening, did you ever hear Carmel say anything about wanting to get even with Coach Briscoe for what he had done to Maria?"

"No, sir. All I ever heard him say was that he would be glad to get out of Kilgore when the school year was over, so he wouldn't have to put up with Briscoe anymore."

"Do you know if Maria ever told Carmel about Briscoe's use of the N-word?"

"No, sir. I don't know one way or the other. She was really private about what went on between her and Carmel. My guess is that she didn't tell him because she knew it would have hurt him. But I don't know that for sure."

"I'm almost through, Ms. Dacus, but I have one more subject to ask you about."

She nodded.

"What, if anything, do you know about Maria's father, Raul Juarez?"

"Maria's father and mother divorced years ago. He moved to Houston and only came to Kilgore every now and then. I've seen him a few times since Maria and I have been running together."

"You said Maria and you became close friends when you were in the fifth grade. That would have been seven years or so ago?"

"Yes, sir."

"And in those seven years you've seen Maria's father in Kilgore a few times?"

"Right."

"Do you know the last time you saw Raul Juarez in Kilgore?"

She moved her head from side to side, focused her eyes on the ceiling. "It would have been after Easter of this year."

"How are you able to pinpoint the date?"

"Maria and Carmel went to see her dad during Easter break. It didn't go well. Her dad was an ass to Carmel, so they came home early. A week or so later, I was at the convenience store in Kilgore, the one that has a Whataburger restaurant, and I saw Maria's dad at the checkout counter. He didn't see me, and I didn't say anything to him. I hoped he was in town to apologize to Maria, but when I asked her about it later that day, she said he hadn't contacted her. She didn't even know he was in town."

"You said Raul Juarez was an ass to Carmel. What did you mean by that?"

"Maria told me her dad didn't approve of her being with Carmel because he was Black."

On cross-examination, Jesmyn Thompson wasted no time spinning Eugenia's testimony to Briscoe's advantage.

"Ms. Dacus, so what you're telling the jury is that only two months before the shooting in the classroom, Carmel Sideout threatened Coach Briscoe?"

"He didn't threaten him. He was just standing up for Maria," Eugenia said, the fire in her eyes again.

"Carmel would have attacked my client if Benjamin hadn't gotten between them, right?"

"Coach followed us outside. He was rubbing Carmel's nose in it. Carmel just wanted him to back off, to leave Maria and him alone."

"I understand that's how you feel about it, Ms. Dacus. But don't you realize that domestic issues, romantic relationships, are the most dangerous and volatile human dynamics of all? Don't you know that people kill each other over love every day?"

"Carmel wasn't a killer, ma'am."

"Ms. Dacus, you testified that you do not know if Maria told Carmel about the racial slur Coach Briscoe used about Carmel?"

"Yes, ma'am. I don't know one way or the other. My guess is that she didn't."

"Exactly, Ms. Dacus. It's only a guess. It's also possible, isn't it, that Maria did tell Carmel about it?"

"It's possible." Eugenia's voice was a whisper.

"And if you add a racial slur to the mix, don't you see that Carmel had two scores to settle with Coach Briscoe?"

"That's just not the sort of person Carmel was, ma'am."

"I have no more questions for this witness, Your Honor."

While Eugenia Dacus made her way out of the courtroom, I got up and walked to the rail near Sarah Gorsky. She rose and leaned close to me. "What's Marcie's temperature today, Sarah? Is she in or out?"

She whispered back. "It's hard to know with that girl, Etch."

I nodded at her and went to the lectern.

"We call Marcie Brumbaugh, Your Honor."

When the back door opened, I saw Marcie outside the courtroom standing next to a young man, holding his hand. She released her grip, smiled at him and waved goodbye as she entered the courtroom.

That momentary exchange between her and the young man told me what I needed to know about Marcie Brumbaugh. Plan A had become Plan B.

Marcie took the stand, brimming with air-head, her fingernails painted with smiley-face emojis, Destin flip flops on her feet.

"State your name and occupation for us, please."

"Marcie Brumbaugh. I am Ms. McEntyre's assistant at Kilgore High School."

"Are you still employed at the high school or did you leave that job recently?"

"I'm on a leave of absence, what with the shootings and all." I thought I heard a slight giggle in her voice.

"Does Ms. McEntyre know you're on a leave of absence?"

"I haven't discussed it with her, Mr. Danielson."

"So, you just took it on yourself to take some time off?"

"Yeah. Cool, huh?"

"You were on the job at KHS from January until after the shootings?"

"Yes, sir. I didn't miss a day, but I was tardy a few times." This time I definitely heard a giggle.

The jury members were not amused at her performance. I could tell they wanted to know where I was going in my questioning of this strange young creature.

"Do you know a man named Merlin Hostetler, Ms. Brumbaugh?"

"Of course. He's my fiancé."

"Since when?"

"Since yesterday, Mr. Danielson."

"Merlin Hostetler is an assistant coach at KHS and a witness in this case, isn't he?"

"Yes, sir."

"And you are telling us that yesterday you and he became engaged?"

"Yes, sir. Isn't that grand?"

"I don't suppose that you and Merlin put your heads together yesterday about your testimony in this case, did you?"

"No, sir. Not our heads. Maybe a few other body parts." She laughed aloud at her joke.

"Ms. Brumbaugh, you and I have spoken before, correct?"

"Yes, sir. At school and then later with my lawyer in Canton and at your office."

"At the meeting in Canton, you told me you saw Merlin Hostetler with the toy BB gun that ended up in Carmel Sideout's backpack on the day of the shooting?"

"I told you that, but it was just because I was mad at Merlin. We'd had a spat."

"But you're over your spat, now?"

She raised her left hand to display her engagement ring.

"You also told me that day in Canton that Coach Briscoe gave Merlin Hostetler the assignment to plant the gun in Carmel's backpack, didn't you, Ms. Brumbaugh?"

"I was confused and hurt when I said that, Mr. Danielson. You know how it is."

"No, I don't know how it is, Ms. Brumbaugh. We are trying Coach Briscoe for murder and we need to know the truth. Did you see Merlin with the gun?"

"I don't remember."

"Did he tell you Briscoe directed him to plant the gun on Carmel?"

"I don't remember that either."

"Three weeks ago, did you meet with Mr. Poteet and Raul Juarez in Lafayette, Louisiana to discuss Coach Briscoe's case?"

Before she could catch herself, she blurted out, "How did you know that?"

"Did you meet with them, Ms. Brumbaugh?"

"I'd have to check my calendar and get back with you on that one, Mr. Danielson."

I passed the witness.

Jesmyn Thompson remained seated. She flipped through the notes she had taken on a legal pad while Marcie was on the stand.

"Any cross-examination, Ms. Thompson?"

"No, Your Honor."

The judge addressed Ms. Thompson and me. "Counsel is this a good time for our morning break?"

"I have one more witness I'd like to call before that, Your Honor. It should be a quick one."

"That's fine, Your Honor," Jesmyn Thompson said.

"All right. Call your next witness, Mr. Danielson."

"We call Merlin Hostetler, Your Honor."

Coach Hostetler was decked out in a three-piece navy suit, a starched white shirt, a KHS necktie cinched tight at the collar. He showed a mouthful of white teeth when he smiled at the jury.

"I understand congratulations are in order, Coach Hostetler."

He looked at me with a question mark in his eyes.

"Marcie Brumbaugh says you and she are recently engaged."

"She told you that?"

"That and other things."

The smile left his face.

"Mr. Hostetler you have been an assistant coach at KHS for the last two school years?"

"Yes, sir."

"And you coach alongside Jim Briscoe?"

"Yes, sir. He's head boys basketball coach, and I'm his assistant coach."

"Are you good friends with Coach Briscoe?"

"I'd say so."

"Does he set you up with women?"

"I don't know what you mean, sir?"

"I mean, doesn't he introduce you to girls?"

"No, sir. Not really."

"He introduced you to Marcie Brumbaugh, didn't he?"

"I guess so. But I already knew who she was. I'd seen her in the principal's office."

"But you never went out with her until Coach Briscoe arranged it, did you?"

"No, sir. But it just worked out that way."

"Let's talk about the shootings, Mr. Hostetler."

"OK."

"A month or so ago, Marcie told me she saw you with the gun Carmel had in his backpack. Did you have that gun at some point?"

"I think she told you that because she was mad at me then. We'd broken up. I never told her I had that gun. I never laid eyes on it."

"She also told me you said Coach Briscoe directed you to plant the gun on Carmel. Did you say that?"

"Like I said. She was mad at me. I think her imagination got the best of her."

"Did Coach Briscoe tell you to plant the gun on Carmel?"

"No, sir. I never saw the gun and never planted it on anyone."

"All that's just Marcie's imagination running wild?"

"Must be."

Jesmyn took him on cross.

"So, to make things clear, Mr. Hostetler, is it your testimony here today that you have never seen the gun Carmel had on him on the day of the shootings?"

"That's right. I may have seen pictures of it on TV, but I've never seen it in person."

"And Coach Briscoe never asked you to plant the gun on Carmel?"

"No, ma'am. He never did that."

"And you don't have any idea how the gun came to be in Carmel's backpack?"

"No, ma'am."

She passed the witness.

"Anything on re-direct, Mr. Danielson?"

"One more thing, Your Honor."

"Mr. Hostetler why did Mr. Poteet meet with you at your apartment three weeks ago?"

"He never came to my place, Mr. Danielson?"

"Would you like to confer with your attorney before you try that answer again, Merlin?"

I looked at Ron Braxton in the back of the room. He dropped a stack of papers on the floor and knelt down out of sight to pick them up.

"No, sir. Mr. Poteet came by to tell me goodbye. He said he was going out of town for a while."

"You and he are friends?"

"We talk at school."

"And the subject of the shootings never came up in your goodbye talk with Poteet?"

"Not that I recall, Mr. Danielson."

"I don't suppose he delivered the gun to you on his way out of town, did he?"

Merlin hesitated for a second before he answered. I suspected that he wondered if we had videoed Poteet coming in his apartment that day.

"You'll need to answer my question, Merlin."

Merlin looked at Briscoe.

"Coach Briscoe can't help you answer, Merlin. Did Poteet give you the gun."

"Uh, no sir," he said, choking on the words.

Chapter Forty-Six

After the morning break, Raul Juarez took the stand. He was the epitome of a Houston mid-level executive, tan sports coat, brown slacks, pressed heavy-starched white cotton shirt and red tie. His build was compact, five-ten, one-seventy-five. His hair, styled in a Brutus cut, was as black as his eyes, his fawn brown skin the color of the coarse sand on a Galveston beach. He carried his brief case with him to the witness stand and placed it on the floor when he sat down.

"State your name, please?"

"Raul Juarez."

"Mr. Juarez, I know Maria Juarez was your daughter. I am sorry for your loss."

"Thank you, sir," he said without emotion. He had a TV-anchor air about him, his accent mid-western without a trace of Texas in it.

"What line of work are you in, Mr. Juarez?"

"I am district manager for the Houston area of Concrete Suppliers, Inc. We provide concrete to construction sites in the greater Houston area."

"How long have you held that position?"

"I was promoted to district manager seven years ago. I moved from Kilgore to Houston when I accepted the job."

"How long did you live in Kilgore?"

"Ten years, give or take."

"Mr. Juarez, how did you come to know Coach Briscoe?"

"When I lived in Kilgore, I managed the Tyler office of Concrete Suppliers. The company encourages its managers to become involved in civic affairs, and I joined the athletic booster club for KHS. Mr. Briscoe was a coach, so I got to know him from visiting with him at booster club meetings and at ball games."

"Did you and Coach Briscoe become friends?"

"I think it's fair to say that we did."

"You and Maria's mother divorced about the time you took the job in Houston?"

"Yes, sir. She didn't want to leave Kilgore, so I moved by myself."

"Maria would have been about ten or eleven years old when you moved to Houston?"

"Yes, sir."

"How often did you see her after you left town to take the district manager position?"

"The job has me working sixty hours a week or more. But I've seen her when I could. I would come to Kilgore every month or two, stay in a hotel for the weekend, and Maria and I would knock around together. When she got her driver's license, she made a few trips to see me in Houston."

"We've heard testimony about a trip she made to see you in Houston during the Easter break this year."

"Yes. She brought Carmel Sideout with her."

"Had you met Carmel before?"

"No, sir. I had talked to Maria about him often on the phone, and she wanted me to meet him."

"How did that go, Mr. Juarez?"

"Not well. Carmel and I didn't really hit it off, and Maria decided she wanted to go home early. They came in on Good Friday and left the same day."

"That meeting must have really gone badly to make them leave so soon. Did you and Maria have a fight?"

"I wouldn't put it that way. I'm a businessman, Mr. Danielson. Maria is my only child and I wanted her to be with someone who could provide for her down the road. Carmel, and I don't mean to speak ill of the dead, struck me as a dreamer, a guy who had no definite plan for his life. I didn't want Maria shackled to a guy like that, one who would be content to allow her to work night and day while he figured out what he wanted to be. I am not a person to mince words, so when I told them how I felt, they packed up and left."

"Did it matter to you that Carmel was Black?"

"Only because I thought that would make things even harder for the two of them if they decided to marry."

"So, Maria and Carmel left on Good Friday. Did you ever visit with her again before the shootings?"

"No, sir. I wish to God I had. But I had no way of knowing my time with her was running out." He bit his lip.

"But between your last visit with Maria and the day of the shootings you did visit Kilgore, didn't you? One of the witnesses we have heard from already said she saw you at a Kilgore convenience store."

He cut his eyes at Briscoe. "I had to make a flying trip to Kilgore to address a work-related issue."

"I thought the East Texas office of Concrete Suppliers, Inc. was in Tyler."

"Yes, sir. It is." He folded his hands and watched them as he spoke.

"Your trip to Kilgore wasn't business-related was it, Mr. Juarez?"

"No, sir."

He cut his eyes at Briscoe again, and Briscoe looked straight ahead as if he was oblivious to the entire exchange I was having with Juarez. "You came to town to meet with Coach Briscoe, didn't you?"

"He had called me and said he needed to talk in person. I thought it had to do with Maria's work at school, so I took a day off and came to Kilgore."

"Why did you lie about it a second ago?"

"It's pretty simple, Mr. Danielson. I am testifying in a murder trial where a friend of mine is the accused and my daughter is a victim. I see how this could go. I feared you would twist my meeting into something it wasn't."

"So you decided the best thing to do was to lie about that innocent meeting, to cover it up and not tell us about it?"

"I apologize to the Court."

"We don't want your apology, Mr. Juarez. I'm not buying what you're selling. Your meeting with Briscoe was about Carmel Sideout and how you could get rid of him, wasn't it?"

"I didn't want to get rid of him, Mr. Danielson."

"What did you want?"

"Briscoe said he had a prank planned, one that would teach Carmel a lesson and take his ego down a notch or two. I thought it was a good idea."

"Briscoe used the word 'prank'?"

"Yes, sir. And that's what I thought it was, a practical joke. Carmel would be suspended for a few days, that's all."

"And maybe Maria would come to her senses and dump Carmel?"

"That would have been a home run," Juarez huffed, his arrogance floating to the surface.

"Tell us how this practical joke was supposed to work. I assume Coach Briscoe laid out the details for you, didn't he?"

"He said he had arranged for someone to plant a toy gun in Carmel's backpack. Briscoe was going to find the gun during class and make a big show of disarming Carmel. Then he would haul him to the principal's office and watch him squirm."

"And what was your role in the prank, Mr. Juarez?"

He stiffened. "That's what I meant earlier. I knew you would try to put this on me. I didn't have a role. Coach just wanted me to know about it."

"He had you come to Kilgore just to tell you about it? He could have done that on the phone, couldn't he?"

"He wanted to deliver the news to me in person."

"Let's go back to the plan a minute. There's still one piece I can't figure out, Mr. Juarez. Coach has someone plant the gun in Carmel's backpack. That means Carmel doesn't know it's there. How is Briscoe supposed to orchestrate the deal so that Carmel discovers the gun while he's sitting in Briscoe's class?"

"Briscoe just told me he would find it. I thought he might do a random search of everyone's bags or something."

"Or he could have had a time bomb in place, couldn't he?"

"I don't follow what you're saying, Mr. Danielson."

I pulled a sheet of paper out of a file folder.

"May I approach the witness, Your Honor?'

"You may."

I walked to the front of the witness stand with the paper in my hand. "Do you have a cell phone, Mr. Juarez?"

"Of course."

"One or two?"

I saw his right hand slip to his side until it came to rest on his briefcase.

"One."

I laid the piece of paper on the railing in front of him. "Take a look at what I've marked as Exhibit 15-P, Mr. Juarez."

His eyes grew big when he saw the hand-written exhibit.

"Remember when you and Mr. Poteet drove to Lafayette to meet with Marcie Brumbaugh?"

He looked down when he answered. "I remember."

"You gave your cell phone information to the waitress at the hotel to qualify for a complimentary stay?"

"Yes, sir."

"And there are two cell phone numbers on here, aren't there?"

"Yes, sir."

"And one of them is the burner phone you used as part of Briscoe's practical joke, isn't it?" I turned and nodded at Dave Schmerz. He reached for my cell phone on the table and pressed send. I put my index finger to my lips to call for silence in the courtroom. Three seconds later, Juarez's briefcase buzzed as a cell phone vibrated inside it.

Juarez grabbed his briefcase, plopped it in his lap, removed the buzzing burner phone and turned it off.

I walked back to the lectern. "And that's how you set the whole thing in motion, isn't it, Mr. Juarez?"

He latched the briefcase and set it on the floor again.

Jesmyn Thompson on cross-examination attempted to break the spell in the courtroom.

"Mr. Juarez, you loved Maria and would never have done anything to hurt her, would you?"

Juarez was contrite now, a frame of mind I doubted he had often experienced.

"Never. She was my only child, my pride and joy."

"So, when Coach Briscoe told you about the prank he had in store for Carmel, you took him at his word, didn't you?"

"Yes, ma'am."

"In all the years you have known Coach Briscoe have you ever seen him mistreat a student?"

"No, ma'am. The kids think the world of him."

"And Coach Briscoe never mentioned anything to you about attacking Carmel or any of the other students, did he?"

"No, ma'am. He said his practical joke was designed to embarrass Carmel. That's all."

She checked her notes. "Mr. Danielson has mentioned the trip you and Mr. Poteet made to visit Marcie Brumbaugh in Lafayette. The purpose of that trip was actually so the three of you could compare notes and confirm that Coach Briscoe never hinted to any of you that there was anything violent or dangerous about the practical joke?"

Juarez picked up on her theory. "Yes, ma'am. That was it exactly. We all saw it the same way and thought Carmel must have done something unexpected in class that day that made Coach have to defend himself."

"Something like brandishing the gun and making a show of it?"

"Yes, ma'am. That must have been what happened."

I was on my feet by the time Jesmyn sat down.

"Mr. Juarez, you've already testified that Coach Briscoe told you the gun he planned to have someone plant in Carmel's backpack was a toy, right?"

"Yes, sir."

"Do you really expect the jury to believe that even if Carmel brandished that gun in class Coach Briscoe was justified in using deadly force against him?"

Juarez studied the jury for a few seconds before he answered. "The kids in the class didn't know it was a toy. Maybe Coach thought Carmel had panicked them, and someone was about to get hurt."

"Someone was about to get hurt, all right. And it was Carmel Sideout, the man you kicked out of your house a few weeks earlier, the man who made the terrible mistake of falling in love with your daughter. You knew that was Briscoe's plan all along, didn't you?"

"No, sir. I didn't know. I didn't know." He pleaded with the jury with his eyes, but they had turned their heads away from him.

Chapter Forty-Seven

After Raul Juarez left the courtroom, the bailiff stood in front of Judge Merrell's bench to get her attention. The judge leaned forward and exchanged a few words with him before she addressed us.

"I have just learned that my presence is required to handle an emergency matter in one of the other courts. I must adjourn our proceedings in the Briscoe case for the day. We will take it up again the first thing in the morning. However, before we go into recess, I would like to hear counsels' opinions on the schedule for the remainder of the trial. Mr. Danielson, what is your estimate of the amount of time until the State rests its case in chief?"

"My best guess, Your Honor, is that we will rest by noon tomorrow."

"Ms. Thompson without revealing your strategy, do you have an estimate of how long the defense will take to present its case?"

"Your Honor, I think we will be fairly brief. I anticipate calling a couple of witnesses, but I think we can have the case to the jury by the end of the day tomorrow."

"Very well," Judge Merrell said. "Mr. Bailiff, please inform the witnesses outside the courtroom that the court is in recess until tomorrow morning at nine o'clock."

By the time we had our gear packed, the jury members and witnesses had cleared out of the courthouse for the day.

"Let's walk over to the coffee shop and debrief before we call it a day," I said to Red and Dave Schmerz, referring to an espresso bar a

226

block south of the courthouse. We rode the elevator to the ground floor and strolled along the sidewalk. When we neared the intersection on the southwest corner of the block, I noticed a maroon Mustang parked in the last spot, a location near Harold Fleming's office where Jesmyn Thompson, Harold Fleming and Coach Briscoe had set up their war room during the trial. I saw the three of them twenty yards or so behind us.

"Do you see that car?" I asked Red.

"I see it, and I don't like the looks of it."

"Me either."

"The high sign is two fingers," Red said. He flashed the peace sign at me and quickened his pace toward the Mustang.

I turned to Dave Schmerz. "I don't have time to explain, Dave. Here's what I need you to do. I have to talk to the driver of that car." I motioned with my head toward the Maroon pony. "You stand behind me, between me and Jesmyn's group. Act like you're admiring the trees until I give you the all clear."

Dave glanced at the car and at the trio coming down the walkway toward it. "Yes, sir."

Red circled around the back of the Mustang and took a position next to the front passenger door. The dark-tinted windows were up, but I could see the silhouette of a person behind the wheel. I walked to the driver's window and tapped on it with the knuckles of my right hand.

Marcus Wellborn lowered the window so that a two-inch slit allowed me to make eye contact with him. I saw a pistol in his hand, a Colt Government Model .45-caliber.

"What's up, Marcus?"

"I can't let him get away with it, Mr. Danielson."

He lowered the window a couple of inches more, and I leaned against the car blocking his view of the group nearing him on the sidewalk.

"Don't throw your life away for Coach Briscoe. He's not going to get away with anything, Marcus."

He cocked the hammer on the Colt. "Move away from my car, Mr. Danielson."

"Here's what is about to happen, Marcus. If I raise my hand, Red will smash your passenger window and fire one shot. That shot will strike you in the head, and you will die instantly."

Marcus cut his eyes at the passenger window.

"If I don't raise my hand, and you put that gun down, this deal will be between us and no one will ever know how close you came to losing your life, ruining the lives of your family and tarnishing the memories of Carmel, Maria, and Benjamin. You've got about three seconds to decide which way life will go for you." I started counting down. "Three, two."

Marcus laid the gun in the passenger seat.

"Unlock the passenger door, Marcus."

He leaned across the seat and followed my command. As soon as the door was unlatched, Red stuck his hand in the car and grabbed the Colt forty-five off the seat so that the web between his right thumb and index finger blocked the hammer from striking the firing pin. He backed away from the Mustang, released the ammo clip, ejected the live round from the chamber and stuck the pistol in the inside pocket of his jacket. He closed the passenger door, moved to the front of the car and tipped his hat at Jesmyn Thompson and her entourage.

"Roll your window all the way down, son," I said to Marcus Wellborn when the danger was passed.

He complied.

I laid my hand on his shoulder. "Go home to your family, Marcus. Go home and make a difference in this crazy world. We're counting on you."

He was crying now. "I'm sorry, Mr. Danielson."

I patted his shoulder. "No need to apologize, Marcus."

He rolled up the window, started his car, backed out of the parking spot and drove away.

"All in a day's work, huh, counselor?" Red said.

Dave Schmerz walked next to us. "Did I just see what I thought I saw?"

"You saw a fine young man standing up for his friends. That's all, Dave."

"I think I need a double-shot of espresso," Red said. "Or maybe three fingers of Wild Turkey 101."

And we strolled down the sidewalk to the coffee shop.

Chapter Forty-Eight

The best bit of lawyering advice I ever heard was a remark attributed to Abraham Lincoln. Honest Abe said that when he was preparing for trial, he spent one-third of his time thinking about what he would say and two-thirds of his time thinking about what the lawyer on the other side would say.

After my near-death experience at the hands of Marcus Wellborn, I sat in the backroom at the office the rest of the afternoon and late into the evening and wondered about Jesmyn Thompson's game plan. She had announced to Judge Merrell that she had a witness or two who would take a half day or so. However, a cardinal rule of trial lawyers is that lying is not necessary, it is mandatory. If you hint to the other side that you will do one thing, do another.

In the Briscoe case, Jesmyn had a couple of maneuvers at her disposal.

She could do nothing or something.

Doing nothing meant resting right after I did. She wouldn't call anyone to the stand, and she would devote her closing argument to poking holes in my case.

Option Two, doing something, meant she would call a witness or two to cast reasonable doubt on the testimony jurors had already heard.

A lot of criminal defense lawyers were firmly committed to Option One: let the prosecution do the heavy lifting and spend your time jabbing at the witnesses on cross-examination. I doubted that Jesmyn was cut from that cloth. The Los Angeles way of lawyering was for the defense to out-do the prosecution, to call a ringer to demolish the State's case.

There was no need for me to rifle through my files to find Jesmyn's star witness. I knew who it would be. That's why I'd laid a trap, and why I prayed to God that Jesmyn Thompson would take the bait.

The next morning when Judge Merrell called the case, I played my card.

"The State rests, Your Honor."

"The State has rested its case in chief, Ms. Thompson. Please call your first witness."

Jesmyn walked toward the lectern, no note pad in hand. She paused, stepped back to the counsel table, picked up a manila folder, and took her position at the lectern.

"The defense calls Brigitte Malcolm, Your Honor."

I glanced at Red who had his poker face on, at Dave Schmerz who suppressed a sly grin.

Brigitte Malcolm entered the courtroom. She carried herself with the confidence of a superintendent about to make a presentation at a school board meeting. For the occasion she wore a black pants suit, no jewelry. She had cropped her blonde hair so that it hung just below her ears. In her hand she held a clipboard, and on the clipboard, I could see a few pages of paper, which I assumed were documents she would reference if necessary.

"State your name and your present employer," Jesmyn Thompson said.

"Brigitte Malcolm. I am the superintendent at Kilgore ISD."

"How long have you held that position?"

"A little over three years."

"Ms. Malcolm are you familiar with the Student Protection Act, also known as the SPA?"

"Yes, ma'am. I have studied it in detail."

"Please tell the jury the purpose of the SPA."

"The legislature, in its infinite wisdom, passed the SPA to address the epidemic of school violence. The SPA's provisions authorize teachers to carry deadly weapons on campus under certain circumstances and shield schools from civil liability if a teacher uses a deadly weapon in response to a threatened or actual case of violence at the school."

"Did Kilgore ISD adopt the provisions of the SPA?"

"Yes, ma'am. The board opted into the SPA at its March meeting this year."

"You said the SPA authorizes teachers to carry weapons under certain circumstances. What are those circumstances?"

"In order to carry a gun on campus, a teacher must complete a state-sanctioned training course and file a certificate of completion of the course with the principal's office at the school where the teacher is assigned to teach."

"Under the SPA, Ms. Malcolm, what conditions justify a teacher to use deadly force in a school violence situation?"

"I have a copy of the SPA with me." She held the clipboard up so the jury members could see it. "The language in the SPA is: A school employee is justified in the use of deadly force whenever he or she has sufficient certainty that a student is about to engage in violence towards another student or is actually engaged in such violence."

"Let's apply the SPA to the facts of Coach Briscoe's case, Ms. Malcolm. First, did he comply with the conditions necessary to carry a gun on campus?"

"No. Not technically."

Ms. Thompson shifted her weight from one foot to the other. "Explain your answer, please."

"Coach Briscoe began carrying a gun on campus in February right after the legislature passed the SPA. I thought he had filed a certificate of completion with Ms. McEntyre's office, but it turned out that he didn't file it until after the shootings in May."

"Do you know if Coach Briscoe had actually completed his required training before he started carrying a gun on campus and simply failed to file the certificate until after the shootings?"

"I don't know that. All I know is that the certificate he filed was dated several days after the shootings. If he had in fact completed the training before the shootings, I haven't seen proof of it. I do know that Coach Briscoe was familiar with guns before the SPA became law."

Jesmyn shifted her weight again. "The SPA uses the language that a teacher must have sufficient certainty that a student is about to engage in violence towards another student to be justified in the use deadly force against the student. Is that correct, Ms. Malcolm."

"Yes, ma'am."

"As superintendent of KISD you believe, don't you, Ms. Malcolm, that Carmel Sideout's actions on the day of the shootings, the fact that he pulled a gun from his backpack and brandished it in class, met the SPA's requirement and gave Coach Briscoe 'sufficient certainty' to use deadly force?"

The jury had a laser focus on Brigitte Malcolm as they awaited her answer to the critical question in the case.

Brigitte looked at Coach Briscoe while she spoke. "It depends on what he knew ahead of time, Ms. Thompson. If he had no knowledge the gun was a toy and thought it was the real thing, then I think his actions may have been justified. If he knew the gun was a fake, he wasn't justified. It's as simple as that."

Jesmyn Thompson shot me a quick look. That split-second glance told me she knew I had sand-bagged her with her star witness. She scrambled to get something positive out of the exchange with Brigitte Malcolm.

"Ms. Malcolm, in the more than three years you've been superintendent at KISD, Coach Briscoe has been employed continuously by the district, hasn't he?"

"Yes, ma'am."

"And during that time, you have recommended three times that the school board extend his contract, haven't you?"

"Yes, ma'am."

"And those contract extensions are an indication that you have been satisfied with his performance as a teacher and coach at KISD?"

"That's part of what those extensions mean. But they mean more than that."

"What else do the extensions mean, Ms. Malcolm?"

"They mean I wanted Coach Briscoe where I could keep an eye on him. I didn't want to pawn him off on another district. I kept hoping he would give me a good reason to fire him. Unfortunately, I waited too long."

Jesmyn Thompson picked up her manila folder, returned to the defense table and sat down.

"Do you pass the witness, Ms. Thompson?" Judge Merrell asked after a few beats passed.

Jesmyn stood. "Yes, Your Honor."

I went to the lectern without notes.

"Ms. Malcolm you just said you wanted to keep an eye on Coach Briscoe. Please explain what you meant."

"I meant that I know what he's made of."

"You've been the superintendent at KISD for a little over three years, but you've known Coach Briscoe a lot longer than that haven't you?"

"Yes, sir. I've known him since I was seventeen years old."

"How did you come to know him?"

"I grew up in Kilgore and attended Kilgore High School. I played on the tennis team and Briscoe was my coach."

"Was that the extent of your acquaintance with him?"

"No, sir. I wish it was, but it became a lot more."

"Did you become involved romantically with Briscoe when you were one of his students?"

She took a deep breath and made eye-contact with the jurors one by one before she answered. "Yes, I did. I was young and stupid, and Briscoe was the hot new coach in town. He lured me in, and I swallowed his advances hook, line and sinker."

"How long did your relationship last?"

"Years. I left for college, and he would come to visit me there. Later, when I worked for Highland Park ISD, he came to Dallas to see me once a month or so."

"How did your relationship end?"

"Briscoe was always after me. He called every couple of days, went on and on about how much he loved me. You know, the usual stuff. About ten years ago, he came to my place in north Dallas. He left Sunday afternoon to come back to Kilgore, and I went to one of our favorite restaurants for a late lunch. I guess he didn't see that coming because when I entered the diner, I saw him sitting in the corner with another woman."

"How did that go, Ms. Malcolm?"

"I confronted him and told him we were through. We took it outside, and he pleaded with me to forgive him. When I resisted, he changed his tone."

"Changed it to what?"

"He told me if I ever mentioned our relationship to anyone, he would ruin my career."

"How so?"

"He knew in the school business it is taboo for a teacher to have a relationship with a student."

"How could that come back on you? You were the student, not the teacher."

"It takes two to tango. He knew school districts would blackball me if they knew I had violated that taboo. They would see me as tainted, and my career would go in the toilet."

"How did you handle that?"

"I kept my mouth shut." She paused. "Until today."

"I am sure the jury is wondering why you would take the job at KISD under the circumstances you just described. Why did you do it?"

"I knew Briscoe would always have the same M.O. I thought if I was his boss, I might be able to keep him in line. When I moved back to Kilgore, he approached me and wanted to take up where we left off. I told him there was a new sheriff in town and showed him the door. That's the way it's been for the last three years."

"In other words, by coming to Kilgore ISD as superintendent you hoped to turn the tables on Briscoe. Instead of him controlling you, you would control him?"

"That's the way I had conceived of it. What I didn't understand was how far Briscoe would go to prove he was still in charge." She faced the jury. "I will regret forever that I allowed Coach Briscoe to remain in the classroom. I should have fired him and seen to it that he never entered any school again as a teacher. Carmel Sideout, Maria Juarez, and Benjamin Cohen didn't deserve that monster." She buried her head in her hands and wept.

After Brigitte Malcolm left the courtroom, Jesmyn addressed Judge Merrell. "Your Honor before I call my next witness, I need a few moments to consult with my client in private."

"All right, Ms. Thompson. Please let the bailiff know when you are ready to proceed. We will take our morning break now and remain in recess until I hear from you."

Red, Dave Schmerz and I gathered in the witness room while we waited on Jesmyn Thompson's next move.

"Will she call Coach Briscoe?" Dave asked.

"Brigitte Malcolm has put her in an impossible spot. The way she spun it, the case hangs on Briscoe's state of mind when Carmel discovered the pistol. Briscoe is the only person who can counter the testimony the jury has already heard. If she doesn't call him the other testimony goes unanswered."

Red piped up. "And if he does testify the jury sees what an asshole he is."

"Yeah. It's a lose-lose for her, but I think she has to call him and try to make the best of it."

We heard a knock on the witness room door.

"Man, that was quick," Red said.

Dave opened the door and the bailiff entered. "Etch, there's a woman out here who wants to speak to you. She says she has critical information about the case."

I polled Red and Dave. "Either of you expecting someone?" They shook their heads.

"OK," I said to the bailiff. "Bring her in."

He shut the door, and, in a minute, we heard a knock again. Red opened the door and a fifty-ish Black woman entered the room. She was wearing a floor-length, royal-purple dress, dark sunglasses. Her jet-black hair was coiled on top of her head, its gold highlights glistening. Although I had not seen her in many years, I recognized her at once. She removed her glasses, shook my hand and gave me a hug.

I announced her to Red and Dave. "Gentleman, I'd like you to meet Carmel Sideout's mother, Ms. Caddo Panola."

She sat down at the conference table. "I know time is short, but I have a few things to tell you about Jim Briscoe, Carmel Sideout, and me."

Chapter Forty-Nine

We had spent fifteen minutes with Caddo Panola when the bailiff knocked to let us know the judge was coming on the bench.

"You stay in here until we call for you," I told Caddo.

We took our places at counsel table, and Judge Merrell entered and addressed Jesmyn Thompson.

"Are you ready to proceed, Ms. Thompson?"

"Yes, Your Honor. The defense calls Coach Jim Briscoe."

There was a murmur in the gallery.

Judge Merrell pounded her gavel. "Ladies and gentlemen, we will have order in the court."

The crowd quieted, and Briscoe sauntered to the witness stand, took the oath and settled into the hot seat.

"State your name for the court, please, sir."

"James Briscoe."

"You are the defendant in this case?"

"Yes, ma'am. I figured you already knew that." He laughed.

Jesmyn did not engage him in banter. "Coach Briscoe you understand that, together with Harold Fleming," she waved her hand at Fleming, "I represent you in this matter?"

"Sometimes, I have had my doubts," Briscoe shot back at her.

"Mr. Briscoe, you and I have discussed the issue of whether you should testify in the case?"

"Yes, ma'am."

"And you are taking the stand today with full knowledge that you cannot be compelled to do so?"

"I understand, Ms. Thompson. I also understand that I am testifying against your advice. You said I should sit on my hands and listen to a bunch of lies without fighting back." He had dropped his smart aleck demeanor and adopted the man-in-charge persona.

Jesmyn folded her hands and allowed them to rest on the lectern while she continued. "Tell the jury about your career as an educator, Mr. Briscoe."

Briscoe leaned back in his chair and lectured the jury like they were high school kids in his health class. "I graduated Stephen F., took a job as assistant football coach in Lufkin. I left there for a position at Mt. Pleasant, and then Solon Prince invited me to come to Kilgore High twenty years ago. I've always received top marks on my annual reviews."

He was proud of himself, too proud, if I read the faces of the jurors correctly. As I watched his performance, I understood full well why Jesmyn Thompson had urged him not to testify.

"Coach Briscoe you have heard the testimony from the witnesses. They painted a picture of you as a person who orchestrated a plan which culminated in the shooting deaths of three students. What response to those witnesses do you have for the jury?"

His face was red with anger. "It's a pack of lies."

"Please set the record straight for us."

"I had no knowledge of any plan. I was going about my business at school when Carmel Sideout pulled a gun in class. I thought he was going to use it against the kids in class. I had a split second to react, so I didn't hesitate. The only regret I have is that I wasn't a better shot. I have nightmares every day about Maria and Benjamin, but time was of the essence, and, unfortunately, they got caught in the line of fire and became collateral damage."

"Is it your testimony that you knew nothing about Benjamin's one-act play, or that Ms. McEntyre had acquired a toy gun as a prop for it, or that Mr. Poteet or Merlin Hostetler planted the gun, or that Raul Juarez had a part in setting Carmel up for a fall?"

"Those are pure fabrications by people who have it out for me. They want to shift the blame for the shooting off themselves and onto me."

"We have also heard testimony about your romantic involvement with Ms. McEntyre and Brigitte Malcolm, and your advances toward Maria Juarez. Are those also fabrications?"

"Ms. McEntyre and I dated for months. It was consensual, and she wanted it. I also had a thing with Bridge Malcolm that was off and on for a while. I broke that off years ago. Eugenia Dacus must have been smoking something that night at the Back Porch. I think she made up the story about Maria, so she could get a little of the spotlight in the case. It worked like a charm for her, too."

"You are saying that Ms. McEntyre and Ms. Malcolm testified as they did to get back at you for breaking up with them?"

"Hell hath no fury," Briscoe said, a smirk on his face.

"Let's talk about your right to carry certificate. When did you receive your firearms training?"

"That's another cluster fuck." He caught himself. "Sorry about the language. I'm a little worked up. The certificate filing was another screwup. I took the training in February right after the law passed allowing teachers to carry. I brought the certificate to Marcie Brumbaugh the day after I received it. She was so scatter-brained that I guess she lost it before she could get it filed. When the shooting happened, and the police investigated my eligibility to carry on campus, I learned for the first time that the high school office didn't have my certificate on file. So, I went back to my instructor, and he issued a duplicate certificate. He dated it the day he re-issued it without thinking about the need to back date it. I was street-legal with the gun on campus from February forward."

I leaned over to Red. "Can you get Dud McGill here pronto?"

"I'm on it." He slipped out of the courtroom along the side aisle.

Jesmyn Thompson continued her direct examination. "Coach Briscoe we have also heard testimony that raises the specter of racism. I'll put the question to you as plain as I can. Are you a racist?"

"That's the most ridiculous charge anyone has made against me in this courtroom. I have never used the N-word in my life. My parents raised me to be color blind, and I've always treated everyone the same. Black, white, red, yellow, purple, it doesn't matter to me."

"I'm almost through, Coach Briscoe. The last thing is the issue of whether you had an ax to grind with Carmel because of the tussle at the Back Porch."

"That was nothing. I've dealt with teenage boys for over twenty years. Their emotions get the best of them sometimes, especially if they need to prove that they're men, not boys. That tussle was just a rite of passage for Carmel. I didn't give it another thought after that night."

"Is there anything else you'd like to tell the jury before I pass you to Mr. Danielson?"

He glared at the members of the jury. "You folks just need to cut me loose, so I can get back to business. All this mess has gone on way too long."

"I pass the witness, Your Honor."

I was on my feet before Jesmyn settled into her chair.

"Mr. Briscoe you want the jury to cut you loose so you can get back to the business of killing students?"

"Cut it out, Etch. You know that's not what I meant."

"Let's take it a step at a time, Mr. Briscoe. Someone planted the gun on Carmel, right?"

"I guess. Unless he figured some way to smuggle it into class."

"And someone planted a burner phone on him?"

"Beats me."

"And someone placed a call to that phone at just the right moment?"

"I guess."

"Well, you didn't place the call to the burner phone, did you Mr. Briscoe?"

"I didn't even know about that phone."

"Because you never talked to Raul Juarez about it?"

"Right."

"And you had no ax to grind with Carmel after the Back Porch fight?"

"It wasn't a fight. Just a misunderstanding. Carmel and I were good."

"You'd always been good?"

"I don't know what you mean, Etch?"

"You and he had a history, didn't you?"

"I just knew him as a student. I wouldn't call that a history."

"Neither would I." I let it drop.

"It's your testimony that you received your right to carry certificate sometime in February, but the high school office lost it?"

"Yeah. And I went to the instructor, and he gave me a replacement."

"You went back to the same instructor?"

"Sure. Dud McGill. He's the only guy in these parts who's authorized to teach the class."

"Is target practice part of the training?"

"It wouldn't be much of a training session if you didn't practice shooting."

"Could you hit the targets?"

"Bullseye every time."

"You know a young coach named Merlin Hostetler, don't you?"

"Sure. I think the world of him."

"You took him under your wing when he joined the faculty at KHS?"

"Yeah. You could say that. I had a lot of experience and thought I could help him."

"Experience in things like manipulating women, for instance?"

"I just introduced him around, Etch. What he did in his personal life was his business."

"I don't suppose you introduced him around to some of the female students at school, did you?"

"He taught classes. He had students of his own."

"Because if you introduced him around to girls who were students, and if he followed the example you set with Brigitte Malcolm, then you might have had something on him, right?"

"I don't catch your drift, Etch."

"Yes, you do, Mr. Briscoe. You knew Hostetler was carrying on with his students, and you blackmailed him into doing your dirty work for you. You made him plant the gun, or else. That's how it worked, wasn't it, Mr. Briscoe?"

"You're crazy."

"And while he was hiding the gun in Carmel's backpack, you had him plant the burner phone, too, didn't you?"

"I don't have to answer crazy stuff like this."

"Yes, you do, Mr. Briscoe. You got up here to strut your stuff, but in so doing you opened yourself up to cross-examination. Answer my question, Mr. Briscoe. You had Merlin plant the gun and the burner phone, didn't you?"

He looked at Jesmyn.

"Your attorney can't answer for you, Mr. Briscoe."

"I didn't know about the gun or the phone, so I didn't have Merlin or anybody else plant them on Carmel."

"I suppose you didn't know about Benjamin's one-act play either?"

"I heard about it the first time here in the courtroom."

"So, you'd have the jury believe that you were in a relationship with Ms. McEntyre for months and she never told you about Benjamin's remarkable play?"

"Not a peep."

"What really happened was when you learned about the play, you realized it provided the perfect cover for you, isn't that right?"

"Cover for what?"

"It provided the opportunity for you to lash out at Carmel and Maria and Benjamin and never have to answer for it. You knew that play would come out after the fact, and you thought it would prove that Carmel and his friends were dangerous, that they were a powder keg about to explode. That's how you had it figured, wasn't it?"

"I didn't know about the play." He clinched his teeth and his jaw muscles bulged.

"But they weren't the powder keg, were they? You were. Isn't that right, Coach Briscoe?"

He slammed his fists on the witness stand railing. "I was in the right, Mr. Danielson. I had sufficient certainty."

"Sufficient certainty that you could get away with murder, right Coach?"

I walked away from the lectern without waiting for his answer.

Jesmyn Thompson motioned for Briscoe to return to his place at the defense table.

"The defense rests, Your Honor," she announced.

"Do you have any rebuttal witnesses, Mr. Danielson?"

I looked at Red who was back at the prosecution table. He gave me a thumbs up.

"We call Dud McGill, Your Honor."

In a minute, a gray-haired man in his early sixties entered the courtroom. He wore a Dallas Cowboys windbreaker, khaki pants and a buttoned Polo golf shirt. He had a thick file folder under his right arm. He took the oath and sat down on the witness stand.

"State your name, sir."

"Dud McGill. I'm a certified instructor for the Texas right to carry program for teachers."

"Sir, did you provide training for Coach Briscoe?"

"Yes, sir. I trained him the day after the Kilgore High School shootings."

"Did you ever provide training for him before that date?"

"No, sir."

"Have you observed Coach Briscoe on the firing range?"

"Yes, sir. Many times. I only trained him once, but I saw him at the range doing target practice. He used to come just every now and then, but this Spring he came often."

"Is he a good shot?"

"Very good."

"Do you know why he came so often to the range this Spring?"

"I didn't discuss it with him, but I figured he was getting ready for a competition."

"He was honing his skills for a big event?"

"That's what I figured, sir."

I passed Dud to Jesmyn.

"No questions, Your Honor."

"Any other rebuttal witnesses, Mr. Danielson?"

"We call Caddo Panola, Your Honor."

When I said Caddo's name, for the first time since the trial started, I saw fear slip into the eyes of Jim Briscoe.

Chapter Fifty

Dave Schmerz opened the witness room door. Caddo walked a straight line toward the witness stand, a course that took her in front of the counsel tables. When she passed near Briscoe, he spit the words at her, "Watch your step, Caddo."

"Control your client, Ms. Thompson," Judge Merrell admonished her from the bench.

"Get your hands off me," Briscoe said when Jesmyn nudged him away from Caddo Panola.

"One more outburst, Mr. Briscoe, and I will have the deputies shackle you," Judge Merrell said.

Briscoe backed a half step away from Caddo who continued to the stand.

"State your name, please ma'am."

"Caddo Panola. I am Carmel Sideout's mother."

The jury members moved closer to the edges of their seats when they heard who Caddo was.

"Ms. Panola, we are in the rebuttal stage of the trial, which means I have called you to respond to Coach Briscoe's former testimony here in court. Do you understand?"

"Yes, sir, Mr. Danielson."

"I asked Coach Briscoe a few minutes ago if he had a history with your son, Carmel, and he said he didn't know what I meant. He said his only contact with him had been in connection with his job as a teacher. Is that a correct assessment of his history with Carmel?"

"No, sir."

"Please explain your answer."

Caddo was calm as she answered, reserved like a family member delivering bad news about a loved one.

"I'm forty-nine years old, will be fifty next week. I grew up in Kilgore and had the best mother in the world. She taught me right from wrong, but I made bad decisions. I didn't pursue my education and chose to go the other route, to build a life on street smarts, to live fast and loose. I held a day job now and then and spent my nights in the clubs. As part of that life, when I was about thirty, I met a young coach who had recently taken a job at Kilgore High School."

"That was Coach Briscoe?"

"Yes, sir. One thing led to another and we became a couple. Coach was always telling me how much he loved me, how we would run away and make a fresh start somewhere."

"Did you run away together?"

"No, sir. That was all just talk on his part. In my heart of hearts I knew he was feeding me a line, but I wanted so bad to believe him."

"How did things end up with the two of you?"

"We rocked along for a while, always meeting in out-of-the-way places, keeping a low profile."

"Why didn't you bring your relationship out into the light?"

"We were in East Texas twenty years ago. Coach told me we couldn't go public until we got out of town, until we found a place that was color blind."

"In other words, he kept his relationship with you secret because you were black and he was white?"

"Yes, sir."

"How long did you maintain your relationship?"

"Until I came up pregnant."

"When was that, Ms. Panola?"

"Nineteen years ago."

At that moment, I thought about what Red had said to me not long ago. There are things that once you know them, you can't un-know. I took a piece of paper in my hand.

"May I approach the witness, Your Honor?"

"You may, Mr. Danielson."

I walked next to the witness stand and handed Caddo the sheet of paper.

"Ms. Panola, can you identify the paper in your hand?"

"Yes, sir. It is my son's birth certificate."

"And when you say your son, you are referring to Carmel Sideout?"

"Yes, sir. He was my only child."

"His birth certificate says the father of the child is a person named Hobo Sideout?"

"Yes, sir. That's what it says, but that was a name I made up."

"Why would you make up a name for your child on his birth certificate?"

"It was an inside joke. Hobo Sideout was my way of saying that the dad was a guy who wouldn't hang around to raise the child. He was a man who was just passing through town and didn't want to be weighed down."

"Ms. Panola, who was the real person behind the made-up name of Hobo Sideout?"

She pointed. "It was the man sitting right there. Coach Jim Briscoe."

A gasp filled the room as jurors and people in the gallery processed her revelation and grasped the horror of it.

"Did Coach Briscoe know he was Carmel Sideout's father?"

"Of course he knew. It was why we split up. He wouldn't have anything to do with me when he learned I was pregnant. He told me to stay the hell away from him. When Carmel was born, he didn't come to the hospital to see him. He didn't acknowledge Carmel to anyone. He left it to me to raise Carmel, so I moved back in with my mother, worked piddling jobs for a while. Finally, I got fed up and I went to the high school and confronted Briscoe. We had a swearing match, and he told me the best thing for me to do was to get out of town. He said Carmel should always be 'our little secret.'"

"Just so we're clear, Ms. Panola, did you ever tell anyone Coach Briscoe was Carmel's father, or did you keep that knowledge bottled up inside you?"

"I never told anyone. Not my mother, not Carmel. They thought Carmel's father was just some one-night stand, a guy passing through town I hooked up with."

"After you had the blowout with Briscoe at school, what happened?"

"I hit the road. My mother said she would care for Carmel until I got my life together."

"Did you ever come for Carmel?"

She was sniffling now. "No, sir. You know how it is. One thing leads to another. Something goes wrong here, something goes wrong there, and the years slip by."

"Did you ever have any more contact with Coach Briscoe?"

She straightened her back and looked at Briscoe. "That's the worst thing about it. I did stay in touch with him."

"Why?"

"To see if it was OK for me to come home."

"Why would you need Briscoe's permission to come home?"

"He told me as long as I was away, he'd keep an eye on Carmel from a distance. But, he said if I had thoughts about coming home, he'd take it out on Carmel."

"What did you think he meant by that?"

"I knew what he meant. He would harm Carmel somehow."

"So, you stayed away from your son all these years to protect him from Jim Briscoe?"

"Yes, sir. I thought when Carmel went off to college, I might could reunite with him, explain why I'd been absent. But Coach took that away from me, too."

"He made sure you and Carmel never got back together?"

"Yes, sir. He killed him before I could have him back."

And with those haunting words of Caddo Panola hanging heavy in the minds of us all, at one o'clock that afternoon, the case went to the jury.

And we waited.

Chapter Fifty-One

Anyone who has spent time in a courtroom knows juries are notoriously unpredictable. They may hang up on a case that looks like a slam dunk, or return a verdict in minutes on a case where the evidence is thin ice.

An hour into the jury's deliberations, the yelling started. Although we couldn't make out the words, we could hear the rumblings emanating from the jury room. When I had tried criminal cases on the defense side, I always took shouting in the jury room as a good sign. It usually meant at least one or two jurors were holding out against the others. Since it only takes one vote to hang a jury, dissension in that room was a harbinger of bad news for the prosecution most of the time.

About three o'clock, the jury sent out a note to Judge Merrell.

She read it silently and called counsel to the bench.

"The jury has sent me a note." She adjusted her thick lenses and scrutinized the note again. "It says, 'Can we give him the needle?' I plan to send them word that they are to follow the instructions I have already given them, and that they are not to consider the defendant's punishment at this stage of the proceedings. Do either of you have any objections?"

Jesmyn Thompson and I shook our heads.

She and I stepped away from the bench. Before we returned to our seats, Jesmyn leaned toward me and whispered, "What's your best number?"

I had anticipated the moment, considered how the case might go on appeal, how an appellate court might interpret the SPA against me and determine the prosecution had not met its burden of proof. "Forty-five," I said.

"Can he plead nolo?"

I nodded.

She went to the table and motioned for Harold Fleming and Coach Briscoe to follow her to a witness room. Three minutes later, she stuck her head out and gave me a thumbs up.

Judge Merrell had not left the bench after our conference about the jury's note. "May I approach the bench, Your Honor?"

"You may, Mr. Danielson."

"We have reached a plea agreement in the case, Your Honor."

She nodded. "Let's get it on the record before I dismiss the jury."

And that is how the case of *The State of Texas versus James Briscoe* concluded with a whimper ten minutes later.

"To the charges against you how do you plead, Mr. Briscoe?"

"No contest, Your Honor," he answered, the words sticking in his throat, a coward to the end.

"The Court accepts your plea, finds that the evidence is sufficient to warrant a finding of guilty to the charges in the indictment and hereby sentences you to confinement in the Institutional Division of the Texas Department of Criminal Justice for a period of forty-five years."

A Gregg County deputy slapped handcuffs on Coach Briscoe and escorted him out of the courtroom.

Never one to linger at the courthouse after a trial, I shook hands with Red and Dave Schmerz, slipped out a side door, took the stairs to the basement and made my escape.

On the way to the office, I called May Ellen.

"It's all over the news, Etch. Congratulations, baby. I knew you could do it."

"I'll be there in a few to pick you up. Let's take a ride."

"I'll be waiting for you, hon."

Twenty-five minutes later, she and I cruised through the old part of downtown Kilgore and turned left toward the edge of town. When we turned the corner nearest the cemetery, we saw a police cruiser stationed at the entrance, its emergency lights flashing. I pulled to the curb, and May Ellen and I joined hands and walked through the front gate. Already, the narrow lanes of the old graveyard were jammed with cars. Soon we saw the crowd gathered near the Cohen plot, the men with their KHS caps in their hands, the women wearing their KHS t-shirts, the students holding hands near the graves of their fallen friends.

Red was waiting for us, as I knew he would be, and he walked with us.

I noticed two people standing arm in arm apart from the crowd in the shade of the old pecan tree. "There's someone I'd like for you to meet," I said to May Ellen. We approached the couple.

"May Ellen Danielson, I'd like to introduce you to Ms. Caddo Panola."

Caddo released her grip on Momma L, extended her hand to May Ellen. "It's not an introduction, Mr. Danielson. May Ellen and I go back a long way."

"It's been a minute, Caddo," May Ellen said, and the two women hugged each other and cried. May Ellen held out a hand to Momma L and she joined them in the embrace.

Red and I were crying, too.

After a couple of minutes, Momma L released herself from the embrace and came next to me. She held out her hand, and I shook it. "You did what I asked you to do, Etch. You cleared Carmel's name. I will forever be grateful to you for that."

"If you hadn't asked me to give it a try, Momma L, people would never have known the truth. I'm the one who's grateful, grateful that you believed in Carmel."

We made our way through the press of the crowd until we stood next to the graves and next to Patty Douglas and Abby Cohen and Eugenia Dacus and Marcus Wellborn. I turned to face the crowd and raised my hands above my head to quiet the mourners.

"Ladies and gentlemen, please bow your heads while Momma L, Ms. Logansport Panola, leads us in a word of prayer."

Momma L grasped Caddo's hand, lifted her eyes to heaven, and prayed for us all.

THE END

About the Author

Stephen Woodfin is an East Texas attorney and author. Kirkus Reviews named his book *The Warrior with Alzheimer's* one of the best books of 2013. *Sufficient Certainty* is his tenth novel.